COLOUR AND THE KABBALAH

Also by James Sturzaker
KABBALISTIC APHORISMS

Colour and the Kabbalah

Doreen & James Sturzaker

THORSONS PUBLISHERS LIMITED
Wellingborough, Northamptonshire

First published 1975

ISBN 0 7225 0283 4 (UK)
ISBN 0 87728 292 7 (USA)

Typeset by Specialised Offset Services Limited, Liverpool
and printed by Whitstable Litho Limited, Whitstable, Kent.

CONTENTS

INTRODUCTION

This book is offered to those interested in the Kabbalah but who have not yet studied its colour aspect, for we feel that to gain a deeper, truer understanding of the subject the differing colours of the Sephiroth and the Paths must be taken into consideration.

For those who have studied the seven rays it is hoped that this work will bring an expansion to their knowledge of colour. It will necessitate, perhaps, a re-orientation of ideas on colour for the Kabbalah can only be understood when twelve rays are related to it. For those Kabbalists who have little knowledge of colour this book may help to serve as an introduction to the occult science and add to their understanding of the Tree of Life.

Many books on the Kabbalah give the correspondences of the four scales of colour but fail to enlighten the student on the most important point, why and how it relates.

In the following pages an attempt will be made to look more closely into these correspondences and to explain the Sephiroth and the Paths in the light of colour symbolism. In doing this we offer our own interpretation and would urge each serious student and fellow Kabbalist to consider the colour aspect, meditate and come to his own understanding, for in the end the validity of the system depends on its relevance for each individual.

Have you ever wondered what colour actually is? Science tells us it is light at varying rates of vibration. Impinging on the rods and cones of the eye it gives us distinct impressions.

Subjective it may be, but a universal human experience it certainly is; and not only peculiarly human, because the other kingdoms of nature also experience, and can respond to, different vibrations of colour.

We at the human stage of consciousness are in a position to appreciate and understand something of the meaning of this wonderful cosmos of colour that is surrounding us all the time, from the moment we open our eyes at the commencement of a new day until we close them again in sleep.

There are several ways in which we can consider colour. The artist who works with it has a deep feeling for it, the psychologist uses it in other ways to gain a knowledge of his patients through their colour predilection. Interior decorators consider its effects and the result they wish to obtain from their use of colour.

In studying the Kabbalah we find that colour plays an important part, in fact it is an integral part of the Tree of Life and the twenty-two Paths.

Before anything was there, there was darkness, yet all was there, silence before the worlds were and a brooding calm. A tiny point of brilliant light appears in the blackness, it grows larger and explodes into a myriad points like itself, they merge and blend, all is brightness.

PART ONE:
THE TEN SEPHIROTH

KETHER

In Atziluth

Kether, the Crown or first sephirah, changes colour very little in the four worlds, as might be expected for the sephirah that is the supreme head of every tree. In the world of Atziluth its colour is brilliance; most people construe this as the great white light and are guilty of misconception. In the world of Briah, Kether is white brilliance; note that a colour is placed in front of the brilliance, but in Atziluth it is not prefaced by a colour. So what is brilliance? This is the first point of light; it is also the archetypal world and as such must contain all colours and be the archetype of all twelve rays. Brilliance then is the perfect combination of all colours; it is something indescribable to man at the human level of consciousness. This is the thirteenth ray where all others meet and blend; this is the true point that the Master D.K. meant when he said, 'This is the point where there is colour and yet no colour, just an infinite point of peace'. Here are all the twelve rays with their qualities, vices and virtues, in potential, that will be met with on the way down the Tree.

In Briah

In the Briatic World, Kether is white brilliance, the positive and powerful active force going out. It has now taken on a colour since leaving the world of Atziluth and becomes one of the twelve aspects, not quite so pure as when it was part of the brilliance. Kether on the Tree in Chokmah, which is the first half of the Briatic World, is overshadowed by the pure soft blue which is the colour of this sephirah in Atziluth. This is a high octave of the blue ray and on this octave is the free spirit, uncontaminated as yet, on the way down, and purified and released from form on the return. Were it not for the tranquillity of the blue ray the powerful force of the white would rush out beyond control and form would be non-existent. The blue of Chokmah is required as the guiding but not all-restricting ray. Binah is the sephirah of restriction with its black ray from Saturn, its Mundane Chakra. The over-shadowing colour of the sephirah is crimson, an octave of the red ray, impulsive and active. It is in the second half of the Briatic world that the madly rushing force is controlled. The World of Briah is the first phase of creativity or creation. First the force of Kether is channelled and slowed and then ensouled so that the process of formation can take place. From the Mundane Chakra of Chokmah, the sphere of the Zodiac, the other aspects of the brilliance now move out to combine with the white brilliance as it moves into the formative world of Yetzirah.

In Yetzirah

In the World of Yetzirah there are six trees. The colour of the sephiroth on each tree is exactly the same; the difference lies in the basic Atziluthic colour of the sephirah in which the Tree stands. The first sephirah in the Yetziratic World is Gedulah or Chesed, and its basic colour is that of the purple ray. It is the octave of deep violet, and although a royal ray, at this octave it has the quality of greatness; there is also pomp and pride and forceful power as opposed to the more gentle persuasive power of the lavender.

The pure Atziluthic perfection of Kether has now disappeared and impurities have infiltrated into the pure white brilliance to a greater extent than in Briah. The power of the white brilliance is, however, still sufficient to modify the deep violet, and by its absorption to a certain degree, succeeds in transmuting it to a lighter shade and a higher octave of the ray. With this transmutation fresh qualities are brought forth, such as tranquillity, gentleness, poise, honour, and humbleness. These are qualities that can be recognized with the sphere that is the objective plane of consciousness associated with the Masters.

Geburah has for its basic colour in Atziluth a golden orange, and from the Mundane Chakra streams out the influence of the primary red.

The golden orange octave holds the qualities of pride and conceit, self-pride and inflated ego. The primary red adds to these qualities those of fire, vigour, energy and force. Here is truly the avenging sphere of justice or Karma, and it is only the white brilliance of Kether that prevents it from being a sephirah of terror.

Kether's own ray subdues in great measure the violent reactions of these lower octaves of the red ray, so that at the level of Kether in Geburah the octave becomes a rosy pink that brings the attributes of constant affection, and a magnetic healing power. This holds out hope that Karma or universal law is just and gives not only hope, but the promise of fulfilment.

Dropping still lower on the basic Tree, there is the sephirah, Tiphareth, and here the white brilliance of Kether is influenced by the Atziluthic colour of this sephirah, which is a clear pink rose, a higher octave of the red ray. This is brought to an even lighter pink with the white brilliance.

The high octave of the red ray holds the qualities of love at the highest point of human physical perfection in Assiah so that at the level of Tiphareth in Atziluth it becomes that complete affection for the whole, entirely unselfish to the point of sacrifice for the benefit of the whole, it also holds the quality of complete forgiveness.

The overall colour of Netzach is amber, a high octave of the orange ray. This influence on the white brilliance of Kether in Netzach produces a medium yellow ray with its mental and spiritual activity. At the level of Assiah this would apply to human beings, but at the Kether level of Netzach in Yetzirah, it applies entirely to the lower mental level of consciousness and aspects of understanding. Here is the realm of hidden wisdom as brought through by the white brilliance of Kether, that can shed light in dark places. The yellow ray at this level can bring in an illusory form of knowledge, false ideals and ideas which makes this sephirah a sphere of discrimination.

Discrimination of the correct wisdom is aided by the blue ray of Love and Wisdom which sends out its influence from Venus, the Mundane Chakra of Netzach, and so the true light of Kether in Netzach is uncovered.

Kether in Hod is the next stage of the Yetziratic World to be considered and the basic colour of this sephirah is a violet purple. As with Netzach there are two rays impinging on Kether from the sephirah; the violet purple and the yellow ray sending through its influence from Mercury, Mundane Chakra of Hod.

The yellow gives activity and zeal. There is also adoration and spiritual dedication from the octave of the purple ray. It also adds the quality of reverence within rigid confines and that touch of quiet complacency. From the yellow ray influence there is more mental activity, and at this level mainly in the sphere of spiritual work.

It could be considered that the majority of these influences are ideal qualities, which in some circumstances they are; but in Hod, the sephirah of rigid form, there can be the adverse effect.

The very fact of rigid form limits these qualities to a narrow field of vision with an element of stubbornness that will not bend or yield from a given position. It is only when the white brilliance manages to break through with a momentary illumination that the activity and zeal of the yellow ray aids in the eventual break-through from the restrictions of the rigid form.

Yesod, the last sephirah in the World of Yetzirah, has for its basic colour indigo. Here again there is a quality of devotion, a devotional form of love; but this form of love at Kether in Yesod is very different to Kether in Gedulah.

From the Moon, Mundane Chakra of Yesod, there is the influence of the grey ray. It is on the higher octave of the ray as it is silver grey, but its purity is detracted from by the touch of green tinging it.

It is at Yesod that the emotions come into play for the first time. Here is the desire world at its height. These are some of the basic attributions of Yesod and part of the purpose for its existence.

The indigo ray gives the desire to worship. The pomp and circumstance aroused by devotional emotions leads to an emotional religious pride which can result in an emotional jealousy of the particular religion's faith aided by the tinge of green from the Mundane Chakra which also gives the envy of and for power.

From the grey ray there flows the influence of peace and calm, spiritual harmony and balance. The white brilliance, highest octave of the white ray, brings to Kether in Yesod the attributes of creativity, morality, and faith from reason.

All of these form the conflicting emotions of Yesod, more of the negative than the positive, on the face of it, but with the strength of goodness embodied in the silver grey and white brilliance, the rays can be merged and computed through a whole gamut of emotions until the balance is found and a perfect emotional level of consciousness is formed.

In Assiah

The perfect archetype of the Atziluthic World is now far removed from its state of perfection as it becomes part of the physical world. The colour has now lost its brilliance and is just white, but it is flecked with gold, the highest point of the yellow ray.

Kether in Malkuth is now influenced by the yellow ray, Atziluthic background colour of Malkuth in Assiah, and from the Mundane Chakra, which comprise the four elements, flow the red, blue, green and yellow rays to further influence Kether. The four rays from the Mundane Chakra are the primary octaves of their respective rays.

In the World of Assiah Kether can be said to have the influence of all the rays, six directly and the other six indirectly, from the computations and interplay of the direct six.

This is how it should be, because Malkuth or Assiah on the basic Tree is the finished creation of the Atziluthic archetype, Kether; not the perfection of the first thought, but containing all in varying states of perfection that was first visualized; the only thing not present is the brilliance.

With the various rays now densified, they also have their impurities and are not in perfect balance with each other. The basic purpose of Kether in Malkuth is to bring all the rays into balance with equal strength, so that they cancel each other out and become the thirteenth synthesizing ray, brilliance.

When brilliance at Kether in Malkuth has been achieved, it will cease to be at that very moment, as perfection is not part of the Tree except at Atziluth.

CHOKMAH

In Assiah

Chokmah is the supreme point of wisdom in the world of Assiah or the sephirah of Malkuth on the basic Tree. The basic colour of Chokmah in Assiah is white, but it is flecked with red, blue and yellow, the three major rays of the lower worlds. Overshadowing the Tree in Assiah, and having an effect on Chokmah, is the pure yellow ray of Malkuth.

The white ray is expansive and creative; it also influences and encourages faith from reason. From this ray expansion is given to the quality of wisdom that stems from the sephirah itself. With the creative quality of the ray, wisdom is used in a creative manner, and it is from this aspect of the white ray that a firm foundation is created which leads to the state of consciousness where faith from reason is born.

At this point in Assiah the initiate is preparing to move through Kether in Assiah to the Yetziratic World. To take this step and leave the physical world for the last time requires a certain amount of courage. It is from the red ray that the initiate can draw this quality and also the same ray will give stimulation.

From the yellow ray running into Chokmah and issuing from Malkuth the spirit is given creative activity as opposed to the creative ideas of the white ray. This gives the initiate the spiritual yearning to advance towards the next stage of his journey to conscious spiritual union with the Ultimate.

One danger lies in the red and yellow rays, that of over-stimulation, and it could lead to the initiate making a rash or impetuous move. To avoid this he must call upon the calm steadying influence of the blue ray.

Once full control of all the rays has been accomplished the initiate can move forward with a quiet courage and confidence toward the world of Yetzirah and progress steadily up the Tree in Yesod until once more he reaches the sephirah of Chokmah.

In Yetzirah

Yesod, the first sephirah in the Yetziratic World on the path of return, has for its overall colour the indigo ray. It is against this background that the Chokmah colour of bluish pearl grey streams out.

The initiate now finds himself urged on by desires and emotions; two qualities of the astral plane of consciousness, which is the Yesod sphere of consciousness.

With a strong influx of the indigo ray from Yesod a strong devotional emotional influence takes over the initiate. He is lost to all other ways of thought, and were it not for the blue and pearl grey rays could remain in this state for an indefinite period of time.

The pale blue, a high octave of the blue ray with its quality of spiritual wisdom, can be called upon and influence the initiate toward the true wisdom of the sephirah Chokmah.

With the high octave of the grey ray bringing the influence of stability the emotions are brought under control, and the devotional aspect is directed towards the true wisdom and its development.

Through the exercise of these rays the initiate now moves toward the lower mental plane of consciousness, progressing ever forward until he reaches the sephirah of Chokmah on the Tree in Hod.

Although the sephirah retains the same flashing colours or rays throughout the whole of the Yetziratic World, the background ray or colour changes from sephirah to sephirah on the basic Tree.

In Hod the background colour to the Tree is violet, and

this octave of the purple ray contains the virtues of humility, reverence, and spiritual dedication.

With the quality of devotion developed at Chokmah in Yesod, and now the quality of spiritual dedication, the initiate tends to become so single-minded that for a time the wider view is lost to him.

Salvation from the predicament in which the initiate finds himself is found in the quality of humility which is continually streaming from the violet octave of the purple ray. When humility is fully developed within, then the limited narrow view of the Hod state is recognized.

Once more the wider view opens out as the realization dawns that even Chokmah in Hod is only a tiny speck far removed from the ultimate end of the journey, and the reverence incubated by the violet octave fills the consciousness.

Now the step across to Netzach is possible, and with reverence and humility the initiate commences to climb the Tree in Chokmah to reach the sephirah of Wisdom in this particular state of consciousness.

In Netzach the whole Tree is enveloped in amber, a medium octave of the orange ray. Contained within the amber octave is mental vigour, justice and wholeness.

Once having seen the wider view, and now in the greater freedom of Netzach, there is the temptation to let the mental vigour take control and run riot, for even this level of consciousness is still only at a lower mental level.

The amber octave has to be brought into full use so that in the wisdom of the blue ray and with the stability of the pearl grey octave, justice and wholeness can be recognized for what they are and can only be at the lower mental level of Netzach.

The initiate now faces in awe the tree in Tiphareth which is bathed in a pink rose, a high octave of the red ray. On this high octave such qualities as constant affection, comfort, and unselfishness are found.

Seeking the wisdom of the higher mental plane he slowly

and sometimes hesitantly climbs the Tree towards Chokmah, passing through many trials and taking a further initiation in the process. Now, on reaching Chokmah in Tiphareth, he has attained to adeptship.

From the Sephirah of Chokmah he takes the wisdom which is also present in the blue ray, and from the pink rose develops universal love. There is now the yearning to send this universal love down through all the lower planes of consciousness.

Now the pearl grey octave must be brought into play so that stability aids in directing with true wisdom the universal love and not just an uncontrolled outflow of Chokmah energy.

The Tree in Geburah is the next stage of the higher mental plane to be faced, and here the blue and pearl grey of Chokmah is bathed in the orange glow of Geburah.

Self-control and reliance are two of the main qualities that emanate from this octave of the orange ray, and it is at Chokmah in Geburah that these two qualities are perhaps needed more than at any other time on the journey through the various planes of consciousness.

At this point a searing experience is reaching its conclusion, where self-control and reliance based on the individual mental body has been completely shattered.

The pearl grey octave must now be called upon to regain stability, and by the use of the blue ray of wisdom, a link is made with the wisdom aspect of Chokmah. It is at this stage that self-control and reliance can be re-established through the use of the orange ray.

In acquiring the two qualities through the Chokmah wisdom, they are now developed on a different basis, that of universal law and the cosmic forces, and no longer on the individual mental body.

Moving on from Geburah the Tree in Gedulah has now to be conquered. Overshadowing the whole Tree is the deep violet octave of the purple ray. It is against this background that the blue and pearl grey of Chokmah in Gedulah operates.

The lesson taught at this level of consciousness is dedication, a virtue of the deep violet octave, dedication through wisdom and right use of cosmic forces within universal law.

Making full use of the sphere of the zodiac, the Mundane Chakra of Chokmah, dedication to the service of all on the lower levels of consciousness is developed and that service is supplied through the celestial spheres.

With reliance on universal law and a stability and love from the rays of Chokmah, the last Gedulah qualities are perfected and the Master is now ready to cross the abyss into the World of Briah and the two supernals.

In Briah

On arriving at Binah, the first Tree in the World of Briah, the Master has reached the point of no return. The Sephirah of Chokmah is now grey with the crimson background of Binah.

The influence of the crimson, a high octave of the red ray, is to give joy to life. Not the life understood at the lower levels, but that true life of freedom within universal law.

Crimson also provides the required stimulation to cast aside all shreds of form with its confinements and deviations and from the high octave of the grey ray peace and harmony is obtained.

With the new-found freedom the eternal spark commences the last stage of the journey which has taken it in many forms across time and space through many planes of consciousness.

The Tree in Chokmah is the last stage and the grey ray of Chokmah is penetrated by the pure soft blue of Chokmah. Here a double Chokmah force is felt, that of Chokmah in Briah with the grey ray, and that of Chokmah in Atziluth with the pure soft blue.

From the pure soft blue, the highest octave of the blue ray, the eternal spark is filled with selfless love, the true pure cosmic love for the oneness; and from the grey ray, peace and harmony. The spark is now prepared to take its place on the

Atziluthic Tree.

In Atziluth

The pure soft blue of Chokmah is now iridescent from the brilliance of Kether, the Atziluthic World. Brilliance is the synthesizing ray composed of all other rays.

From all the various forms and experiences passed through, the wisdom of all the rays in turn has been absorbed. At Chokmah in Atziluth, the spark is perfected wisdom based on the particular scheme of manifestation.

BINAH

In Assiah

Against the yellow background of the World of Assiah – Malkuth – the grey and pastel pink rays of Binah are highlighted, and standing out starkly from the lighter coloured rays is the black ray of Saturn, Mundane Chakra of Binah.

Although the rays of the sephirah change within the differing sephiroth and Worlds, the black ray will be constant from Assiah to Atziluth.

At the level of Assiah the grey is a medium octave of this ray and provides the qualities of endurance, persistence, and a desire of the soul to struggle for freedom. From the pink, a high octave of the red ray, comes the understanding of love at the highest point of physical affections.

To prevent the physical affections getting out of hand and developing into weak sentimentality, the black ray of restriction and absorption is brought into use, so that the affections are restrained and weak sentimentality absorbed.

From the interaction of these rays a true understanding of love and affection is gained, which helps the pink octave of the red to impress its other quality, that of forgiveness.

There is, however, a danger from the black ray, which at the level of Binah in Assiah is only a medium octave of the ray. The ray inclines to obscure the spiritual and enhance the more material or mental level of the initiate.

It is because of this tendency of the black ray that the yellow ray of creative activity and spirit must be harnessed and used, enabling the initiate to break out of the obscurity and adjust his mental body to the more spiritual path and so enable him to move forward to the Tree in Yesod.

In Yetzirah

On the return journey Yesod is the first sephirah and Tree in the World of Yetzirah with the indigo ray as its overall colour. The sephirah Binah has now changed its rays from the grey and pastel pink to dark brown, a low octave of the brown ray.

A basic quality of the indigo ray is devotion. This is not necessarily spiritual or religious devotion, but to whatever the emotional and mental bodies are applied. This can be quite an obstacle to surmount at Binah on the Tree in Yesod because the low octave of the brown ray produces the quality of biased thought.

If, before the true understanding at this level of consciousness is developed, emotions and thoughts are taken on the wrong path, the initiate with biased thought and devotion towards the path will find it difficult to break away into new spheres of thought.

It is in this situation that the black ray with its restrictive quality can be brought into use, and by right application can place a restriction on both the devotion and biased thought, so that these two qualities do not completely rule the mental and emotional bodies.

Once the limitation has been placed on the indigo and brown rays there is the opportunity for the initiate to develop the idealistic aspect of the indigo ray, and with the quality of fortitude, also from the indigo, he gradually obtains the true Yesodic understanding of Binah and can prepare for the further progress which brings him into the sphere of Hod.

Hod is a sephirah of consolidation and construction, two aspects of form of which Hod is the ruler in the World of Yetzirah. The ray of this sephirah is violet, a medium octave of the purple ray, which in itself is a royal ray symbolizing rulership at its many different levels.

Against this background of violet is the dark brown of Binah and the yellow ray issuing forth from Mercury – Mundane Chakra of Hod. The yellow ray, if brought into use by the initiate, can be merged with the dark octave of the brown ray, and by merging transmute it from the dark brown to a more medium octave of the ray.

From the violet octave the initiate develops to the full the quality of adoration, and in the first instance it is adoration in the creating of the form and the form itself.

Consolidation of the rulership of the lower mental body over the emotional body, and this very act in itself, can bring concretion and a fixed form of mental activity. It is now that the yellow must be brought into play to create within the mental body spiritual activity so that the adoration can develop on a different and wider pattern.

The lower mental understanding now commences to develop and the initiate is reaching the stage where he has to move forward and go through the experiences of the Tree in Netzach until he reaches Binah, where his understanding of the lower mental world has to be completed.

The dark brown ray of Binah is now bathed in amber, a high octave of the orange ray. This blending of the two rays produces a coppery brown, a reasonably high octave of the brown ray which produces confidence and a quietness in activity.

At this level the brown ray takes on in full, and at a high level, its studious aspect. Knowledge is now increasing, and the amber gives mental vigour to such a degree that the initiate begins to lose control of the lower mental body, and the black ray must be brought into use to restrict it to reasonable bounds.

Once the lower mental body is under control Binah in Tiphareth can be tackled. The initiate is now in the higher mental plane of consciousness, and although Binah is still governed by the dark brown ray, it is against a background of pink rose, a high octave of the red ray.

Saturn still sends out the black ray, and from the sun – Mundane Chakra of Tiphareth – streams out golden orange, a high octave of the orange ray.

The pink rose numbers amongst its qualities tact and also healing power of a magnetic nature. These are qualities that the adept now takes unto himself, and in joy and love for all humanity, which also comes from the pink rose, he sends the healing power flowing down the Tree to all life quite indiscriminately.

Karma, or universal law, cannot be flouted in this way and the adept has to understand where healing can be given and karma lifted, and where it must be allowed to run its course. Help in this respect can be obtained from the brown, which on the higher octaves has discrimination as one of its attributes, and also from the restricting influence of the black ray.

Ever evolving, the adept proceeds to Geburah and in due course of time to Binah on the Tree in that sephirah. The dark brown of Binah is now set in the orange ray of Geburah, which changes it to a golden brown, or can do if the orange ray is employed correctly, and cutting across is the red ray from Geburah's Mundane Chakra – Mars.

Golden brown, the high octave of the brown ray, bestows upon the adept understanding, knowledge and concentration, and from the orange ray he can develop self-reliance.

Full knowledge of universal law is now open to him, providing he concentrates and absorbs the understanding of these cosmic laws. The adept must exercise his self-reliance and so create confidence in his own ability to do this. By drawing on the black ray he will be aided in the absorption of knowledge, while at the same time his higher mentality will be restrained from straying away from the subject in hand. The black ray aids concentration.

All that is required at this point is the stimulation to carry the task through. This can be obtained by judiciously drawing upon the red ray. From this ray can be obtained the vigour and energy required, but care must be taken not to draw too heavily on it in case more force is obtained than required and all the adept's efforts up to this level of the Tree be shattered.

Having balanced the forces and achieved the goal, the adept enters into Mastership and moves into the sphere of the Masters – Gedulah – where his training can be completed and when he reaches Binah in Gedulah his purpose and journey in the World of Yetzirah is nearly completed.

Deep violet now overshadows the brown ray of Binah and raises the black ray of Saturn to a much higher octave. To understand true humility is one of the lessons to be learned at Binah in Gedulah.

Although humility is a quality of the deep violet, which is an octave of the purple ray and is developed at the lower levels of the Tree, it is at a lower level of understanding. The Master realizes that even at this high state of consciousness the only aspect that makes him different to all other sparks of the Ain is his spiritual progression, but that apart he is no greater or smaller in the whole scheme of things than a densely clothed spark of the Ain dwelling at Malkuth in Assiah. This realization is the true humility.

The higher octave of the black ray is brought into use, so that humility is not taken to the extreme where the Master's higher mental body loses its strength, and in so doing loses all sense of proportion. Were it not for this restricting influence that is always at the Binah level it would be nearly impossible for any spark to pass beyond this point and return to its original source.

With the dark brown ray. transmuted to the mid-brown octave there comes the quality of studious absorption, and so the Master's understanding develops and in the course of time enables him not only to complete his journey through the Tree in Gedulah, but completes the preparation for his step across the abyss to the World of Briah and the Tree in Binah.

In Briah

From Binah emanates a crimson glow. This is a medium

octave of the red ray which surrounds the whole Tree in Binah. The ray of Binah in Briah is now black, having replaced the dark brown of the Yetziratic World.

The black ray will remain with the sephirah, not only as Binah in Binah, but also as Binah in Chokmah. With the black flowing from the Mundane Chakra this is now the predominant ray, counteracted only by the crimson from Binah on the main Tree.

It is from the crimson that the spark must draw, and by combining this ray with the black ray, produce magenta, an octave of the amethyst ray which gives the desire for spiritual experience.

To obtain the experience the Master knows that the last renunciation has to be made at this point, and the high octave of the black ray is brought into play, and from it the latent powers, still undeveloped, are brought out and used. With the last of the latent powers developed, true understanding of the need to lose the personality dawns.

From the crimson is drawn the power to increase and strengthen the individuality, at the same time using the black ray, not just to restrict, but to completely absorb the personality, and with the completion of this task the final freedom from form and compulsory restriction.

The pure spark now enters the Tree in Chokmah and progresses upward to the Binah state of consciousness: although compulsory restriction no longer exists, the black ray still covers Binah on the Tree in Chokmah, but the ray of Chokmah itself is the pure soft blue.

At the Chokmah level of consciousness the black ray of Binah is at its highest octave, and from it streams the true esoteric wisdom. This is the last lesson the spark has to learn from the sephirah of Binah, to understand the true esoteric wisdom and to have voluntary control over itself and the powers within itself, now consciously recognized.

Selfless love, conscious wisdom of innocence, and true spirituality are the qualities contained in the pure soft blue, highest octave of the blue ray. These are qualities which the spark must possess to enable it to complete the journey it has taken across time and space.

Eventually, with the right use of both the blue and black and the merging of them to produce the highest octave of the indigo ray, the spark completes the last stage of the journey. From the indigo ray comes the last quality, devotion to purity, that enables the transition to be made from the Tree in Chokmah to the Tree in Kether.

In Atziluth

Brilliance surrounds and interpenetrates the whole of the Tree in Kether – World of Atziluth – and the ray of Binah is crimson, but not the crimson of the lower levels. It is now sparkling with the brilliance and with a purity that can never be outside Atziluth. From this ray comes the joy of life and love for all life.

The black ray is still sending out vibrations from Binah's Mundane Chakra, but like the crimson it is a sparkling black and its powers of restriction or control are those of voluntary control taken by the spark with the joyousness of perfection in life.

GEDULAH

In Assiah

Gedulah, the last sephirah in the Yetziratic World, is probably the most important, if only for the fact that it is the last stage on any Tree in any World of the lower planes. From this sephirah on the return journey the abyss has to be crossed and Gedulah is the last aspect of training prior to the crossing.

In the World of Assiah or Malkuth the sephirah is influenced by a deep azure blue, which is the predominant ray of the sephirah, but running through it are thin rays of yellow. The yellow ray is accentuated by a further yellow from Malkuth bathed in its Atziluthic colour.

The Amethyst ray also has great influence on Gedulah. This ray stems from Jupiter – Mundane Chakra of the sephirah, and will be influencing the Gedulah consciousness in every World. This ray never changes, although the others change World by World.

From the high octave of the blue ray the initiate can draw the qualities of patience and gentleness, two of the attributes he must develop to the full if he is to extract himself from the World of Assiah and its physical limitations.

Aid towards progress can be obtained from the yellow ray of creative activity, which can also be turned into a ray of spirituality providing the initiate chooses to use it in this direction.

The choice of how to use the creative activity can always be correctly made if the amethyst ray from Jupiter is employed. This is the spiritual ray and is always in attendance at this level of the Tree if called upon.

It is evident from the qualities available that the initiate should have no difficulty in successfully absorbing the lessons of Gedulah in Assiah by a judicious use of the rays that abound at this point on the Tree of Life.

Once the lessons have been absorbed and put into action the abyss can be crossed and the initiate is well on his way to the World of Yetzirah.

In Yetzirah

On reaching the World of Yetzirah the initiate makes progress up the Tree in Yesod until he is once again at the Gedulah level. The azure blue and yellow have now given way to a deep purple, a low octave of the purple ray. This ray will remain throughout the whole of his journey in the Yetziratic World.

It is from the changing rays of. the different sephirah that the initiate must rely for his progression. The Tree in Yesod is completely enveloped in indigo, Yesod's Atziluthic colour.

The purple ray is a royal ray, but at this low level of the Tree, and also a low octave of the ray, it can have vices that are so easy to slip into.

Some of the vices that the initiate could develop from this ray are pride, greatness, and a pomposity of which he may not even be aware. To avoid the pitfalls of the purple ray, use must be made of both the amethyst and the indigo.

Indigo must be used for its quality of devotion and the amethyst for its spiritual quality, so that a spiritual devotion is initiated, and with its development the vices of the purple ray will not only be subdued, but in course of time, conquered.

The greatness which the purple ray bestows can now be turned into spiritual greatness as opposed to egocentric greatness, the difference being a spiritual emotion instead of egocentric emotions.

Emotions are now controlled, bringing the initiate to the

realization that he is not his emotions but much more, and with this dawning truth he moves forward towards the Tree in Hod.

Hod has violet for its Atziluthic colour, which is a slightly higher octave of the purple ray than that of Gedulah in Yetzirah. Its qualities are also those of a higher plane of consciousness.

From the indigo ray the initiate receives a cautious characteristic which, if he is not careful, can develop into a fixation that will hold back his progress. It is now that he can call in the forceful power of the purple to drive him forward, and while proceeding with caution, prevent him becoming overcautious and coming to a halt.

Progress in Hod is slow, the lower mental body finding it difficult to expand outside the bounds of orthodoxy, but the forceful power drives him on within those bounds until he reaches their limit. It is then by use of the amethyst ray that he can see a vision beyond those boundaries, and reaches out towards it, ultimately reaching the Tree in Netzach.

At Gedulah in Netzach the visionary power of the amethyst ray now floods out and the initiate sees stretching before him a completely new plane of consciousness, free of limitations.

Amber clothes the Tree in Netzach, and from this high octave of the orange ray the initiate draws mental vigour which he combines with the forceful power from the purple ray. Consecration, one of the characteristics of amethyst, floods the initiate's mental body, and he spiritually consecrates himself to the ideals of service to humanity.

Through service he develops and progresses his own spiritual being, while at the same time his mental capacity is expanding and with the visionary outlook the higher mental body now commences to take over and the journey through the Tree in Tiphareth begins.

In the transition from the lower mental to higher mental plane of consciousness a struggle within takes place, and it is only the spiritual vision obtained from the amethyst ray that keeps him firmly on the path he has chosen to take.

From Tiphareth a ray of clear pink rose beams out, and the purple of Gedulah is transmuted into a magenta, an octave of the amethyst ray that creates a desire for religious or spiritual experience.

It is the spiritual experience of Gedulah in Tiphareth that teaches the initiate how the quality of greatness, obtained from the purple ray, can become true greatness.

Humility is a characteristic that also comes from the purple ray. This is the true greatness, the sinking of self for the benefit of all life, and once this lesson has been learned the Tree in Geburah calls the initiate with an irresistible pull.

Now at the stage of adeptship he prepares to learn the lessons of Gedulah in Geburah so that he may move forward to the state of Mastership.

Still there for his use are the purple and amethyst rays, but now there is also the overall ray of Geburah, the orange ray, to bring a fresh influence and give further impetus to the adept on his journey across time and space.

From the orange ray the adept can learn self-control and reliance, also the meaning of orderliness. By drawing on the amethyst ray he can reach attainment in mystical powers.

Through the merging of the amethyst with the purple ray a higher octave of the purple is produced from which can be absorbed the qualities of sensitiveness and generosity. There is also an influence of progressiveness emanating from this octave of the purple ray.

By the right use of the mystical powers obtained through the amethyst ray the adept can make an orderly progress through Gedulah and the remainder of the Tree in Geburah, moving across the Tree to Gedulah and the Tree contained within that sephirah.

The purple ray of the Yetziratic Gedulah now has the violet ray for a background. Violet is another octave of the purple ray which, at the level of Gedulah in Gedulah, is all-powerful. Only the amethyst from Jupiter cuts across the powerful royal ray.

A combination of violet and purple produces an octave of that ray, which, if drawn upon, creates a protective influence and gives understanding; two qualities that are essential to a master. It is also essential to absorb from the purple ray the quality of rulership.

It is the quality of rulership that is the main lesson to be learned at Gedulah in Gedulah. A rulership that is commanding and holds attention, but at the same time has understanding that blends into a balanced justice, gaining respect from lesser mortals, and forging a link of love between Master and pupil.

In no respect must the rulership be overbearing; neither must it be obvious. By judicious use of the amethyst ray the rulership of the purple can be developed into the friendly Master-pupil, or even an elder brother relationship.

Once the Master has developed these attributes to the full he is in the position to work for a period of cosmic time from this high level of the Tree, or maybe voluntarily descend to the lower levels for the specific task of helping humanity.

The time eventually comes when the Master's work at this level is completed and he crosses the abyss to the World of Briah.

In Briah

On the path of return the first Tree to contend with is that in Briah, where again the sphere of Gedulah is reached. Binah itself is clothed in crimson, an octave of the red ray.

Blue is the ray of Gedulah in Binah accompanied by the ever present amethyst flowing from Jupiter. The blue ray produces the quality of selfless love and this is the culmination of the lessons of Gedulah.

With the background influence of Binah, the great mother of the Tree, for the gathering together, absorbing and returning to its source, the Master finds that at Gedulah in Binah he must bring together all the qualities he has developed through his experiences on the journey up the Tree of Life.

By using the rays and merging the blue into the amethyst he produces an octave of the purple ray from which he can draw the quality of understanding, which is augmented by the Binah influence of this same quality.

Once the Master has brought the qualities together he must now use his attribute of understanding. Once this is absorbed into his eternal spark he is then prepared to use the crimson octave of the red ray to burn away all that is no longer required and what may impede his progress.

Using the crimson ray he commences the task of elimination. It is as the process of elimination carries on that the true understanding is developed of its purpose. Now he knows why all had to be absorbed into the eternal spark. When the elimination process is completed there is very little but the spark left, and through his highly developed understanding, the Master knows that what is left will be discarded at the level of the supernals on the Tree in Binah.

Drawing on the crimson for desire and impetus and on the amethyst to increase the spiritual desire, he progresses toward the top of the Tree in Binah and makes the crossing to the sphere of Chokmah.

Now the personality of the Master has gone and it is a spark of the whole that moves up the Tree in Chokmah to reach Gedulah in that state of consciousness.

The blue of Gedulah and the amethyst of Jupiter remains, but the crimson of Binah gives way to the pure soft blue ray of Chokmah. This is the highest octave of the blue ray.

With the blue predominant, both universal love and wisdom are the influences waiting for the spark to fully develop and by employing the Amethyst ray and drawing on its main quality the spark becomes near perfection through spiritual love and wisdom.

Once this state is acquired it is but a short step to Kether, the World of Atziluth, and in due course to Gedulah in Kether.

In Atziluth

In the World of Atziluth the last Tree is climbed and the last sephirah called Gedulah experienced.

The background of the Tree is brilliance, the synthesizing ray that blends all others into itself to become just pure light. Against this background the violet of Gedulah in Atziluth sparkles and really becomes alive. In a similar manner a living ray of amethyst beams out from Jupiter.

An indescribable spiritual humility comes from the combination of these two rays, and impregnating the spark brings it to perfection, the Gedulah archetype of perfect quiet strength with the true compassion that transcends the highest form of love.

GEBURAH

In Assiah

Geburah is the sephirah of severity, punishment, fear, and the symbol of death. It is the universal corrective. It is natural therefore, that in the World of Assiah – Malkuth on the main tree – that the rays of this sephirah are red and black.

The red ray is further accentuated by the Mundane Chakra of Geburah – Mars – which is also on the red ray. This mixture of red and black is set against a background of pure clear yellow, the Atziluthic colour of Assiah.

In the World of Assiah physical justice emanates from Geburah, and at this low level it is a very rough justice emanating from the red ray of will and power.

At the low level of Assiah it is the will and power to rule at all costs whether it be the rule of law or the rule of violence, and in its process it brings out the vices connected with power to a greater or lesser degree.

The rough justice would be even more harsh were it not for the black ray with its restrictive quality, and even this has its vices more than its virtues, albeit used in most cases unconsciously.

These adverse aspects only rule unconsciously where no true spiritual path is being followed. Once the student in the school of life takes the first step on the spiritual path the will and power is exercised with greater care and the better qualities brought out.

As the student gains more understanding the black is operated more, so that the will and power become controlled. It is at this point in his experience that the student calls upon the yellow ray with its quality of activity, an activity that can be employed at every level of consciousness.

With increasing mental consciousness the administration of justice is modified from rough to not so rough. He is now reaching the stage where the creative activity influence of the yellow ray can be drawn upon.

From the yellow ray the creative activity can be used in either direction, good or evil, according to the user; hence creative activity could be brought into being and used for organized crime by the head of a ring who, through the red ray, desired to rule and have power within the crime world.

The student who eventually arrives at the commencement of the spiritual path will use the creative activity in a manner beneficial to humanity and absorb the spiritual influence from the yellow ray. Now an improved form of justice is meted out by him and he in turn reaps the reward in the type of justice levelled upon him.

Even with this advancement the student's idea of justice is still in rigid confines through the merging of the black and yellow rays which, through merging, produce an octave of the orange ray.

Having once reached the highest standard of employing the Geburah principle through the use of its rays, the student is ready to move forward until he reaches the World of Yetzirah.

In Yetzirah

At Yesod, the first sephirah on the return journey in the World of Yetzirah, the sephirah of Geburah is a bright scarlet, a medium octave of the red ray. This ray will remain with Geburah throughout the whole of the Yetziratic world.

The black ray has now no activity within the sephirah and the rays that are to combine with the bright scarlet of Geburah are indigo, the ray of Yesod on the main Tree, and silver from the Moon – Mundane Chakra of Yesod.

Embodied in the bright scarlet octave of the red ray is the

energy of the other octaves, but in this particular octave the energies are in the lower directions. There are also the vices of self-pride and inflated ego attached to this octave.

The emotional nature of Yesod is inclined to highlight these vices, and it is at this stage that the student finds it so easy to slip into the role of rulership through the will and power influence, and to have great pride in his accomplishment, the first stage in the inflation of ego.

A vicious circle now develops as the inflated ego gives satisfaction to the emotions, which encourage further inflation of the ego, and through this circle the self-pride also grows. The cycle is only broken by the silver, a high octave of the grey ray which is lowered at this level of consciousness to a medium grey octave.

From this middle octave comes the incentive to the soul to struggle for freedom. It is in this struggle through a greater grasp on the grey ray that the quality of idealism creeps in, also from this middle octave.

Once idealistic thoughts have been implanted the self-pride disappears and the ego commences to decrease. Slowly the student commences to take control of the emotions and reaches upwards to a more mental level.

From the indigo ray the emotions are still being fed by religious superstition which comes from this ray, but it has a twofold effect. First, it plays on the emotions to the degree that it makes it more difficult to subdue the ego, and at the other end of the scale, the second aspect of this octave of the indigo ray, the aroused religious superstition makes the student think that ego and pride are unforgivable sins, and so he sets to work to remove them and so resumes his journey back on the path until he comes to the Tree in Hod.

The bright scarlet has now for companion rays the violet purple of Hod and yellow from its Mundane Chakra – Mercury.

The self-pride now takes on a different aspect. It is the pride in his religious achievements, his knowledge and faith. This in turn brings into play the ego, that form of ego which says I have found the true religion, here am I, amongst the saved, why are you not like me.

There is also at this plane of consciousness a belief in Divine justice, but this aspect of Geburah in Hod is one of limited comprehension. It is a justice bound in the narrow confines of Hod rigidity, conforming to a pattern that is synonymous with the religious beliefs.

It is barriers such as these that the initiate has to break down, but such can be the stubborness and stupidity of the lower mental body that it is not an easy task, and the pompous quality of the purple ray adds to the difficulties.

From the scarlet octave of the red ray the initiate can obtain the surging power to push forward. First he feels an unconscious irritation as periodically he comes up against the boundary of conformity, and then as he commences to draw upon the yellow ray the desire for activity becomes even greater.

The yellow ray has the attribute to quicken and make more alert the mental body. As it does so the initiate consciously realizes the irritations of the red ray and the will to break the narrow confines of Hod strengthens.

Now making full use of the red ray driving force and the intellectual yellow, the initiate moves away from his rigid stand. With reverence and spiritual dedication, both attributes of violet – another octave of the purple ray – he conquers Geburah in Hod and in due course of time has to deal with Geburah on the Tree in Netzach.

Amber, a high octave of the orange ray, is now the all-pervading background to the scarlet of Geburah, and penetrating through the two is the blue ray from Venus.

Still in the lower mental plane of consciousness the scarlet can have a pull in the direction of lower energies, and the initiate can waste a lot of time following useless and ineffectual causes. At this stage of consciousness the irritant of the scarlet can make him treat lightly of intellectual matters, and he is inclined more to the simple beauty of harmony through an idealistic mental trend.

It is from the blue ray that these qualities of beauty and harmony spring. The initiate is only using the love aspect of the ray overlooking the wisdom aspect. It is only when the influence of the amber begins to take effect on him, and he captures from it the quality of mental vigour, that he understands the need for wisdom.

With the use of both aspects of the blue ray – love and wisdom – true discretion is developed, and an understanding of justice which had evaded him in the lower spheres. Justice could only be done by the achievement of perfect balance, and this necessitates the blending of wisdom with harmony and beauty.

From the amber comes the quality of wholeness. Wisdom tells him this can only be obtained from within, and then only if impurities are rectified. To reach that state of consciousness he must make sacrifices, and with this dawning awareness he moves on through the Tree in Netzach to that in Tiphareth.

The bright scarlet of Geburah is now joined by the pink rose of Tiphareth and the golden orange of the Sun. At the Tiphareth level the red ray is predominant, pink rose being a high octave of the red ray.

Progress for the initiate is now very much slower due to the amount of the red ray streaming out. To control this is no easy task, but to be controlled by it is quite simple. Golden orange is his salvation, with its qualities of geniality and receptiveness.

Once the initiate commences to use the golden orange with its qualities, then the mental body is open to the full conscious influence of the rose pink with its attributes of comfort and unselfishness. Now he commences to sacrifice some of the ideas and ideals that had meant so much to him but had prevented him from finding a true balance.

Beauty, the initiate realizes, is something far higher and deeper than what he considered beauty to be at the Netzach level. Through the use of the rose pink the initiate is aware that beauty is a spiritual thing extending beyond the range of

Malkuth or Netzach.

By blending the golden orange with the red ray a more medium octave of the orange ray is brought into being with the quality of self-control. Now he is in a position to gain that perfect balance, but although obtained, there are still past karmic debts to be paid.

With a balanced view of justice he is fully aware that the spiritual goal can never be reached until he has worked out all his karma, and so he prepares to move forward to the cosmic seat of justice – Geburah.

Having passed through the initiation of Tiphareth the adept is now faced with Geburah on the Tree in Geburah. The whole of the Tree is surrounded and impregnated by an orange glow, the Atziluthic colour of Geburah. The bright scarlet of Geburah's Yetziratic colour is added to by the red that streams from Mars.

With the self-control of the orange ray and trust, a further quality of the orange, the adept prepares to meet his judgement and accept the justice meted out by the cosmic and unalterable Divine law.

Understanding, as he now does, the adept works and co-operates with the red ray and thereby is able to draw from it the will to go through this phase of experience, and though he does not avoid the justice of Geburah he can transmute it.

Once he gains victory over Geburah a further initiation is completed and the adept that entered the Tree in Geburah now leaves it as a Master to enter the Tree in Gedulah.

At Geburah on the Tree in Gedulah the bright scarlet has a background of violet, Gedulah's Atziluthic colour, and from the Mundane Chakra streams forth the amethyst.

The Master is now in the sphere of the Masters and the Masters' work, part of which is to send out to the lower planes of consciousness guidance and help in every possible way. Now the Master fully controls the scarlet and blends it into the amethyst flowing from Jupiter, so that he now controls a medium octave of the amethyst ray.

Qualities that are available from this particular octave of

the amethyst are those of altruism, idealism and the visionary. These are essential attributes that the Master must possess, but they can be dangerous if acted upon in the full expansiveness of Jupiter.

It is here at Gedulah that there can be the same idealism as at Netzach, but on a much higher plane of consciousness. To conquer the Tree in Gedulah the Master must carry out the Masters' work to the point of perfection.

From the violet he absorbs the quality of spiritual dedication, also humility, and it is the humility that aids him to carry out his tasks in a discretionary manner. Although much has been gained from his many experiences and the Master has developed powers and gained knowledge, he realizes that even this state is a lowly one in the scheme of things and the law of justice must take its course.

His task is to guide and help others as they pay their karmic debt, and by sending the right influences down through the lower planes, prevent others creating a karmic debt.

After carrying out this task over a period of cosmic time he has earned the right to move forward on his own evolutionary path. With the will and power from the red ray and spiritual dedication from the violet, he progresses from the higher mental plane to the Buddhic level, where he commences to conquer the Tree in Binah.

In Briah

Now the scarlet octave of the red ray floods the whole of Geburah on the background of scarlet, the Atziluthic colour of Binah.

With its influence towards the lower energies the Master is pulled back towards the peace and comparative calm of Gedulah by the strength and power of the scarlet.

Inward conflict now takes place as he struggles to go forward knowing that it is the right course, but progress is slow and the desire to return to the Tree in Gedulah is stronger. From the high octave of the black ray, given out by

Saturn, comes the meditative quality, and through this the Master realizes that pure justice demands he return this way just as he came out through Binah.

With the use of the black ray he develops the last of his latent powers and through this is able to extract from the red ray the will to destroy his personality through allowing the purging fire of the same ray to take away the last impurities, the greatest of which was desire, a desire to retain his personality.

Once this desire is removed he can move on through the Tree in Binah, meeting and conquering other obstacles until at last he is free and as a spark of the whole he moves to the Tree in Chokmah.

Chokmah is a mass of pure soft blue which tones the scarlet of Geburah into a light amethyst from which the spark obtains final spiritual attainment, and from the pure blue the spiritual sedative. It is from Chokmah that the spark views all the experiences it has been through, and how the cosmic justice has followed it in every phase and experience of its journey across time and space.

The spark now prepares to take the last initiation in the lesson of universal or cosmic justice. All around from the sphere of the zodiac the spark is bombarded by the twelve rays as the Host of Angels working in Chokmah send them streaming out through the Tree. Nevertheless the blue of Chokmah and the scarlet of Geburah are the predominant rays playing on the spark.

The ray forces at this level are extremely powerful and although transmuted as they go down the various planes of consciousness, can still be devastating, even at the lowest level if wrongly used. The spark sees and understands the need for pure justice, which is the perfect balance of all the rays.

With this understanding the eternal spark completes the last stage of perfection in Geburah by balancing the red ray of will and power with the transmuting quality of the blue and is now ready to move into the Atziluthic world.

In Atziluth

Geburah on the Tree in Kether has now changed from the scarlet red to orange which is against the background of brilliance, the Atziluthic colour of Kether, which is the Atziluthic World.

The spark now becomes the perfected aspect of justice and though retaining its individuality, merges with all other sparks that have reached this same level.

Brilliance is the ultimate thirteenth ray which all other rays spring from and to which they return. It is also the ultimate perfection of the whole, only the orange ray distinguishes the Geburah aspect of the whole. This is a scintillating orange by virtue of the brilliance and as such embodies all aspects of the orange ray in all the octaves and at every level of consciousness, and so all the qualities, practical knowledge, receptivity, wholeness, self-control, orderliness and justice are blended into one.

All the sparks that have reached Geburah on the Tree in Atziluth have absorbed these qualities and are the centre which gives the perfect archetype of justice.

TIPHARETH

In Assiah

Tiphareth is the sephirah of harmony and balance. It is the centre of The Tree or The Universe. Many of the paths on The Tree either come down or go up and meet at Tiphareth, which makes it a very important centre. This is the meeting place, not only of the higher and lower mental planes, but the bridge between the higher and lower worlds.

In Assiah, Tiphareth responds to a golden amber, a high octave of the orange ray, but it is influenced by the four rays which emanate from the four elements – Mundane Chakra of Malkuth.

From the world of Assiah – Malkuth – the yellow ray provides the background to all the other rays. Although the student is in the physical world the plane of consciousness is a high one and when he touches this state a vision of how the universe operates opens up before him, showing the intrinsic harmony that governs it.

The golden amber gives practical knowledge and receptivity with wholeness and geniality, and the yellow provides the qualities of well-being and helpfulness. All these are the lessons of Tiphareth, which the student must learn and develop.

Even at this level in Assiah the first rays the student heeds are those of the elements. Red, the fiery will-power ray, blue, the love wisdom ray, yellow, ray of creative activity and the green of harmony through struggle and conflict.

It is from these rays that the student can fall from the

grace of Tiphareth unless he can conquer the vices inherent within them sufficiently for him to fulfil his task and experience the sephirah. Even at this high level vices exist. It is still only the physical world – Assiah.

The yellow gives the influence and has the power of creative activity in any direction the student desires. Because of this it is perhaps the most important ray at this stage of his evolution. From the red ray he obtains the will and desire to rule. Tiphareth is the sphere of a king and a child, but quite often the student only accepts the king aspect through the desire of the red.

Even the blue bestows its vice, that of the selfish love that gives out in the hopes of a return that will be more beneficial than what has been given; in other words, the love of self or benefit to self. The green ray brings with it greed, envy and jealousy. All or any one of these can bring failure to the student's attempts to conquer Tiphareth in Assiah.

It is only when the student commences to use the golden amber octave of the orange ray that he makes progress. With its receptivity and great organizing ability the power of this ray works for the benefit of the whole, through its own quality of wholeness, rather than for the love of power itself.

Here is the first indication to the student of sacrifice, which is one of the attributes of Tiphareth, the sacrifice of self for the whole. The student does however need more than this ray to aid him, but once he has absorbed the influence of the golden amber, the yellow ray of illumination and creative activity is brought into use and the mental body becomes more attuned to using the rays.

Now the student can control the rays and by a careful blending of the red with the blue he produces an octave of the purple ray which possesses the quality of humility.

Still a king, but of a different nature, now emerges. It is a king born of a spiritual nature with the humility of a child. The struggle and conflict of the green ray is over and its quality of harmony is achieved, and from the golden amber influence a great warmth of feeling and compassion is poured out which embraces the whole of life.

Tiphareth in Assiah has been conquered and the student moves on through Assiah to the World of Yetzirah.

In Yetzirah

At the first Tree in the Yetziratic world, that of Yesod, the student progresses through many experiences until he reaches Tiphareth, where the golden amber has given way to a salmon pink, a high octave of the red ray and the background colour is now indigo. Interspersing these two rays is the silver of Yesod's Mundane Chakra – the Moon.

The task of conquering Tiphareth in Yesod is perhaps more difficult than Tiphareth on any other Tree, due mainly to the fluidic state of consciousness in which this Tree exists. Yesod is governed by the water element, and although this has its stability it also has its moving tides.

Indigo, Yesod's Atziluthic colour, is a very devotional ray and as such can have a very strong emotional appeal which adds to the fluctuations at this level of being. The student has the task of obtaining balance and harmony, while at the same time being fluidic. The words of the poet Tennyson sums up the position very well.

> When such a moving tide as this
> Too still for sound and foam
> Turns again Home.

The devotion of the indigo ray can through its emotional side give the student an appreciation of beauty which is also a quality of Tiphareth. Once he has gained this appreciation he can from Tiphareth view both the higher and lower emotions, his first step towards balance.

From the salmon pink the qualities of high affections and love can be obtained, and it is when he tunes into this ray that he begins to see the need for harmonizing the emotions, and so he brings into play the silver octave of the grey ray coming from the Moon.

At this low level of the main Tree the silver is not pure but is a light grey; still quite a high octave of this ray, and amongst its virtues is that of stability and harmony.

Through the use of this ray the student now blends the lower and higher emotions to a point of balance and peace at Tiphareth in Yesod. With the emotions under control, so that only the beauty and balanced love is expressed through them, he is now ready to face the rest of the Tree in Yesod, and in course of time moves on to Hod.

Hod is enshrouded in violet purple, a medium octave of the purple ray. The salmon pink of Tiphareth is still there and these are now joined by the yellow ray which issues from Mercury.

At Tiphareth in Hod the initiate is now at the centre of the sephirah of splendour and stellar light. His task at this point is to sacrifice this glory and splendour for the humble path of spiritual progression. He has also to sacrifice all his preconceived ideas and follow a fresh train of thought.

With the rigidity of a conditioned mind this poses a problem for the initiate, and it is only when he commences to use the yellow ray and bring its creative activity influence to bear upon his lower mental body that the barriers of the mind commence to weaken and eventually break down.

Once the barriers are down the mental body is now free to follow fresh impulses. The love impulses from the salmon pink draws him now to a wider view, and the yellow activity gives the stimulant to search for it.

From the use of the violet the initiate develops the quality of humility and spiritual dedication. Now he can, in full, sacrifice all previous ideas that held him prisoner in a narrow groove and pave the way to freedom from the Tree in Hod and advance to the state of Netzach.

Netzach has for its overall colour amber, a high octave of the orange ray which the initiate can manipulate in conjunction with the salmon pink and the blue, which comes from Venus, part of the Netzach influence.

The lower mental body at Tiphareth in Netzach has to turn to higher things, and one lesson to be learned in this particular experience is that love without restraint and discrimination is just as bad as not having the quality. The salmon pink has to be balanced and this is where the blue ray can be useful if the initiate will draw upon it, and by its use have love with wisdom, the blue being the love/wisdom ray.

The influence of the amber ray instils into him a sense of wholeness and justice. Only then he realizes, through the blue and amber, that love, however pure, if uncontrolled leads to weakness and becomes more of a liability than an asset.

With ever-increasing wisdom and wholeness, once more, he brings balance and harmony to his being, with love and justice blending into harmony, enabling him to see the higher vision and make for it.

At Tiphareth on the Tree in Tiphareth he has to balance the higher and lower mental bodies until he can see the beauty and harmony of them both, in their individuality and blended into a wholeness with each playing its part.

Clear pink rose, Atziluthic colour of Tiphareth, now blends with the salmon pink of the Yetziratic Tiphareth, and through the high octaves of the red ray shines the orange of Tiphareth's sun.

From the pink octaves the adept can obtain healing power of a magnetic nature and it is this power that he brings to bear on the two mental bodies, welding them into a oneness and yet each retaining its own individuality.

By this action the adept balances them both and there is a united mental body that can retain the quality of wholeness produced by the orange ray.

In his accomplishment the adept has to make sacrifices in as much as he has to discard certain aspects of both bodies, and although they are the vices of those bodies they are not always seen in that light.

Moving ever forward, the adept successfully ascends the Tree in Tiphareth, moving all the time towards Tiphareth on the Tree in Geburah, where – with the salmon pink – the orange of Geburah are his tools, also the red ray of Mars, part of the Geburah influence.

Geburah, as the symbol of death, must by this virtue also

be the symbol of re-birth and the adept must realize that one is complementary to the other, and to achieve true Mastership he must be prepared to sacrifice one life to attain another.

Although this may appear obvious and sounds simple to do, when the moment arrives there are doubts and uncertainties which can still be there, even at this high level of consciousness.

Only the true balanced outlook of life and death can enable even an adept to make this sacrifice knowingly and willingly, and to do this the full use of the rays must be made.

From the red ray he can draw the will and power required for his task. From the pink he takes the quality of comfort, and from the influence of the orange ray he can obtain self-control and practical knowledge. With these attributes he develops the balance needed to go through the purging experience of Geburah and eventually emerge into the new life of a Master of the Wisdom.

The journey takes him ever onwards and upwards until in Gedulah, the sphere of the Masters, he reaches Tiphareth on the Tree in that sephirah.

Rays that are to have influences useful to the Master at this point of his journey are the salmon pink of Tiphareth, deep violet, the Atziluthic colour of Gedulah, and the amethyst from Jupiter.

Although Gedulah is on the higher mental plane of consciousness, it is still part of the formative world, and as such, still holds a certain amount of form. At Tiphareth in Gedulah the Master has now to prepare for, and commence to discard, the formative world.

Temptations to remain at this level of the formative world are subtle. Part of the Master's work at Gedulah level is to help those below, and it is through this that the temptation comes, to stay and help. A perfect justification for desiring to remain at Gedulah.

The love for all humanity that the Master has developed is also another subtle temptation to stay, and the last temptation is the power that he now holds at this level of being and which will dissipate in its use as he progresses on his path.

Through the use of the violet octave of the purple ray, spiritual dedication can be developed, and through this the power complex and temptation can be overcome. With the spiritual dedication attribute urging him to further progress on the journey towards the ultimate he also develops humility from the amethyst ray.

In true humility he recognizes that more than he are helping the lower levels, and that he has reached the stage where he can help far better by proceeding to still higher spheres where there is less limitation.

Now in his humility and with spiritual dedication he has to acknowledge that his tremendous love for all levels below him is still not the ultimate, but only the highest point of love in the physical and formative worlds.

At this point he has come to, and is prepared to make, the Tiphareth sacrifice of power and love, and with the amethyst ray sending out an influence of mystical attainment the Master makes the sacrifice and proceeds up the Tree to the point where he is prepared to leave Gedulah.

In Briah

In Briah the Master's first experience is on the Tree in Binah with its overshadowing colour of Crimson, a very high octave of the red ray. The sephirah Tiphareth in the Briatic world now responds to a yellow gold – another high octave, but on the yellow ray – and working in with these rays is the black, which emanates from Saturn.

The Master is now faced with a number of different tasks. First he must learn to balance the form and the formless. From the black ray he can experience restriction and know the frustration of an overplus of this ray, just as his experience of the unrestrained yellow activity ray makes him realize the need for restraint, and it is from these experiences that he learns to handle the rays and create a fine balance that shows the form fluidic enough to be – at the same time – formless.

The purpose and need for Binah is now clearly seen and placed in true perspective. Once this is seen, then the high point of love expressed by the pink octave in Gedulah is transmuted to that higher state of compassion which is restricted into correct channels by the black ray, so that the pure justice of the red ray is not disrupted and the universal law of Karma operates smoothly with the aid of the yellow activity ray.

This is the true compassion that can transmute Karma, inasmuch as it eases the burden, making it bearable by a smooth operation of payment of karmic debts. The Master learns that unrestricted compassion increases Karma for both giver and receiver.

Having achieved this balance between restriction of form and the formless, the Master is now prepared to move on towards the sephirah of the formless.

Chokmah, the second sephirah in the Briatic World, knows no form but through all experiences the eternal spark does know balance. At Tiphareth on the Tree in Chokmah the sephirah retains its golden yellow ray, but the crimson of Binah has now at Chokmah changed to a pure soft blue, high octave of the blue ray.

From the sphere of the zodiac – Mundane Chakra of Chokmah – stream all the other rays. The spark now becomes a mediator and all efforts are directed towards sending out and keeping the rays in perfect balance and harmony.

At the heart of the Tree in Chokmah the spark beholds the beauty and harmony of balance which is the basic quality of Tiphareth on all Trees in every World. It also beholds how it requires the cross of sacrifice to achieve this balance.

In Atziluth

In the archetypal world the brilliance of Kether sets the whole Tree shimmering with a vibrating, scintillating light which illuminates the clear pink rose of Tiphareth on the Tree in Kether. From the Four Holy Living Creatures flow out the red, blue, yellow and green rays.

The spark now perfectly balanced at Tiphareth in Kether appreciates the beauty of colour and how the harmony of the rays is formed at the commencement of their projection from the three major rays, red, blue and yellow, controlled by the stabilizing green ray of harmony, which is obtained through the struggle and conflict of first the separation of the rays, and later through their merging. It is in these processes that Tiphareth holds a key position as the perfect archetype of beauty, harmony and balance.

NETZACH

In Atziluth

In the Archetypal World Netzach is the perfection of the arts, idealistic philosophy, imaginative inventions and the realm of abstract thought.

On the Tree in Atziluth, Netzach has the colour of amber and the ray from its Mundane Chakra is blue, and the overall background colour of the Atziluthic World is the brilliance of which all other rays are but aspects.

The amber octave of the orange ray gives to Netzach that higher vision and level of receptivity that Hod lacks; receptivity to new thoughts and ideas coming in, aided by the blue ray of Love, and at this level of the Tree, in particular, the Wisdom aspect; and although at a low level of the Tree, the brilliance of Atziluth still gives great clarity of the universal thought and mind.

In Briah

The first aspect of Briah on the way down the Tree is Chokmah with its overall colour of pure soft blue and it is on the Tree in this sephirah that Netzach is next considered.

Netzach's own overall colour has now become emerald green. The sephirah obtains its new ray from the effects of rays flowing down from Gedulah (blue) and from Tiphareth (yellow), the two merging at Netzach.

From the Mundane Chakra of Netzach the blue ray flows forth and will continue to do so all the way down The Tree. All other rays may change from tree to tree, but the

Mundane Chakra, Venus, remains with its flow of Love and Wisdom.

Tolerance, adaptability and love of nature are qualities that spring from this octave of the green ray, and where it merges with the blue ray of Chokmah, creating another octave, there are the qualities of tact and diplomacy.

A further quality of the emerald octave of the green ray is ambition, with the wisdom of Chokmah accentuated by the blue ray. This can lead to the wrong form of ambition as it can be applied for the sake of power, the Wisdom being used to obtain it. Even the love aspect of the blue ray would not counteract this, as in the free flowing atmosphere of Netzach – and with the as yet uncontrolled force of Chokmah – it could be a selfish love that would justify its actions. Only on the way back up The Tree, when it would be controlled by the conscious consciousness, would the right aspect of love and wisdom prevail, and the consciousness would absorb, and incline more to, the gentleness of the pale blue.

It is because of this free-flowing, uncontrolled force that Binah plays a part in the Briatic world. The basic colour of Binah is crimson and Netzach on The Tree in Binah is brought under its influence. This is an octave of the red ray, Netzach also having a restricting influence of the black ray from the Mundane Chakra of Binah, which is Saturn.

This black ray, merging with the green and blue rays, produces a very dark blue verging on indigo, which possesses the qualities of the lowest and darkest octave of the blue ray, a very interesting mixture considering that Binah is the sephirah where the first major deviation takes place with the advent of controlling form, nebulous though it may be at this high level of consciousness.

On this high octave of the indigo ray are the qualities of foresight, coldness, clarity of thought, construction and caution. If these qualities are examined closely, it will be seen how they are part of the Binah influence.

At the lowest octave of the blue ray there is again

selfishness; here also is religious fervour, very near to the utterly devotional quality that is very apparent on the lower octaves of indigo, aided by the exciting crimson.

Indigo is itself a synthesizing ray on one of the higher octaves of colour and again this is truly a Binah characteristic: the bringing together into form and synthesizing or blending all these qualities into a whole, ready for transfer to the World of Yetzirah.

In Yetzirah

The first stage in the formative World of Yetzirah is the sephirah, Gedulah. The Atziluthic ray for this sephirah is deep violet and it is on this background that the Tree in Gedulah is placed, and into this merges the yellow and green rays, which are now the colours of Netzach throughout all the six sephiroth in Yetzirah.

From the deep violet octave of the purple ray stem the qualities of spiritual dedication, humility, and reverence; just the qualities that would be expected in the sphere of the Masters.

Bright yellow green is the actual colour of Netzach in Yetzirah, and the bright yellow octave of this ray gives out the influence of happiness and friendliness so appropriate to Gedulah and to the wider view of Netzach. It also brings out the wisdom of the intellect, which is another Netzach trait associated with the lower mental body, of which this sephirah is part; the wisdom aspect is further developed from the blue ray of Netzach's Mundane Chakra.

The bright green aspect brings out the qualities of charity and understanding which are undoubtedly part of the Netzach sphere of influence. These latter qualities are not directly characteristic of bright green but flow out because the blue ray changes it to a light pastel green.

The true influences of bright green are jealousy, and unconsciously greedy, and these are qualities that can flow from the sephirah Netzach, particularly at the Yetziratic level.

Orange is the overall Atziluthic colour of Geburah, and is the middle octave of the orange ray from which flows the influence of energy which, in the World of Yetzirah, could be in lower directions. It also contains the characteristics of self-pride and an inflated ego.

These adverse qualities are mitigated to a degree by the blue ray emanating from the Mundane Chakra of Netzach, and when the two rays merge they produce a combined ray which has the influence of spiritual phenomena and religious experiences which could be the karmic implications of the adverse qualities of the orange ray; a true transmutation through the love-wisdom ray, and the self-control of the orange.

The merging of the green and yellow rays add strength to the blue ray, but the individual characteristics of both will also show through according to circumstances and reactions.

Clear pink rose as the overall Atziluthic colour of Tipareth, replaces the orange ray of Geburah as we examine Netzach on the Tree in the sephirah of sacrifice. This octave of the red ray holds within it the qualities of blind trust and immaturity that can lead to reckless sacrifice – which serves no good purpose. The yellow ray also adds to mental activity with quick decisions, not always correct. It is left to the wisdom aspect of the blue ray to prevail over these qualities, and aided by the calming influence of the green ray, a balance can be attained in all the aspects of Netzach. The pink must be merged with the blue so that the yellow ray can direct its creative activity in the right channels, with the green providing harmony that results in the Victory of Netzach.

On the Tree in Netzach the bright green/yellow has a background of amber, the colour of Netzach in the Atziluthic World, and this gives geniality, receptivity, mental vigour and justice.

It is probably from the amber influence that Netzach obtains its philosphical qualities, with the wider view that marks it the extreme opposite of Hod. The yellow ray of creative activity is susceptible to the amber influence and becomes receptive to new ideas, a typical Netzach quality.

The blue ray responds to the geniality, and the green to the idea of justice. Mental vigour is accentuated by the yellow ray combining with the amber and gives ultimate victory to the deeper philosophy which forms a large part of the Netzach philosphy.

Netzach on the Tree in Hod has for its background a violet purple which is one of the higher octaves of the purple ray. From this octave flows the principles of spiritual dedication, reverence and adoration.

These qualities incline to a concretion of form and the yellow ray, active within that form, tends to give an over-bearing attitude of intellectual superiority that is supported by the quality of rulership which is an aspect of the purple ray. This is the answer to the pomp and splendour of the Church, limited within its own intellectual dogma and spiritual dedication to that dogma.

This all portrays the true atmosphere of Hod, which is one of the concretion of form, and as such, worships with dedication, the form more than what is contained within it.

In Yesod, the last sphere on the way down of the formative or Yetziratic World, has for its overall background ray the Atziluthic colour of indigo. The octave of this ray at the level of Yesod holds the qualities of blind devotion. With the yellow ray creating activity, there is the tendency toward devotional fanaticism for any sphere of idealism, broad or narrow.

The green ray, throwing in its influence, can add strength and conflict at this level of consciousness through the blind devotion. The redeeming feature of Netzach in Yesod is the silver ray, somewhat grey at this low level, bringing a calming influence, although at this octave of the ray, there is the quality of deception there. This is not surprising as this ray emanated from the Moon, Mundane Chakra of Yesod.

It is this silvery grey mixing with the green that brings out the emotion of jealousy, and indeed with the devotion of the indigo ray can develop into a devotion of hatred as might be found in a witch on the black path. This is indeed a sphere of trial and conflict and were it not for the wider application of philosophical thought and the quality of victory belonging to the sephirah of Netzach itself, there would be little hope of release from the whirling maelstrom of conflicting illusory ideas.

A modicum of wisdom and emotional love flows through from Venus bringing a ray of illumination, and with the quieter influence of the grey ray, brings an aspect of sanity and true realization to Netzach in Yesod.

In Assiah

Netzach in Assiah is the culmination of all the other stages down The Tree and it is now far removed from the idea of Netzach in the World of Atziluth, where it was conceived in amber. At the level of Assiah it is olive green flecked with gold; the gold being the last tiny semblance of the Atziluth colour. It is, however, against the yellow Atziluthic background of Malkuth. From the Mundane Chakra of Malkuth stream forth the red, blue, green and yellow rays of the four elements.

Netzach now has the influence of all seven, as the three primaries merge and blend with the fourth ray, green, but predominant is the yellow ray of creative activity that keeps not only the spirit of the sephirah moving, but of all life that makes up the world of Assiah.

The olive green brings in the element of struggle and conflict accentuated by the green ray from the Mundane Chakra of Malkuth. The red gives energy and impulse, and the blue exercises its love influence. All these rays are working at a low level and it is the task of the Netzach qualities to overcome the lower impulses and raise them to the mental level from the mud of Assiah.

HOD

In Assiah

Hod in Assiah has a predominance of yellow over all the other rays that influence this sphere at the physical level. There is the overall colour of Assiah which is the yellow ray, this ray also streams forth from the Mundane Chakra of Hod – Mercury – and from the air element of the Mundane Chakra of Assiah itself.

The sephirah Hod is yellowish brown flecked white at this level of The Tree. The other colours or rays that have an influence on the sephirah are the red, blue and green rays which stem from the Mundane Chakra of Assiah or Malkuth on the main Tree.

It can be seen that this overall picture indicates activity at many levels which might be expected in the physical world, the yellow ray creating the activity. The blue ray brings the love and wisdom, even though at a low level, just as the red gives will and power, that is of a very material nature. The brown ray gives to the sephirah a studious element, mainly in the field of material progress.

All these influences are operating within the crystallized ideas of Hod and conforming to the form and standards of the day. The situation, however, is not so depressing as it looks. There is the white ray flickering dimly through to keep the spiritual aspect still alive, and with the aid of the yellow ray, whose other aspect is that of the creative spirit, the Brown ray can be diverted from the study of the material to a spiritual study. The blue ray of love and wisdom can be expanded from the personal to the benefit of others.

Even the red ray can be diverted into the fields of exploration where the will and power can aid the pioneer in his task and the destructive side of the ray channelled to destroy the barriers that impede progress, and it is these two opposites of all the rays that – through the green ray – bring struggle and conflict into the sephirah.

In Yetzirah

The overall Atziluthic colour of Yesod, the first point of the Yetziratic World on the path of return, is indigo. This is the devotional ray, but at this level a fairly low octave of the ray.

Hod in Yetzirah has now changed its rays to red-russet and retains this colour throughout the whole of the six trees, the only variation being that of the Atziluthic colour behind and overshadowing the Trees in the different sephirah.

The red-russet brings in the influence of the red and brown rays, apart from the qualities of their merging into one. The red ray incites devotional fervour and the brown ray the studiousness that can lead to a deep meditational devotion. The red-russet combination provides knowledge, but it is without wisdom. Here can be seen the limiting influence, the quality of Hod.

Basic emotions, the qualities of Yesod bound within the limitations of Hod, can develop into an explosive situation, and it is from just such a situation that this force flows down into Assiah, developing there into the fervent devotion to a religion or an idea. It could have been one such explosion of this type of influence that brought the Christian Church in with such fervour, and from the influence of the red ray in a later explosion of this influence from Yesod, came the Inquisition.

It is only when the yellow ray with its intellectual wisdom penetrates from the Mundane Chakra of Hod with sufficient power to predominate for a period, that the Hod influences in Hod can be felt in the lower world of Assiah.

The Atziluthic colour of Hod is a violet purple, a medium octave of the purple ray with spiritual dedication and adoration as two of its qualities. Here is the situation of Hod in Hod and so the form is very rigid and the only means of outlet from this rigidity is the double force of the yellow ray of activity which influences from the Mundane Chakra of both Hods. It is this restricting influence of form that flows down into Assiah and holds within limits that Yesodic emotional force.

Just as, in many instances, the red ray can be a destroyer ray, in this instance it helps to create. The amount of red that flows in is just sufficient to create the quality of zeal, and in this case it is for the construction of form, which keeps uncontrollable forces in check, preventing them being too devasting and shattering.

At this level of The Tree Hod performs very similar functions, at a lower level of consciousness, to that of Binah at the higher level, and it is because of this that universal law endows it with the yellow ray to give a creative and active intellect; otherwise the restricting power would be so great that the forces essential to creation would be bound within its limitations, free to flow neither up nor down, and life would become stultified.

With the yellow ray qualities and the depth of study from the brown ray, it is possible for life to flow through to Netzach aided by the quality of adoration from the violet purple. Where in some instances this quality could be applied to a God or Master, in other instances it can be the adoration of knowledge, and with the red ray creating the influence of the explorer, the life force can plumb the depths of Netzach.

Hod on the Tree in Netzach is overshadowed by the Atziluthic colour of amber adding further to the quality of intellect, and with the brown ray aiding in the absorption of study Netzach becomes a centre of idealism, philosophy and the further reaches of the mind, which leads upward to Tiphareth and the commencement of the higher mental realms.

The overshadowing colour of Tiphareth is a clear pink rose, a high octave of the red ray. Here are the qualities of universal love and forgiveness, although at the Hod in Tiphareth level they are somewhat far from this ideal state due to the primary red of Hod lowering the octave. The brown, too, can bring in the absorption of self, but with the yellow ray from Hod's Mundane Chakra there are periodic bursts of spiritual activity that enables the true love, which more often than not brings sacrifice in its wake, to break through, and the Geburah level is attained.

Orange is the basic colour of Geburah, and it is now this ray that merges with the red-russet of Hod and the yellow flowing in from Mercury. Self-control, trust, reliance, are the attributes of this octave of the orange ray and this is the purpose of Geburah, to teach these qualities by virtue of its corrective attitude. The red ray with its impulsive characteristics is toned down and becomes controlled in its fire and drive by the restraining influence of the orange ray. The yellow ray of activity is also channelled into the activity of the spiritual being, but at the same time it activates the russet, so preventing this octave of the brown ray becoming too introspective.

On the Tree in Gedulah deep violet is the predominating over-all background to the Yetziratic colours of Hod. Here is an octave of the purple ray that gives out the influences of humility and reverence. At this level of The Tree this is the true reverence for all life, far removed from that imperfect reverence of a God which does not prevent the worshippers from slaying fellow man, which is the type of reverence to be found in Assiah, where it is largely influenced by material and emotional desires.

At this level of consciousness there is the true humility that realizes how small everything is in the universe and therefore the true spiritual reverence is born activated by the yellow ray of spiritual purpose.

The brown ray helps to bring the sober realization of the true state of all that makes up life and the red ray provides the driving force to bring the influence of humility and reverence to every aspect of the one life.

In Briah

The Tree in Binah is overshadowed by crimson and apart from the yellow ray of its Mundane Chakra, Hod now gives out the qualities of the orange ray.

It is from this ray that the idea of form becomes so strong and difficulty is found in discarding the personality. Crimson, an octave of the red ray, has the effect of inflating the ego and the quality of self-centredness, increasing the difficulties of dispensing with the personality.

With the yellow ray and its element of air the crimson is fanned into flames and the spiritual activity aids in the realization that the personality must be burnt away before further progress can be made. This is part of the work carried out by the crimson under the able direction of the yellow ray, and with this achieved, Chokmah becomes the sphere of activity.

The orange sphere of Hod is now surrounded and impregnated by the soft pale blue of Chokmah. This high octave of the blue ray endows Hod with wisdom, selfless love and kindness. It is also the octave that endows all within its reach with a spiritual sedative. The fire of the red ray that influenced Hod for so long has now dissipated and the only activity lies within the yellow ray, which activates all the qualities in the path of pure spirit.

With the stabilizing influence of the orange ray there is an active but balanced wisdom, a selfless love and kindness so well balanced in its activities that it penetrates through all the aspects of Chokmah, spread out by the sphere of the zodiac, Mundane Chakra to Chokmah, without becoming weakness. Here is true wisdom and perfect love and kindness.

In Atziluth

Hod has now changed its personality ray to a violet purple which merges with the brilliance of Kether – the Atziluthic World. The merging of these two produces lavender, the higher octave of the purple ray. Tranquillity, gentleness, poise; these are the attributes given to Hod. Here is the perfect Archetype of spiritual form poised in perfect tranquillity in the sea of brilliance which we know as Atziluth.

YESOD

In Assiah

Yesod, the sephirah of emotions, the astral etheric state of consciousness and the foundation of the physical universe. All things have their structure built and held together by the etheric web and Yesod is the etheric network or foundation behind all life.

The emotional side of Yesod springs from its Mundane Chakra, the Moon. It may possibly be the reason humanity reacts to the ebb and flow of the Moon, some more than others because Yesod is the perfect replica of Malkuth, but on this more fluidic state of consciousness.

On the Tree in Assiah, or Malkuth of the basic Tree, Yesod is governed by citrine flecked with azure. Azure is a fairly high octave of the blue ray and citrine is a composition of the yellow and green rays. Malkuth responds to the yellow ray and the four elements – Mundane Chakra of Malkuth – add to those rays, plus the red ray.

There is a very strong illusory aspect to Yesod and the citrine colour is the underlying cause. This mixture of the green and yellow rays also brings in the qualities of fickleness and deceit.

To counteract these adverse qualities the flecks of azure contain the qualities of sincerity, and honour; but what is more important about the azure is the urge it creates for spiritual maturity. This struggle can be aided by the yellow ray of creative activity, providing the student can at this stage of his development take hold of – and use – the rays to his own benefit.

From the green ray can be obtained harmony once the student understands how to balance it. This ray is however, one of struggle and conflict, which in the early stages of following the path of wisdom will give him much trouble. There is a great emphasis on the green ray at this point in Assiah, due to the flow from the earth element of the Mundane Chakra.

Not until the student can still his emotions, a difficult task at Yesod in Malkuth, will the struggle and conflict lessen sufficiently for him to make further progress.

From time to time the blue ray from the Mundane Chakra penetrates to the consciousness of the student and it is in one of these moments that he becomes calm from the influence of this soothing love-wisdom ray. In the calmness he takes all he can from the wisdom aspect of the ray.

Now he can to a small degree control the rays and so he draws more and more on the blue and the azure octave until the emotions are more under control. It is then the student makes use of the green ray, but the harmony aspect of it, and his first struggle for spiritual maturity is nearly over. The vices from the citrine are quelled and the yellow ray is now turned into the correct channel of creative activity.

It is a long way from Yesod through the remainder of the Tree in Assiah but in course of time it is accomplished and the world of Yetzirah is entered.

In Yetzirah

In Yetzirah the first Tree the initiate has to conquer is the Tree in Yesod, so he is now faced with the task of conquering Yesod in Yesod. Emotions are at full stretch, with no physical body to anchor him or through which he can work.

The rays have now changed and the initiate has to work with new forces. Indigo, the Atziluthic colour of Yesod on the basic Tree, forms the background for the deep purple of Yesod on the Tree in Yesod. From the Moon the silver ray sweeps out to lighten the indigo and deep purple.

Deep purple is a ray of forceful power. It is also a ray of integrity. From the indigo comes the qualities of blind devotion and also caution. The silver at this level is not pure and is more of a very light silvery grey, still a very high octave of the grey ray.

The initiate's danger at this stage is to draw too much from the deep purple and become too forceful and overbearing, and the blind devotion of the indigo is far from helpful with this particular attitude.

It is the light grey that offers the initiate salvation. From this ray he can gain stability. Once this is achieved he can gain fortitude from the indigo ray. This ray also has an idealistic quality to its nature, and this the initiate can take when he wants to. It is probably not until he has had many incarnations at Yesod in Yesod that the idealistic quality is absorbed and the forceful power is controlled and directed into the right channel, that of driving the initiate to conquer, not just Yesod on the Tree in Yesod but the whole of the Tree in that sephirah.

Hod is the next sephirah on the basic Tree with its Atziluthic ray of violet purple. Still on the purple ray, but this time a higher octave, Yesod is still the same ray as is the Mundane Chakra of Yesod. The yellow ray, however, now comes into play, issuing forth from Mercury.

Originality and knowledge are two of the qualities sent out by the yellow ray; and from the violet, adoration and spiritual dedication. Although the qualities of the violet are admirable, they can lead the initiate into trouble if he is not careful.

In Hod, the first sephirah on the lower mental level and only the second sephirah of the Yetziratic world on the journey up the Tree, there is a rather limited vision, and this limitation can direct, so easily, the qualities of spiritual dedication and adoration in the wrong direction.

To avoid becoming rooted in these two qualities of the violet ray the initiate must make originality from the yellow ray his keynote, and through this keep his mental body pliable; at the same time he must not discard either the quality of adoration or spiritual dedication, but keep them evenly balanced and apply them as and when required.

Originality in itself can cause many wild ventures and so the initiate must also use the balancing quality of the light grey octave of the grey ray, and once having achieved balance, not an easy task in the conditioned sphere of Hod, he can then draw upon the knowledge quality of the yellow ray.

Combining originality with knowledge he can overcome Yesod in Hod and attain to the true glory of Hod and move forward through the remainder of the Tree in that sephirah and eventually come to the Tree in Netzach, the only other sephirah entirely based in the lower mental plane of consciousness.

At Yesod in Netzach the initiate meets with completely different experiences and circumstances. This is the sephirah of energetic activity and victory. One aspect of the victory of Netzach is that over the lower mental body, and it is towards this end that the initiate must work by controlling the Yesodic influence of Netzach.

The deep purple of Yesod is now enveloped in the Atziluthic amber of Netzach with the blue of Venus shining through. With the blue ray of love making its influence felt, Yesod is a difficult sephirah to conquer on this tree as the lower mental body is inclined to be swayed by its emotions.

From the deep purple octave the qualities of overbearing and forcefulness can now be brought into use and the positive aspects of these qualities used. If applied with discrimination they can control the love aspect of the blue ray and turn what could be a weak sentimental love into a true form of love without weakness.

Amber supplies justice and mental vigour. The first quality has to be balanced with love and the initiate will find the second quality, from the amber, of untold value in exercising control of Yesod in Netzach and this will bring him the victory he requires, that he may move forward to the experiences that await him at Yesod in Tiphareth.

At Tiphareth, Yesod still retains the dark purple, but the overall background colour has now changed to a clear pink rose with orange glinting through from the sun.

The initiate's task is now to raise himself from the lower mental plane of consciousness to the higher plane, and it is at Yesod, which even in Tiphareth is still lower mental, that he must commence the task.

Mental reactions on the lower plane are still very strong and tend to pull the initiate and hold him at this level of thought. The reaction to lower mental ideas is emphasized through the overbearing quality of the purple. 'I am so right' is the attitude of the lower mental body.

The quality of reliance which comes from the orange ray, if just accepted for what it is, in its pure state can also adversely affect the progress of the initiate. With the tenor of thought adopted through the purple the initiate has taken reliance and becomes self-reliant to a point of self-assuredness.

Trust is another quality obtained from the orange ray and this also can have its dangers because the initiate can be lulled into the false security of trusting himself and then becomes even more assured of his own judgements.

All these subtle traps await the initiate at Yesod in Tiphareth and true to the quality of the sephirah his mental body sways between the influences of the lower and higher mental plane of consciousness.

From the light grey octave he eventually uses the quality of harmony and once this is attained between the higher and lower mental bodies he can, with the self-reliance, use the orange ray to his benefit instead of letting the ray use him to his detriment.

With trust and reliance his mental body turns towards the higher planes and now, with the aid of the purple ray, he becomes just as forceful in his mental outlook towards the higher level as he was previously towards the lower.

The overbearing aspect of the purple ray has still to be

overcome, but once the desire is turned towards the higher mental, this presents very little difficulty. The initiate now makes use of the high octave of the red ray, and through the pink transmutes the overbearing quality to the point where he can go forward to his present goal, the higher mental plane.

Geburah is the first sephirah of the higher mental plane on the return journey and it is Yesod on the Tree in this sephirah that the adept has now to face.

The deep purple of Yesod now merges into the orange of Geburah and the red ray issues forth from Mars. With the low octave of the purple ray the adept is rather limited in his scope and this is typical of the Geburah influence, as it is the sphere of rigidity amongst other things.

Yesod, with its fluidic movements, strains against this rigidity and tries to move the immovable. These are the conditions and influences the adept finds himself in and also has to resolve. The first realization he has is that of being alone in this set of circumstances, knowing that only he can resolve them and no-one can help him, even those at the same level, because like himself they are trying to resolve their own difficulty.

Through all the varied experiences on his journey there has always been some form of guidance, even preparing him and warning him that this stage in his journey would eventually be reached. Now he has to rely on his own abilities and knowledge.

With the influence of the will and power from the first ray he is inclined to plunge straight in without thought, and using that will and power, backed up by the forcefulness of the deep purple, he tries to take Yesod in Geburah by storm, only to find himself driven back to his starting point.

The red ray holds the quality of emotions, and with the Yesodic experience the adept for a period of time is thrown off balance and it is then that he remembers and calls upon the light grey octave of this ray and gains tranquillity and balance. With this steadying influence he commences to make use of what rays are available to him.

Tuning in to the orange ray he develops its qualities of self-control and trust. Once this is accomplished he views the corrective powers of Geburah in a different light and feels true humility in the presence of its influence.

Conquering the Yesodic emotions, and also this aspect of the red ray, he faces Yesod in Geburah with a different attitude and realizes that the way to conquer Yesod in Geburah is not by force but by humility and accepting the cosmic laws.

Turning again to the violet ray, he draws from it the virtue of spiritual dedication and now equipped with the right qualities and attitude of his mental body he commences again the task of conquering Yesod in Geburah, but he makes it a submissive conquest and so paves the way to conquering the whole tree in Geburah, from whence he proceeds to the sphere of the Masters.

Gedulah, the last sephirah in the formative world, now waits for the Master to conquer the Tree in that sephirah. Arriving at Yesod in Gedulah, the Master still has for his use the deep purple and the light grey, while deep violet – Atziluthic colour of Gedulah – replaces the orange of Geburah. He can also call on the Amethyst ray of Jupiter.

Yesod in Gedulah creates complications, because adding to the Yesodic influence are the qualities of Gedulah, grace, sentiment and feelings. The Master's task is to control these within the sephirah of Yesod so that the qualities can be used with balance, discrimination and within the bounds of Universal law.

The first effort in this direction is to negate the forcefulness of the purple ray, and this can be done by avoiding its use and counteracting its influence by making full use of the light grey and drawing upon its quality of Peace.

Stability is another virtue of the light grey that the Master finds useful in his conquest of Yesod in Gedulah. Tuning in to the violet, an octave of the purple ray, he absorbs from it the idealistic quality, and through this he can understand what is the ideal of Yesod in Gedulah and commences to work towards this end with true spiritual dedication, obtained from the violet octave of the purple ray.

With the control of Yesod in Gedulah the Master's feet are well placed on the path up the Tree in Gedulah from which he will cross the abyss into the World of Briah and the supernals.

In Briah

In Briah all the rays change, except for the light grey octave from Yesod's Mundane Chakra. Yesod in Binah is violet, and Binah itself throws a crimson glow over the whole Tree within its sephirah, and from Saturn issues the black ray.

It is at this point on the basic Tree that the etheric and astral structures were created. Here the emotions first took shape, but they are at Yesod in Binah, a more exalted and reverential kind, held within limits by the black ray and having spiritual dedication from the violet.

The crimson, a fairly high octave of the red ray, endows the emotions with the potential of impulsiveness and instability that develops at the lower levels. It is this potential that the Master must completely eradicate if he is to complete his return journey.

As the potential will always be there through the Atziluthic colour of Binah, which the Master cannot remove, he only has one answer to his problem, and that is to dismantle his astral and etheric bodies; not an easy decision to make, but nevertheless, one that he must make if he wishes to reach Chokmah.

With the spiritual dedication of the violet ray and developing the last of his latent powers from the high octave of the black ray, he employs these two qualities to achieve his object and so move into the mental plane of Binah.

At long last the Master completes his journey through the Tree in Binah, and now free of all form and personality, the individual spark moves through the Tree in Chokmah. The violet ray remains, but the ray from the Moon, no longer polluted, is silver, the highest octave of the grey ray, and the whole has a background of a pure soft blue, the highest octave of the blue ray.

The spark is now in perfect control of the emotions and Yesod in Chokmah presents him with no difficulties. Spiritual dedication from the violet is now complete. Tranquillity and spiritual harmony from the silver adds to the spiritual sedative and wisdom taken from the pure soft blue.

Now, face to face, the desire of the spark is to be the original face or the perfection of Kether. Swiftly moving along the tree in Chokmah the spark reaches Yesod in Kether.

In Atziluth

All the rays can now be used, as they are all pouring forth from Kether. This is the sephirah of ultimate perfection and so Yesod in Kether. Indigo is the ray of Yesod in Atziluth, the silver octave of the grey ray remains, but behind the whole is the ray of brilliance, perfection of all the rays.

Here is the emotional perfection, from the highest octave of the indigo ray, devotion to purity, from the highest octave of the grey ray, spiritual harmony, which is also due to the perfection of the etheric and astral bodies.

The spark is now the archetypal blueprint of all that is embodied in the emotional, astral and etheric web.

MALKUTH

In Atziluth

Malkuth in the Atziluthic World is the perfect archetype of Assiah, the physical world as it should be in a state of conscious perfection. The basic background ray is the pure white of Kether, the Atziluthic World, and the colour of the Sephirah is a pure yellow.

In these two rays are a combination of purity and spirit, with also the very positive influence of the white ray. The yellow ray is also a ray of creative activity and this is indicative of Malkuth at this level.

There is the positive force of Kether pushing out the archetypal plan into manifestation and all creative activity is directed towards bringing this aspect of the Ain force through into the creative world. The spirit, which the yellow ray symbolizes, has to be formed and clothed for the completion of the physical world which is to become spirit clothed in matter.

The Mundane Chakra of Malkuth is the four elements, Fire, Water, Air and Earth; in other words, the four holy living creatures, The Lion, The Man, The Eagle and The Bull. In this Mundane Chakra are four rays of importance, Fire – red, the ray of will and power; Water – blue, the ray of love and wisdom; Air – yellow, the ray of creative activity; and Earth – green, the ray of harmony through struggle and conflict.

From the fourth ray – green, which is neither positive nor negative, hot nor cold, alkaline nor acid, comes. that balance which should make Malkuth the completed perfection of the archetype visualized in Kether.

Red, blue and yellow are the three main aspects of the Divine or Ain force at the lower level, and so in Atziluth is born the concept of the perfect world of matter.

In Briah

The concept now commences on the first stage of becoming reality in the creative World of Briah, the first aspect being in Chokmah, and here the rays change. The background of the white ray gives place to the blue ray, which at this high level is a pure soft blue, and the clear yellow of Malkuth itself is replaced by four rays, citrine, an octave of the yellow ray, olive, an octave of the green ray, russet, which is on the brown ray, and black, which in Briah is on the higher octave of the ray, having more of this ray's virtues than vices. Through all these changes, however, there remains the constants of the Mundane Chakra of Malkuth, red, blue, yellow and green.

Although the pure white of Atziluth is no longer there, the perfection is still there to a very great degree through the Mundane Chakra of Chokmah, which – as the sphere of the Zodiac – contains within it all the rays. There is, however, the predominance of certain rays from the other factors already mentioned. The citrine and olive octaves bring in the first imperfections as both are possessed of the quality of deceit. Citrine has also the vice of being fickle. Russet, as an octave of the brown ray, holds within it the first stage of egoism, and the black ray gives to it latent powers and a secretive quality, as the second stage of creation commences in Binah, through its Mundane Chakra, Saturn.

The force of the black ray has increased, having two effects, one of deepening the esoteric aspect of the sphere and restricting at this level of consciousness the vices, but the second aspect is that of also restricting the qualities of the pure spiritual by commencing to enfold that same spirit in form so that the clear direct line of communication prevailing in Atziluth, and to a major degree in Chokmah, becomes clouded.

In Yetzirah

With the completion of the creative aspects the forces of the formative world, Yetzirah, come into play, and the four rays of Malkuth are flecked with gold – one of the higher octaves of the yellow ray – which endows Malkuth with the qualities of health and well-being and the attribute of being helpful. All other rays remain unchanged.

In the world of Yetzirah Malkuth goes through the six aspects of this world without any change in its own rays, but is affected by the differing rays from the basic colours and Mundane Chakras of each of the six stages.

The basic ray of Gedulah at this level of consciousness is a deep violet, one of the lower octaves of the purple ray. This is the ray of rulership, and at this octave of the ray there is pride and the quality of greatness. Pomp and splendour are vices of this octave but these are held in check at the Gedulah level through the influence of the amethyst ray flowing out from Jupiter, the Mundane Chakra of Gedulah. The amethyst ray with its high level of spiritual quality expands in true Jupiterean style all the spiritual qualities of Malkuth at its present state of formation, and overrides the vices, although they too are expanded with the Jupiter influence. This effect is brought about by virtue of the amethyst ray expanding with each expansion emanating from Jupiter, even though it be the adverse qualities expanding. It is here that the need for a spiritual belief first becomes consciously inherent in the sephirah.

Geburah is the second stage in the formative World of Yetzirah, and here Malkuth has the background of bright orange, the Atziluthic ray of Geburah, and from its Mundane Chakra, Mars, flows the influence of the primary red. Through the action of the red ray, the ego – first brought in by the Crimson octave at Binah – now becomes inflated, accentuated by the will and power of the primary red. In this sephirah Malkuth is endowed with force, vigour, energy and determination, further encouraged and supported by the orange ray.

Malkuth on the Tree in Tiphareth has now a basic background of pink rose. This is another octave of the red ray, and this octave has for its qualities the highest point of physical love, affections and forgiveness.

It is in this sephirah of the formative world that Malkuth is endowed with the quality of sacrifice which, with the other rays having their effect, can take many forms. The influence of the red ray from the Mundane Chakra of Malkuth could mean at the physical level a sacrifice through impulse. The blue ray would influence a sacrifice of love, while the green ray would demand a sacrifice to bring harmony from a conflict. The yellow ray sacrifice would be one of spirit. All the other rays influencing Malkuth would have their own particular sacrificial aspects.

The qualities of the pink rose are such that to develop and possess them in their full perfection, sacrifice must be made in some way, otherwise the qualities of the ray will be distorted.

After Tiphareth the next stage in the formation of Malkuth is on the Tree in Netzach, and here the basic overall colour is amber and the Mundane Chakra sends out the blue ray. The combined influence of these two rays give the qualities of intellect, love and wisdom. The sephirah at this stage in its formation has a predominance of the blue ray, which adds wisdom.

Development of the intellect – with the mental conflict that results from it – is the result of this formative stage of Malkuth, not quite the result envisaged in the archetypal plan, but Malkuth is now at a distance from the archetypal level and denser form not only restricts but distorts communications, and the harmonious plane for mental spiritual activity is despoiled, although a great degree of freedom for this particular aspect of thought still remains, and it is at this point in its formation that Malkuth receives the attributes that earn it the titles of 'The Breaker of Foundations' and 'The Gate'.

Now the formative process continues on the Tree in Hod and the overall influencing colour of amber gives way to one of violet purple. Again there is the mixture of two ray influences, with the yellow streaming out from Mercury, the Mundane Chakra of Hod, giving a predominance of the yellow by virtue of the yellow that comes from Malkuth itself and the Mundane Chakra of Malkuth.

This is the stage where the desire for study, a quality of the yellow ray, is born. The preponderance of this ray, however, is only active within a limited groove. This is caused by the restriction of the black ray emanating from Malkuth itself. The excess of yellow endows Malkuth with the vitality or zeal to free this limited thought, the determination to keep the concepts of thought progressive.

The one ray of hope at this point is the impulsive quality of the red, which from time to time aids by impulsively bursting through the rigid confines and letting the thought or mental activity flow through to Netzach.

The last stage of the formative process takes place on the Tree in Yesod, where the emotional field is attached to Malkuth. The basic overshadowing colour is now the indigo ray, one of the lower octaves of the ray.

This is the Devotional and religious thought ray. At this low level it inclines towards the emotional type with much pomp and splendour. It could also tend towards the superstitious through the emotions, but here the black ray curtails it and the blue influence from the Mundane Chakra also helps to keep a sober attitude, but there is in most instances a stubbornness which springs from the indigo ray combined with the red ray influence, which – like the blue – comes from the Mundane Chakra.

The red is the ray of leadership with fire and drive and were this at the mental level of the Yetziratic World instead of at the emotional level and without the restriction of the black ray, it would indeed be the ruling force of harsh dictatorship.

The green ray from the Mundane Chakra of Malkuth also adds to the emotional aspect generated by the red ray, and as this is the lowest point of the Yesodic Tree, Malkuth in Yesod is a sphere of conflicting emotions, which with the yellow ray of activity is inclined to move quickly from one emotional state to another.

In Assiah

Malkuth in Assiah is now complete with the dense covering of the physical world. The ray now predominant is black with flecks of the yellow ray interpenetrating and an overall background of yellow from the World of Assiah itself.

From the Mundane Chakra of Malkuth stem forth the red, blue, yellow and green rays. With the intermingling of the rays, black and yellow exercise the greatest influence. This leads to a great deal of activity from the yellow ray but at a very low level of materialism, the black ray influence.

Short of going down into the Qliphoth, Malkuth in Malkuth is the lowest point that can be reached. The one opportunity that is left to raise the level of consciousness from this low state is to channel the fire and drive of the red ray in the right direction and to do this make use of the wisdom of the blue ray so that the yellow ray, symbolic of spirit and activity, can break through the restriction of the black ray of materialism.

PART TWO: THE TWENTY-TWO PATHS

THE FOOL

In Assiah

The path of The Fool is the first path on every tree throughout the basic tree and represents the indestructible eternal spark coming out of the Ain. At each tree this is the commencing point at the particular level of consciousness that the tree represents.

Having reached the World of Assiah – or the physical world – on the outward journey, the student that the spark has become commences the path of return.

It is in the World of Assiah that the student's journey will commence on every path, as this is the conscious starting point for the majority of humanity, the way out being mostly made in a state of unconscious recognition and the remainder of the journey being beyond recollection at the stage of physical conscious imperfection.

In the World of Assiah the tree is engulfed in yellow, the Atziluthic colour of Malkuth. From the path itself flows emerald green flecked with gold and the Mundane Chakra supplies more of the yellow ray.

The yellow ray as the third ray of creative activity is also the creative aspect of spirit and is associated with the element of air, which is again symbolic of spirit. In every sense the ray depicts this as an eternal spark of the Ain setting forth on its journey across time and space.

Harmony through struggle and conflict is the keynote of the green ray, and where this particular octave of emerald green is concerned it denotes harmony, balance and discrimination.

It would appear on the surface that the spark is all set for a perfect start in the World of Assiah, but from the four elements – Mundane Chakra of Malkuth – apart from the yellow and blue rays there are the green and red rays to contend with.

As the rays from the elements are of the primary colour the green has vastly different qualities from the emerald green octave. They are jealousy, ambition and – unconsciously – greed. From the red ray comes will and power, energy, quick temper and strong emotions.

The spark endowed with some admirable qualities has many hurdles to face and overcome if he is to completely tread this path of The Fool. Another hazard that is to be faced is that of deceit, a quality that comes from the yellow and green rays combining into a greenish yellow.

Will and power are the first qualities to be drawn upon by the majority, the general idea being that a strong will backed by power, both physical and of authority, will achieve any end and so the spark becomes the blind fool.

It is not until a number of incarnations have been spent in this manner that the eyes of the blind fool are opened to his folly and he looks in other directions. He is now in a position where the blue ray of love and wisdom can bring its influence to bear upon him.

Once the influence of the blue ray is accepted the eternal spark has taken the first step towards being a student of the ancient spiritual wisdom and commences to make use of the yellow ray with its quality of creative activity in this direction.

From the emerald green octave of the green ray the student can stabilize himself and gain both harmony and balance and the red ray still can give him power, although tempered by the blue ray there is still the will to do, but controlled and directed towards the right goal.

The path of The Fool in Assiah has been trodden and its lessons learned, the student now moves towards the Yetziratic World and the path of The Fool on its first tree, that in Yesod.

In Yetzirah

Indigo, the Atziluthic colour of Yesod, is the background against which the blue and emerald green of the path of The Fool operates. The rays of the path will remain constant throughout the whole of the Yetziratic World, and the yellow ray from the element of air which governs the path is constant through all four worlds.

The student also has the use of the grey ray through the silver octave, which flows out from the Moon, although at the level of Yesod it is more a light grey octave.

In Yesod, as in Malkuth, the emerald green can aid the student in obtaining stability and harmony if he chooses to make use of the ray. The merging of this octave of the green ray with that of the blue is also a benefit to the student as this mixture of blue/green sends out the qualities of strength, and trustworthiness. All excellent qualities, but all holding dangers if taken to excess, and in Yesod excesses become very easy to indulge in and difficult to cure because of the stubbornness which the indigo ray can impart to the student.

From the indigo also comes the quality of devotion and at this level it is a blind devotion which is inclined to accentuate the stubbornness that leads the student into futile endeavours which – through the activity of the yellow ray – he follows with zeal.

It is not until the student allows the emerald green and light grey to influence him that he can commence to tread the path of the wise fool. Up to this point he has been the blind fool tempted by his own desires and only investigating and following those paths that gave satisfaction to his desire nature.

From the emerald green he develops the quality of discrimination and from the light grey, stability. Once he has stabilized himself then he is in a position to exercise the discrimination taken from the emerald green. Strength and trustworthiness from the blue and emerald green merger is now turned into the true direction, that of becoming the wise fool and completing his journey along this path.

Exercising the devotional influence of the indigo ray he becomes devoted to the task of treading, with success, the path of The Fool. This he now does, secure within himself and in harmony with his desire body, for his desire now is to make progress in the journey across time and space.

When next the student meets the path of The Fool it is on the tree in Hod. In Hod he has the same path rays to work with, but the indigo ray of Yesod is replaced by violet purple, a medium octave of the purple ray, and in place of the light grey, yellow issues forth from Mercury.

Hod is the sephirah of Glory and this attribute is well supported by the purple ray, which is the ray of rulers at any level of consciousness, and all the responsibility and glory that goes with rulership. What the student must be careful of is seeking glory; and also, when attaining glory, that it is the right aspect.

The danger on the path of The Fool in Hod is to be a blind fool, blind to reason, basking in the glory of being so right, full of the misplaced self-confidence that comes so easily to the lower mental body that has reached the peak of its own narrow limits.

In this condition the lower mental body so easily accepts the qualities of the purple aspect of the ray, forceful power, pride and greatness, at the same time ignoring the more desirable qualities of the violet octave. Even if the violet is contacted it is usual at this stage to pick up the wrong qualities of this octave, adoration being one of those qualities, and this is turned into self-adoration.

The other quality taken from the violet is that of magnanimity and it is easy to see how the lower mind in its present state would use that quality. It would not be spiritual magnanimity, but the type associated with the great 'I am' or that of self-righteousness.

There are many lessons to be learned by the student and it can be a slow process. The first change can be made when the influence of the yellow ray is able to penetrate the innermost recesses of the mind and stirs it into an activity that breaks open the fixed ideas a little.

From the blind fool the student now becomes the fool's fool. Through the yellow ray activity he commences to see things in a different light, but although he knows differently he does not act upon it, but lets the purple ray hold dominance.

Once more he must call on the rays of the path, first the emerald green, from which he obtains discrimination and balance. With a more harmonious and balanced outlook he deliberately draws on the blue ray and contacts the influence that makes him struggle for spiritual maturity.

From this ray he also develops honour and sincerity; with the development of these qualities the student now looks more to the violet octave of the purple ray, from which he draws the more positive qualities of humility and spiritual dedication.

A wise fool now emerges, and accepting the purple ray with its aspect of rulership he treads the path of The Fool with humility and spiritual dedication until he reaches the end of the path, ruling his mental body with the true spiritual qualities and achieving the glory of Hod.

The student is now prepared to move to the tree in Netzach and climb his way up to the path of The Fool in that sphere of consciousness. He now finds that with the rays attached to his path he also has the amber of Netzach to work with.

Amber is a high octave of the orange ray. There is also the blue ray connected with Venus. This amplifies the blue of the path and it is this excess of blue that he must learn to balance.

Netzach is the sephirah of victory and idealism. The blue holds the quality and influence to make the student a hard worker and through this influence he does work hard to attain victory for his ideals, but as a result of wrong choice the blind fool finds it a hollow victory on many occasions.

From a different aspect the student treads the path of The Fool, entering on the path in the state of conscious imperfection, always aiming for conscious perfection. Treading this path (which is the first and last of each tree in each sephirah), is not easy for him.

This path is one of opening up and when the student reaches The Fool in Tiphareth, full realization of what is involved brings him face to face with the path he is treading and the task involved if he is to return to the levels of the supernals.

On the path in Tiphareth the student has moved into the higher mental plane of consciousness and is in the position where he can look back over past experiences and gain an idea of what is ahead of him.

However at the highest point of Tiphareth there is still a pull from the lower mental plane of consciousness, which covers the lower half of the tree in Tiphareth. The clear pink rose of the sephirah is not always helpful because of its quality – the highest point of physical affections. This is more inclined to pull the student towards those lower planes of consciousness instead of being the incentive to progress to higher levels, where he can use this quality to much greater advantage.

The orange ray from the sun can bring with it a benign influence which – allied with the rose pink – can make the task of progressing further away from the lower planes even more difficult.

Now the student must draw upon the quality of the path itself, that of the pioneering spirit. Once he has developed this he is prepared to take the quality of trust and self-control, which in turn gives him the confidence to step forward and make the first move towards the conquest of the path.

This step forward must not be in blind trust, but in trust born of reason and knowledge, otherwise the student would still be the blind fool. Two choices lie before him and if he is the wise fool he will draw upon both choices. From the blue aspect of the path he can obtain wisdom and from the path itself he can add to that wisdom as it flows along from Chokmah, which lies at one end of the path.

The element of air, which is the path's main influence, projects for his use the yellow ray of creative activity and at this level of consciousness it is spiritual activity. Combining this with the wisdom he has accepted he can tread the path of The Fool in complete trust and confidence.

Having overcome and trodden safely the path of The Fool in Tiphareth the adept must now commence to climb the tree in Geburah until once more he comes up against this path. In Geburah the tree is overshadowed by the orange ray, the Atziluthic colour of Geburah

The red ray from Mars also has an influence on the path of The Fool in Geburah. With the emerald green and blue of the path itself and yellow from air, its ruling element, the adept is now well provided for in the ray influences he can use.

One of the main lessons the adept has to absorb at this stage is the wisdom of justice. From Chokmah at one end of the path flows wisdom and from Geburah comes the justice. On his path of return the adept has had experiences of many aspects of justice in his steady climb up the tree in Geburah. Now the ultimate lesson must be understood.

Red – with its influences – is the first obstacle the adept must overcome. From this octave of the red ray comes unwanted influences such as impulsiveness, fiery reactions and impatience. There are other qualities of this ray such as energy, force and vigour which can be vices or virtues according to the use made of them.

With the impulsiveness and fiery reaction from the red the adept is inclined to harsh justice and employs both energy and force in the wrong way. The streak of impatience is accentuated by the activity influence of the yellow ray.

From the orange the adept obtains the quality of power. This again is a quality that can be used two ways, so even with all the ray forces at his disposal the path of The Fool is not an easy one for the adept to tread.

As he takes the power from the orange ray he comes into contact with the qualities of self-control and reliance and as he absorbs these influences a fraction of the Chokmah wisdom permeates his mental body giving him not only food for thought, but in due course of time bringing him to a standstill.

During this pause the adept realizes the need for both the blue and emerald green rays to strike the right balance. Using the self-control provided by the orange ray he sets to work with the blue aspect first and then the emerald green.

From the blue he obtains the characteristics of honour and trustworthiness and these qualities bring home to him the hard fact that he has been not just a blind fool, but with all the experience he has previously gained, a fool's fool. Now he must redeem his honour and justify the trust of those on lower planes of consciousness.

The adept now draws from the emerald green the quality of discrimination so that he may dispense justice wisely and truly in accordance with universal law. It is at this point along the path of The Fool that he finds the value of the mixture of the rays as they appertain to the path; so he makes use of this combination and obtains the qualities they supply, which is to be strong and friendly.

The adept now fulfils his destiny of the path of The Fool in Geburah and becomes, as this first path implies, perfection at this level of consciousness in dispensing justice with wisdom. Having learned this lesson he now must be able to accept justice meted out to him, but he is well prepared for this with the self-control from the orange and the wisdom from Chokmah.

The experiences in Geburah and in particular the treading of the path of The Fool fits him for mastership and the ability to tackle the tree in Gedulah, the last tree in the world of Yetzirah. It is on this path in Gedulah that the Master has to learn the wisdom of universal love, the compassion that transcends all other forms of love, fully embracing, but without involvement.

Deep violet, an octave of the purple ray, covers the tree in Gedulah and the blue aspect of the path is reinforced by the blue ray from Venus. The emerald green is still there for the Master's use with the yellow ray.

From the violet the Master obtains the quality of adoration, but with the excess of the blue ray and its characteristic of sincerity and the love aspect of the blue ray he can employ adoration the wrong way and in his sincerity of love for all creatures fix his adoration upon them and so follow the path of the blind fool, blinded by his tremendous love.

When he learns the lesson of this he is inclined to turn to the wisdom aspect of the blue ray and develop a cold detached outlook which dispenses love by calculated measurement and with great magnanimity as if bestowing great favours. Penetrating through this attitude is the yellow ray with its creative activity and slowly it makes its presence felt and the master realizes he is being a fool's fool. The way is clear and plain before him, but he has ignored it.

With the realization that he is treading the path the wrong way he turns once more to the blending of the blue and emerald green rays to draw upon their influence and become helpful and friendly. Now he turns to the emerald green and once more attains balance and employs the discrimination that comes from this ray.

Once balance and discrimination are his it is then he can call again upon the violet ray and extract from it the humility that aids him in employing his adoration to the universal forces and the laws that are embodied in the whole scheme of manifestation at every level of consciousness.

The wise fool emerges and through his balance and discrimination he strikes the true balance between his other two attitudes. Discarding the blind love, he develops compassion with a true understanding that replaces the cold aloofness with a detachment full of warmth and understanding, without ties of involvement.

With this change the Master can now work with full

sincerity of purpose and employ the creativity activity of the yellow ray to the full and with a right purpose. His task now completed, he faces the crossing of the abyss.

There is at this stage a certain amount of reluctance on the part of the Master to leave his work in Gedulah and sever his ties with the lower worlds. At this level of consciousness he knows that once across the abyss he has taken the path to the point of no return.

The violet octave and the yellow ray are the two aids he can call upon. The violet to give him the required spiritual dedication and the yellow for its creative activity. Making use of them both he crosses the abyss to the tree in Binah and the Briatic World.

In Briah

From Binah there is the glow of crimson, a high octave of the red ray. It is against this background that the sky blue of the path of The Fool stands out. The black ray of Saturn and the yellow ray of Ain also influence the path on the tree in Binah.

A state of near conscious perfection has been reached by the Master, who aeons of time before had come through this same sphere where the first awakening of the spark had taken place, and the phase of conscious imperfection had commenced.

The long journey across time and space is nearly at an end. The Master has made his way up the tree in Binah and now has only the path of The Fool to tread to release himself from all but the ultimate 'ring-pass-not'. Once again – even at his state of consciousness – doubts assail him, the pull of personality can still be detected.

Self-pride, a quality of the crimson octave of the red ray influence, creeps in, not the self-pride as expressed at the lower levels, but pride in his work and ability to help those climbing the lower levels of the tree. The restrictive action of the black ray momentarily prevents him from seeing the wider vision and the greater aid that can be given to the whole scheme of things by reaching the ultimate of perfection.

A feeling of frustration with the black ray restriction eventually develops through the activity influence of the yellow ray and so the Master turns to the sky blue octave from which he obtains a spiritual sedative; also from this octave of the blue ray he obtains the quality of selfless love. Now he can see the need for dispensing with the personality.

With determination, which he draws from the red ray, he once again gives his attention to the black ray, but now he draws from it the quality and influence of latent powers and through these dispenses with the last restrictions. The spark now moves freely towards the tree in Chokmah, the other half of the Briatic world.

Pure soft blue, the Atziluthic colour of Chokmah, replaces the crimson of Binah as the background ray to the sky blue of the path. The yellow still flows out from the element of air and from the sphere of the Zodiac all the other rays are present.

Blue predominates the whole sphere of consciousness and the universal love and wisdom, the basic qualities of this ray, are here in their perfection. As the spark makes its way along the path of The Fool in Chokmah it scintillates with compassion and is brilliant with wisdom.

The latent wisdom born in the spark at this point on the outward journey is now stirred into full activity by the yellow ray. Here is the positive aspect of conscious perfection unfolding into full flower and with the full consciousness of wisdom develops the full compassion that embraces the whole of manifestation.

All cosmic forces are there for the use of the spark and the spark now in its wisdom employs them to help in the work of bringing the whole universe into that ideal state of perfection.

For a period of time, with the influence of the yellow creative activity ray, the spark is devoted to the task in hand until in due course of time it has to complete the last section of the long journey, this time to the path of The Fool in Kether.

In Atziluth

Brilliance is the all-pervading ray in Atziluth and the path of The Fool on the tree in Kether now reflecting the yellow ray is vibrant and alive. The yellow ray from the path's ruling element is also sparkling in reflection from the brilliance.

At this level of consciousness the yellow is no longer creative activity but pure spirit, in other words the creative side of the life force; if for no other reason, yellow must be the predominant ray on the path of The Fool at this point.

This is the first path on the outward journey and so holds within its subjective nature the archetypes of all that is to be in unconscious perfection. It is the first path the pure spark of spirit treads. It is also the last path the spark moves along, but now as a changed spark. It is still pure spirit, but now it is the conscious perfection containing all the qualities or the essence of all the qualities, both positive and negative.

The end of the journey has been reached and the 'I' in the individuality sense takes its place in the formation of the ultimate archetype, sparkling in the brilliance of perfection.

THE MAGICIAN

In Atziluth

The path of The Magician in Atziluth is yellow and the overall background is pure brilliance, which gives to the yellow ray a sparkling effect. The yellow ray is symbolic of spirit, related to the element of air with attributes of creative activity and mercurial movement and mental perception; this sums up the perfect archetype of The Magician.

This is the Atziluthic conception of the perfected Fool on the completion of his journey, the full conscious perfection. Only two rays influence the path of The Magician at this level, brilliance of Kether and the yellow which is not only the ray of the path, but also of its governing astrological influence, Mercury.

The Intelligence of Transparency is clearly shown and easy to interpret, with the pure brilliance giving to the mental activity of the yellow ray a transparent scintillating yellow that is beyond the vision of the human mind.

In Briah

Chokmah in the world of Briah – with its ray of soft blue – is the next background for the path of The Magician, which although retaining its yellow ray of Mercury, changes its own ray to purple.

The purple ray has the quality of rulership and on the lower octave can be overbearing and full of pomp and splendour that would be inconsistent with the path of The Magician at this high level, and it is here that the pure soft blue of Chokmah comes into play and has the effect of toning down the purple or transmuting it to lavender – a high octave of the purple ray – so that in spite of the tense activity that is typical of Chokmah and the yellow ray flowing through from Mercury, there is a calm control that can exercise the full wisdom of the Chokmah plane of consciousness.

On the path of The Magician in Binah the purple ray is impregnated with crimson, the overall colour of Binah and an octave of the red ray. Again the overbearing qualities of the purple ray are transmuted by the effect of the crimson merging and creating an octave of the amethyst ray.

The yellow ray flowing in from Mercury and meeting with the crimson is transmuted to an octave of the orange ray, the ray of the concrete mind. Here is the first restriction on the mental body, and yet with that restriction comes understanding, both qualities of Binah. The amethyst ray brings with it the first conscious idea and understanding of spirituality. This is also a ray of ceremonial magic, which is a state of subjective experience on this path.

In Yetzirah

The path of The Magician leaves behind the purple ray for that of the grey, which remains the ray throughout the whole of the Yetziratic World. There is still an influence, however, from the purple ray, deep purple being the overall Atziluthic colour of Gedulah (Chesed), the first sephirah of the Yetziratic World on the way down.

The merging of the grey with the purple produces a violet, a higher octave of the purple ray than the purple itself. The influences flowing through from this octave are humility, reverence and spiritual dedication. All these qualities are activated to a high degree by the action of the yellow ray.

These are indeed the qualities of Mastership and Gedulah is the sphere of the Masters. Here can be seen The Magician at the superhuman level, the spiritual Magician or Master: the clear vision as is so well expressed by the Intelligence of

Transparency.

The Sephirah Geburah presents an overall orange ray background to the grey of The Magician. The grey at this level is one of the middle band of octaves and as such contains the qualities of endurance, persistence, and is symbolic of the soul's struggle for freedom. The yellow ray adds a greater activity to this struggle.

Geburah being the sphere of karma, both the endurance and persistence are required by the spirit when it goes through this phase and at this archetypal level universal law has taken care to build-in the particular rays for the working out of this part of the plan. The orange ray at this octave is responsible for justice and wholeness and in this sense exercises restriction, which is one of the characteristics of Geburah.

From orange to clear pink rose, the Atziluthic colour of Tiphareth. This is a high octave of the red ray, with the quality of universal love that helps the spirit in its struggle for freedom. Here the path of The Magician teaches that the powers obtained have to be used for the sacrifice of self-love, or a love that covers only a narrow field, and that in this power house of the universe all powers are directed and channelled out to every corner of the Yetziratic World.

From Tiphareth the path of The Magician runs through Netzach and here the grey ray meets up with amber, a high octave of the orange ray that bestows receptivity and mental vigour, with the reactions of the yellow ray the mental vigour is expanded to one of high imagination, a quality required for success on the path of The Magician at any level, but particularly so at the Netzach level, where in this lower mental realm imagination is one of the working tools that can raise the spirit to higher levels of consciousness.

Venus, Mundane Chakra of Netzach, sends out the idea of a universal love through the blue ray, but as it merges with the yellow ray an octave of the green is formed and this brings struggle with it as all wider views in the lower planes tend to. This octave of the green ray also brings with it the idea of charity and endows the path with altruism, a quality that is typical of the idealism of Netzach with its philosophy of the wider field. It is in all the activities of Netzach, with all the struggles, that the grey ray can bring out a calming influence.

The overall background colour now changes to violet purple, the Atziluthic colour of Hod, but in this sephirah the yellow ray is predominant due to the flow from Mercury, the astrological influence of the path of The Magician, and also from the Mundane Chakra of Hod, which is also Mercury.

The spiritual side of the yellow ray is, however, restricted through the clouding by the grey ray and the overbearing influence of the violet purple, which is a low octave of the purple ray. Even the grey ray is on a lower octave at this level, due to the merging and resultant darkening by the purple ray. At this lower octave it produces a quality of suppression and hardness typical of the restricting quality of Hod.

The purple gives a forceful power and an overbearing attitude. This, combined with the lower level of the yellow ray, which produces an influence towards physical unity, lowers the tone of The Magician and the powers of this path now become restricted and lean more to work at the lower levels. It is only through the increased force of the yellow ray, which from time to time can break through the suppression and overbearing of the others, that escape can be made from Hod.

Yesod is the last sephirah in the Yetziratic world and the path of The Magician in Yesod is now subject to many fluctuating emotions, which is one of the main characteristics of this sephirah. The all-pervading colour is indigo, but from the Moon, Mundane Chakra of Yesod, there flows a ray of silvery grey, a high octave of the grey ray, and combined with the grey of the path aids in keeping the emotions to a controllable level with its quality of calm. There is also a quality of innocence in the octave of the grey ray, and this can be played upon by the emotions with disastrous results.

The level of indigo is one that produces the superstitious emotions and also stubbornness. This makes it rather difficult for the yellow ray of creative activity to break through. But it can be done and has to be done. It is through the intellectual aspect of the yellow ray that The Magician at this level can attain control.

In Assiah

In Malkuth the path of The Magician is indigo rayed with purple, with the yellow of Mercury still flowing through. In this sephirah the yellow ray is predominant, the overall basic Atziluthic colour of Malkuth being the yellow ray.

There is a great deal of activity on the path in Malkuth, as might be expected with such an influx of yellow, and the flow is further increased from the Mundane Chakra of Malkuth. From this chakra also issues the red, blue and green rays.

This is the one point, other than in Kether itself, where The Magician has the opportunity to control all the rays and through his powers merge them into the brilliance so that the perfect copy of Kether be attained with an added quality, that of conscious perfection as opposed to the unconscious perfection with which the Magician commenced.

THE HIGH PRIESTESS

In Assiah

The path of The High Priestess is a path of balance. She sits between the two pillars before the Temple with the scroll of wisdom in her hand. This path – joining Kether the Crown to Tiphareth, the heart of the universe – has for its astrological influence the Moon, from which it receives a ray of silvery grey, a high octave of the grey ray. The path itself is silver, the highest octave of the grey ray, rayed with sky blue.

In the World of Assiah, which is Malkuth on the archetypal tree, there is the background of yellow. The Mundane Chakra of this sephirah is composed of the four elements which provides the influence of four primary colours, red, blue, green and yellow.

It is because of these four primaries that the calm, tranquillity, and wisdom of the grey ray and the light octave of the blue is detracted from at this low level. Even though the wisdom is not pure, and from time to time the tranquillity is disturbed, the yellow ray of intellect can still penetrate, and even with the green ray causing envy of those further advanced, it is possible for this path to be conquered. The red ray at this octave can be the power of destruction, but with the aid of wisdom from the grey it can be channelled so that its destructive force can be used in the right way and as the wrong influences are destroyed the grey and yellow can construct with the aid of the blue ray.

This appears to be turmoil and struggle and it is the octave of the green ray causing this and yet from its other aspect it can help with the harmony that eventually leads out of Assiah into the World of Yetzirah and to the point where the path of The High Priestess has to be followed in the different stages or planes of consciousness in the Yetziratic World.

In Yetzirah

Yesod, the first objective sephirah in Yetzirah on the path of return, has an overall background of the indigo ray and the path of the High Priestess is now on the blue ray. The specific octave is pale blue, which is a high level octave of the ray.

There is still the silver ray from the Mundane Chakra of the path and this is accentuated by an addition of the silver ray from the Mundane Chakra of Yesod, which is also the Moon.

The indigo ray at this low octave contains the qualities of blind devotion and superstition, both are qualities which spring from the astral plane of Yesod. There can also be a degree of stubbornness arising from the low octave of indigo. This is, however, countered to some extent by the pale blue octave of the blue ray from the path itself, which helps to raise the indigo to a higher octave once it is brought into play.

This higher octave of the blue ray has innocence for one of its characteristics. This is not the innocence of purity, as might be expected, but rather innocence of the truth of the true spiritual teachings of the ancient wisdom due to the effect of the indigo clouding of the pale blue. From this clouding comes the religious faith within narrow orthodox teachings accepted in innocence of the truth.

Were it not for the double strength of the silver ray, this would also be clouded to a dark grey by the effect of the indigo. Even though brought down from the highest octave silver, it still retains some of its higher qualities at the octave of medium grey.

Here is an octave of the grey ray which gives endurance, persistence, and the desire of the soul to struggle for freedom. It is this last quality which enables the initiate to eventually free himself from the astral world of Yesod and reach up to the lower mental plane of Hod.

The all-pervading ray of Hod is violet/purple, a medium octave of the purple ray which inclines towards being overbearing and pompous with the spiritual dedication and reverence. Hod is the sephirah of the concretion of form and as such embraces all orthodox religions with their narrow confines of beliefs, typical in many instances of the characteristics of the medium octave of the purple ray outlined above.

From the blue ray of the path stems religious faith which is also part of the Hod activities and it is only through the effect of the grey ray, struggling for the freedom of the soul, that escape from full crystallization and stagnation is possible. Mercury, the Mundane Chakra of Hod, sends out the yellow ray which is the ray of all spiritual activities and creative activities. This also aids the grey ray in the struggle of the soul for freedom to follow a spiritual path as opposed to a religious way of life.

The spiritual awakening eventually takes place and the initiate is ready to move forward from Hod to Netzach, which although still on the lower mental plane, is just as wide in thought as Hod was narrow.

Amber is the background ray of Netzach and from Venus, Mundane Chakra of the sephirah, flows the blue ray. Amber as one of the higher octaves of the orange ray is noted for its quality of receptivity and geniality, whilst the particular octave of the blue ray contains within it the attributes of sincerity and also inspires the soul to struggle for spiritual maturity.

Netzach is the lower mental sephirah of idealism and it is receptive to all ideas that promulgate the well-being of man. It is with this receptivity and geniality that the Netzach influence can entice the initiate on to wild false trails, albeit in all sincerity. There is here, or can be, a touch of illusion, but of a different nature to the type found at Yesod. One is illusion through emotions, Netzach can be the illusion of the mind.

Spiritual maturity has not yet been attained, but the attempt at Netzach to reach this stage is inspired by the blue ray of the Mundane Chakra and the faith to obtain it comes from the higher octave of the blue ray associated with the path itself.

The silver from the Moon is toned down by the merging of the blue rays and the light grey octave of this ray gives harmony and it is in that harmony that the lower mental body finds its spiritual path in due course of time, which leads it up to Tiphareth.

Tiphareth is the bridge between the lower and higher mental planes of consciousness and the sephirah is flooded with a clear pink rose, a reasonably high octave of the red ray. From the Mundane Chakra of the sephirah flows the orange ray of the Sun.

The orange ray is a middle octave from which issues the quality of self-control and reliance. Comfort and unselfishness springs from the pink rose. Peace and stability stem from the light grey.

With the pink rose merging into the blue of the path an octave of the amethyst ray is produced that holds the quality of the visionary.

At Tiphareth the spark finds its spiritual maturity as the lower mental plane is left behind. The path of the High Priestess in the upper half of Tiphareth is in the higher mental plane of consciousness.

Self-control and reliance are key notes of this sephirah of the sacrificed Gods, the quality of comfort both nurtured and dispensed.

From the sephirah the true visionary sees the goal that is to be reached, here is beauty and harmony and it is in this atmosphere that the spark dwells and attains stability.

The danger at this stage is the peace and harmony which the spark is not inclined to relinquish. But it is also here that realization for the need to sacrifice becomes apparent.

Only by sacrifice can the spark rise again into the higher

realms, and with a peace of mind he sees the higher vision and makes the sacrifice that leads him up to Geburah.

Geburah, sephirah of correction and judgement, the controller of universal law, is ablaze with the orange ray. It is a middle octave of the ray, which has for its attributes orderliness and self-control: both qualities that are required for the enforcement of universal law, the ordered universe, the planets in the course and the organized evolution of man. For this to be carried through, self-control at all levels is required and where it is lacking, Geburah exercises its influence.

Mars, Mundane Chakra of Geburah, gives out the red ray which supplies the force, vigour and energy required to carry out the task of keeping all life, manifest and unmanifest, within the bounds laid down.

The blue merging with the red ray produces an octave of the amethyst ray with its altruistic quality. This combined with grey, ray of spiritual maturity, enables the spark to meet its karmic debts and with full idealism step forth towards the last phase of the higher mental level, which will be experienced in Gedulah.

From the harshness of Geburah to the sephirah of compassion and grace, the sphere of the Masters. On the path of the High Priestess in Gedulah the spark is approaching the point of departure to the point of no return.

Deep violet, an octave of the purple ray, is the overall colour of Gedulah. This octave of the ray is one of humility and spiritual dedication. It also has the quality of reverence, not as associated with the religious reverence for a God, but a spiritual reverence for all life at all levels.

Idealism is a keynote of the amethyst ray, which flows out from Jupiter, Mundane Chakra of Gedulah, and with its quality of expansion the blue ray of the path bestows the quality of compassion. At this high level of consciousness the silver ray is not so clouded and bestows a quiet, peaceful calm and tranquillity.

These are the qualities not only absorbed by the spark, but

also given out by the spark from his high level to all in need on the lower levels. The work of this sephirah experienced and completed, the next stage of the journey is across the abyss to the World of Briah.

In Briah

The path of the High Priestess is now flooded with the silver octave of the grey ray, accentuated by the silver from the Moon. Binah, the first sephirah of the Briatic world on the path of return, is covered in crimson and from Saturn, its Mundane Chakra, flows the black ray.

At this high level or octave of the black ray it holds esoteric and meditative powers, which – combined with the peace and tranquillity of the silver – could lead to inertia were it not for the vital force of the all-pervading crimson of Binah that contains active and impulsive characteristics.

Were it not for the restraining influence of the black ray this impulsiveness could lead to trouble. This is one of the best examples of how the rays act and interact one upon the other, thus providing the right qualities for each stage of progression of the journey from spirit to man and back to spirit.

Now free of even the most tenuous form, the spark in due course reaches the path of The High Priestess in Chokmah. The silver ray is still in evidence, both on the path and from its Mundane Chakra. The predominant colour of Chokmah is a soft blue, a high octave of the blue ray, full of wisdom and selfless love.

The Mundane Chakra of Chokmah is the sphere of the Zodiac from which pours out all the rays. Here we have the whirling mass of force which is Chokmah, but with the qualities of the silvery peace, tranquillity and harmony, the spark withstands and is impervious to the rush of Chokmah forces.

In Atziluth

Blue is now the colour of the path. This is the pure blue

which holds all wisdom and the silver from the Moon gives that tranquillity unknown and incomprehensible at lower levels. Both these rays shimmer in a living colour that emanates from the pure brilliance of Kether.

THE EMPRESS

In Assiah

The basic teachings of the path of The Empress are unity in general and at-one-ment with nature in particular. In the World of Assiah or Malkuth on the basic Tree the path gives forth a bright rose, high octave of the red ray and the green ray with which it is flecked.

Venus is the planetary ruler of the path and gives out the blue ray of love and wisdom. This is very appropriate for this path and it is the one ray that will remain constant, although the others change from world to world.

As The Empress is also the door, love and wisdom qualities play a very important part in its function. The path joins the two Sephiroth of Chokmah and Binah, again emphasizing the unity aspect. This path is the first bridge between active and passive or positive and negative.

Unity expresses and emphasizes balance and harmony. Love can help with the balance and wisdom with the harmony. Rose produces the qualities of healing power of a magnetic nature and constant affection. Harmony through struggle and conflict is a product of the green ray.

To pass through this door is no easy task for the student and in the World of Assiah the rays are inclined to influence the student instead of him using their influence. The yellow of Malkuth has him in a perpetual state of activity, and with the green this is quite often expressed in struggle and conflict.

With the rose creating within him a desire of affection and

the urge to heal the ills of mankind, to bring about unity between nations and the general well-being of man, and at the same time the green ray creating within him conflict of ideas, he finds it difficult to follow a settled way of life.

It is only after much struggle and conflict – and in all probability, many incarnations – that it dawns upon him through the wisdom aspect of the blue ray that he must first obtain unity within himself, to find his own inner peace, then and only then will his objective become clear.

How can he help others to attain unity with each other if he is not in harmony with himself and with others? The student finds it difficult to be at-one-ment with those who follow a different way of life and hold to different ideas. This is the key to the conquest of the path of The Empress and the work of this path, to attain unity with all, although differing from others in many ways.

To attain true unity within himself is a hopeless task if he does not first resolve a line of action that arouses or creates doubts that result in his inner conflict. He must assure himself and be certain that his feelings and ideals are correct.

The first task is to balance within himself the four elements which give out the four rays, red, blue, yellow and green. These are the ingredients of all nature and the path of The Empress is – apart from other things – the state of consciousness that is at one with all nature.

Consideration of the rays connected to the four elements bring to notice the important factor that they are the three major rays plus the ray of balance; but it is this ray of balance, the green ray, that causes all the struggle and conflict, and will do so until such time as the three major rays are brought into harmony.

The green ray is the ray of earth, the element of conflict. Once the student is aware of this he understands that Air – spirit (the yellow ray) must be working with Water – love/wisdom – (blue ray) and the two must be operated by the perfect balance of Fire – will and power – (red ray). Only when these three are perfectly combined will the balance of Earth – harmony – (green ray) be achieved.

To gain his first insight into the mysteries and power of the rays the student must succumb to the blue ray of wisdom, which is one of the two predominant rays on this path in Assiah, through the element of water and from Venus, planetary ruler of the path.

Yellow is the other predominant ray, flowing out from the air element and from Malkuth or Assiah on the main Tree. Having gained wisdom from the blue ray, he now applies it to the use of the yellow ray and directs its activity into spiritual channels.

This is the student's first attempt on this path to control the rays, and though his handling of them by cosmic standards is far from perfect, it is accurate and efficient by the standards of Assiah. With the blending of these rays or the elements the student finds himself in unity with himself. Now he can proceed with confidence, all doubts settled.

Moving forward with his new-born confidence he commences to attain true unity with all life in Assiah and reaches at-one-ment with the whole of nature. The student is now ready to complete his journey through Assiah and commence a new adventure in the World of Yetzirah.

In Yetzirah

Yesod and its Tree now faces the student or initiate and through the whole of his experiences on this Tree he is enshrouded with indigo, Yesod's Atziluthic colour. When he reaches the path of The Empress he discovers the rose has given way to a light green – a high octave of the green ray – but the blue ray from Venus remains with him, as it will do through all the Yetziratic world.

Silver, a high octave of the grey ray, which issues from the Moon, is also available for his use during his sojourn in Yesod. The student or initiate will find this ray invaluable as he tries to find unity and a feeling of oneness in what can be a sphere of illusion.

In Yesod the student or initiate commences to find union

with his spiritual nature, not an easy task to accomplish, nevertheless a task that has to be carried out if he wishes to progress along his journey toward the ultimate, and this he is devoted to doing mainly through the influence of the indigo ray, which is a ray of devotion.

At the level of Yesod the devotion of the indigo ray can be one of blind devotion, which in one sense is an admirable characteristic displaying a great faith, on the other hand it can be dangerous due to lack of knowledge and finish up as misplaced faith. In this respect the indigo ray has its dangers.

In this astral emotional world the student or initiate has to bring about unity of emotions to gain balance and understanding of what are illusions and what is reality. It is also on the path of The Empress in this sephirah that he must come to terms with – and make conquest over – his lower animal nature.

Just as Yesod is the strong foundation on the outward journey in preparation for descent into Malkuth – Assiah of the basic Tree, so it is the strong foundation for the return path and the student must be careful to choose the right foundation or he could plunge down to lower levels of the Tree in Yesod or even back to Malkuth.

The control and harmonizing of the lower nature is the major lesson to complete the victory on this path, which teaches not only to rule but also to be at one with nature.

To prevent the blind devotion of the indigo ray taking a firm grip, he must use the silver ray from the Moon and not only draw from it the qualities of tranquillity and balance, but he must direct it into the indigo ray in order to develop that higher octave of indigo which will give him charity of thought and foresight.

From the light green ray he draws the quality of understanding and from the blue he obtains wisdom. Once he has obtained these qualities to a small degree he is in a position to find a balance whereby he can also utilize the understanding and wisdom flowing from Binah and Chokmah respectively along the path of The Empress.

Hod, the sephirah of form, rigid principles and the perfection and glory of organization at the lower mental level, is the next sephirah in which contact is made with the path of The Empress. Now it is the nature of the lower mental body that the student must bring under control and Hod is the first stage of this task.

The overall ray for this sephirah is violet/purple, and it is in this ray that the path of The Empress is bathed. The light green of the path and the blue ray of Venus still flow out but the silver of the Moon has given way to the yellow of Mercury.

Rulership is now a predominant characteristic, not only from the path of The Empress but also from the purple aspect of the violet/purple ray. From the yellow flows the creative activity that leads the student into a maze of orthodox, organizational, and religious systems that culminate in that rigidity of outlook that finds no place for tolerance.

It is only when the blue ray of wisdom commences to prevail that he sees the folly of any form that does not have a certain amount of pliability. From the light green he develops the characteristic of sympathy and it is this quality that makes him relent on his rigidity of rulership.

Now he commences to understand the nature of his lower mental body and puts the yellow ray to use again, but this time using a different aspect of the ray. First he absorbs its friendly quality and then draws from it the influence that gives him a powerful intellect.

A true ruler commences to develop, one that is finding harmony within his own mental nature and in so doing has developed the first stages of control, which enables him to take a wider vision.

The student or initiate is now ready to come to grips with the Tree in Netzach, the second aspect of the lower mental nature. In the course of time he reaches the path of The Empress clouded in amber, a high octave of the orange ray. Two rays of blue now meet him; one from Venus, planetary ruler of the path, and the other from Venus, Mundane Chakra of Netzach.

A quantity of the blue ray without compensating factors can make the work of the student very difficult and even retard his progress. The quality for being a hard worker is developed without discrimination, and hard work is put in to obtaining many hollow victories.

The wisdom from the blue ray is also employed in following the lines that lead to useless victories. From the high octave of the orange ray the student can, and in course of time he does, absorb the quality of practical knowledge, and by applying this to mental vigour, also a quality of the amber ray, he balances the wisdom aspect to a point where he is able to use the high octave of the green ray.

Green is the ray of nature itself and from this high octave the student develops understanding and becomes altruistic, another quality of the light green. Altruism, with wisdom and understanding applied to the practical knowledge, gives him the victory of Netzach over the path of The Empress and with the nature of the lower mental body correctly ruled he can make for his next goal, which is Tiphareth.

As the path of The Empress is on the higher reaches of the Tree in Tiphareth, the initiate is now clear of his lower mental body and can commence the harmonizing of his higher mental body.

The green of the path and the blue of its planetary ruler are both overshadowed by the pink rose of Tiphareth, and trying to make its presence or influence felt is the orange ray darting out from the Sun, which is the Mundane Chakra of the sephirah.

There are not many pitfalls for the initiate at this level of Tiphareth because many qualities of the sephirah are the same as those for the path. Harmony and balance are the keynotes of them both and the pink rose of universal love is a ray that merges in with The Empress and with Tiphareth.

The main danger of the few that exist at this plane of consciousness is that of pride, which can take three forms.

Pride in achievement, intellectual pride and spiritual pride. The adept can succumb to one or all three of these vices, because this is a quality that is very strong in the orange ray.

Pride can be a virtue as well as a vice if applied in the correct way and this can be accomplished by the use of the green ray to give that calm and balance required to make the most effective use of the higher mental body.

Once calm and balance has been obtained, then the full use of the rose with its capacity for universal love can be employed and directed in the right channels through wisdom taken from the blue ray. Now the adept can turn the quality of pride from a vice to a virtue, which is pride with humility. This is not a pride in himself or his abilities, but a pride in the task itself.

Having reached this stage in his development, no form of sacrifice is too great for the adept because he is attaining the perfection of the path of The Empress, which is complete unity with the whole of life. The at-one-ment is not, however, quite reached; there are further stages of consciousness and experiences still to work through, but the experience of The Empress in Tiphareth is completed.

The Master's next experience on the path of The Empress is on the Tree in Geburah. The green and blue rays of the path are now set against a background of orange, the ray of Geburah in Atziluth, with the power of the red ray pouring out from Mars.

At the level of Geburah the orange ray is a very high octave and produces the qualities of geniality and receptivity, whilst the red ray provides vigour and energy. Through the orange ray with its geniality the Master develops a gentle understanding aided by his receptivity of all the influences about him. There is, however, no weakness in his kindness because, through the vigour and energy of the red, transmuted by the blue and given balance by the green, he has also developed a gentle firmness.

Full realization of the path of The Empress at Geburah is to be at one and united with the whole of nature and life without being engulfed in the whole. A lesson in self-discipline and how to be in harmony with and in the midst of the whole and yet to be apart from that whole in as much as the Master works with it, not for or against it.

This is not an easy lesson to learn as the Master, full of vigour and energy from the red ray, is desirous of working for the whole, a very commendable quality at the lower levels, but on the path of The Empress in Geburah it would in reality be working against the whole. What the Master has to learn is that at this level each aspect of the whole has to stand on its own feet and find its own salvation. No spark of the whole in any guise or form can be given perfection by the Master or any other being. It must be developed within itself.

The Empress in Geburah is a path of testing for all sparks of the Ain force at that level, and it is on their own ability, their strength or weakness, that their rewards in the sense of hopes and fears are realized.

All is available for their needs to make good on the path of The Empress in Geburah if they choose to use the cosmic tools to hand. The red ray for strength, orange with receptivity and practical knowledge, balance and harmony from the green and love and wisdom from the blue ray.

With the end of his journey through the lower worlds in sight, the Master moves forward to Gedulah and steadily climbs the Tree in that sephirah until once more he faces the path of The Empress. The orange and red rays of Geburah have given way to the deep violet of Gedulah and the amethyst of Jupiter.

It is on the path of The Empress in Gedulah that the Master faces his last experience and lesson that the lower worlds have to offer him, that of the duality of love.

In kindness and with the highest motive he gives out to all life a full and expansive love, the expansiveness that could only come from the influence of Jupiter, combined with that deeper love which flows out from Venus.

Part of the work in this sephirah is to give love to the maximum of the Master's potential but it must be given with wisdom. Love without wisdom becomes selfish, love given with wisdom is selfless. This is another quality of the blue ray, which is the one permanent ray of The Empress in all four Worlds.

Love in one form or another is a permanent quality or feature of The Empress at all levels and on all Trees, but it must be controlled lest it pour forth with such a rush that it becomes a destroyer agent instead of a creative agent. It is here that the high octave of the green ray from the path aids by bringing balance to the outpouring.

From the amethyst ray comes a spiritual quality and from the violet spiritual dedication, and with these influences brought to the path the Master learns to give out love endowed with spiritual wisdom, that true harmony may prevail.

Mystical attainment also comes from the amethyst ray, and as the Master develops his powers in this field he realizes the true mysticism of nature, as expressed by the path of The Empress, and how it binds the whole of nature into perfect balance and harmony.

In Briah

Over the abyss is the vision of Binah, its crimson ray reflecting into the abyss, and it is on the path of The Empress in Binah that the Master now sets his sights and takes the leap forward that takes him to the point of no return.

On reaching the path of The Empress in Binah the Master finds that it is predominantly blue. The path itself is sky blue and from Venus also blue, but a little lower octave. The black ray now appears for the first time in connection with this path and so if the Master desires he can, for his use, merge the blue and black rays to give himself an octave of the indigo.

From a careful balancing of the crimson and blue rays an octave of the amethyst can be added to the Master's cosmic tools and he is now in possession of five of the cosmic rays with all the powers they hold.

This is the last Tree where he will be restricted by form, however tenuous, and this is the restriction imposed by the black ray, but this ray also serves another purpose, that of binding or holding together. Here is the true unity of nature with form.

Through the amethyst ray the Master understands in entirety the mystery of nature and develops through the blue ray an even greater love of nature.

The fortitude of all nature through the indigo ray is now revealed to him and this he applies to himself that he may become at-one-ment again at this higher plane of consciousness.

With the blue ray predominant and containing two octaves of the ray, the love of the lower levels gradually turns to pure compassion and this, combined with the humility of the amethyst ray, teaches the Master the need for both fortitude and humility in the nature of life, each being but a small speck in the totality.

Latent powers belonging to the black ray now open up what has been the secretive side of nature, also an aspect of the black ray, where at the lower levels the black ray withheld this knowledge, now the Master controls and uses it to the fullest extent.

What had been a ray of restriction now becomes the cosmic tool for his liberation and he prepares to leave the path of The Empress on the Tree in Binah for the last lap of the journey, the Tree in Chokmah.

In Chokmah the path of The Empress presents the last and widest aspect of nature. The spark now free of all form and restriction is brought into direct contact with the stars and their activities. The blue ray is even more accentuated as the pure soft blue of Chokmah forms the background to the two octaves of blue flowing from the path and its governing planet.

A true understanding of the Wisdom of the Universe and its nature is now possible and at The Empress level of The Tree in Chokmah there is very little chance of the spark falling back. At this point the near pure spark of the Ain consciousness sees clearly and face to face.

As the spark follows the path of The Empress it notes and understands each sign of the zodiac as it wheels round in the sphere of Chokmah. The true nature with the last of its secrets is opened up.

One by one the rays related to their individual sign pass before the spark as they follow their ordered evolution, and each in turn projects its own particular ray down the main Tree, through each sephirah in turn.

The whole nature of life, from the major forces to the minor details, now lies exposed before the eternal spark and it now realizes its own nature, and in so doing is fully integrated into the unity and fullness of the one life.

In Atziluth

The path of The Empress is emerald green on the Tree in Kether; from its ruling planet of Venus the blue still streams forth, and from Kether itself is the scintillating brilliance.

On the Tree in the Atziluthic world this is the perfect archetype of unity, the path joining Chokmah (wisdom) to Binah (understanding). It is the uniting of force and form, bringing together in balance and harmony the two opposites.

Green, particularly this octave, holds within it the virtues of balance and harmony, and combined with the blue of love creates the ultimate in perfection of unity. This is the seed that the spark was endowed with on the outward journey and which has now come to fruition and blossoms forth in full illumination on the spark's return to the conscious perfection of Atziluth.

THE PATH OF THE STAR

In Assiah

Malkuth with its clear yellow colour is full of activity befitting the yellow ray qualities and yellow is also the ray that symbolizes spirit. With the zeal of the red ray from the path itself and also from Aries the astrological influence of The Star, it could be anticipated that this would be a place of consciousness for great spiritual activity.

With the four elements as Mundane Chakra to Mars the spiritual activity is detracted from through the three major and the one balancing ray which flow from the four elements. The merging of these rays creates octaves of all the rays, which unlike the Kether level of consciousness are not perfectly balanced and integrated. There are therefore many impurities that affect the path.

The red and yellow rays are still predominant, the red with its energy, drive and burning desire to get somewhere, and with the spiritual yellow breaking through, his desire is to see and know the answers to life.

Man at this stage is peering through a glass darkly, but he is at least peering through the glass. Spiritual realization is commencing to dawn and his energy and creative activities are devoted to this end, even though at times misguided through the mixed influence of the other rays.

The red ray at this level can make him fiery and it is perhaps fortunate that the yellow breaks in to tone down what could easily develop into unreasonable temper. The yellow ray, however, softens it to a point where it becomes what is termed righteous anger.

With all the conflicts it takes man a long time to conquer the path of The Star and be in a position where he can move slowly forward until he reaches this path in Yesod where the path has to be traversed again, but this time without a physical body, the astral body being the densest level.

In Yetzirah

The indigo ray of Yesod is at this level conducive to emotions of a religious nature. The silver from the Moon is partially absorbed by the indigo so that it becomes a lower octave of the grey ray.

The path itself throughout the whole of the Yetziratic World is brilliant flame, a medium octave of the red ray, and this – combined with the red of Aries – gives a great deal of impulsive emotions, acting directly from an emotional level without first stopping to consider if the action be right or wrong.

With the indigo ray providing the element of superstition, and the impulsiveness of the red to seize upon it, the seeds of emotional religion are sown, which flow down from the World of Yetzirah into the World of Assiah.

The task of the dwellers in Yesod is to use the silver ray flowing out from the Moon and use its qualities to calm the emotions and help subdue the superstitions so that the mental body can take control.

With the completion of this task the spark is prepared to move onward to the sephirah of Hod and the path of The Star in that sephirah.

In Hod the red ray of the path is joined by the violet/purple of Hod with the yellow ray flowing out from Mercury. It is here, through the yellow ray, that intense spiritual activity commences to take form. Lines of communication – another aspect of the yellow ray – are also formulated. The illumination of The Star is breaking through and the means of proceeding from Tiphareth to Chokmah becomes more clear.

The driving destructive force of the red ray aids in the

breaking of the forms built in the early stages of Hod experience, for the purpose of forming a wider concept.

As the red ray merges with the violet/purple, an octave of the inspirational amethyst ray forms. It is the quality of this ray that rebuilds the ideas into a wider concept and by the judicial use of the inspiration given out by the ray the spark can sacrifice what are now to him outmoded forms, free itself from some of the lower mental limitations and commence work in the wider field of Netzach.

Netzach is the sephirah of ideas, a lower form of Chokmah, from which the first abstract thoughts flow. At the Netzach level they are more concrete due to the amber, which is an octave of the orange ray, although not so crystallized as the limiting form of Hod. Also from Chokmah flows wisdom. This comes out of Netzach through the blue from Venus. Again it is not the wisdom known at Chokmah, but the highest that can be found at the lower mental level.

The red and blue merge and produce the amethyst, an octave of the ray that gives out spiritual wisdom, which in turn gives a greater expansion of consciousness that enables progress to be made from Netzach up to Tiphareth.

A clear pink rose, a high octave of the red ray combined with a middle octave of the orange ray, flows from Tiphareth and its Mundane Chakra, bringing to the path of The Star both love and pride, but the true pride of achievement, not the false pride of 'Thank God I am not as one of those'.

The wisdom of Chokmah at the top of the path and the sacrifice of Tiphareth at the lower end imbue the path at this level with both true love and true wisdom. This point of progress is now above the lower mental plane and the higher mental body takes over.

The red ray creates not only the vigour, but a burning desire to probe deeper into the mystery of the seven seals as symbolized on the path. At Tiphareth five of the seals have already been broken. Two remain to be understood, the next being Geburah.

Geburah is the sephirah of many restrictions, one of which is self-control, a quality of the middle octave of the orange ray which covers this sephirah. Self-control is essential if the path of The Star is to be conquered in the sphere of karma. It is also required to withstand the harshness that emanates from Geburah.

The red ray from its Mundane Chakra combined with the flame of the path and the red from its astrological influence can make this a point of destruction, and, in effect, that is just what it is.

With the opening of this seal the full force of retribution is let loose and the spark realizes that all the sacrifices at Tiphareth are of no avail unless and until full retribution has been made and the last imperfection burnt away by the searing destructive force of the red ray. Once these imperfections have been removed the spark is ready to move forward again into the sephirah of Gedulah, the last point in the higher mental world.

Gedulah is deep violet, an octave of the purple ray. This is a royal ray and what could be more appropriate for this sphere of the Masters? This particular octave is a ray of humility and spiritual dedication. Added to this is the spiritual ray of amethyst which flows from Jupiter, the Mundane Chakra of Gedulah.

The flame of the path and the red of the astrological influence gives a burning desire, which combined with the spiritual influences flowing in from the other rays is a desire to help all life, to gain full illumination and see clearly the true life and this is one of the main objectives of the path of The Star, commencing at Tiphareth, the point of sacrifice, and seeing through a glass darkly and terminating at Chokmah where full illumination of wisdom comes through.

Gedulah is the point of the seventh seal and it is the opening and understanding of the wisdom contained within this last seal of The Star that gives again a burning desire, but this time to cross the abyss to the two worlds beyond, the first being the World of Briah.

In Briah

Across the abyss the spark reaches Binah, the first stage of the Briatic World on the path of return. The path of The Star is now flooded with the red ray which merges with the higher octave of the ray – crimson – the overall ray of Binah.

High-powered energies are now released in a flood of activity, curbed only by the black ray which – as it merges into the crimson and red tones – drown and control the destructive power of the red ray. The power of the red is still strong enough to burn away or dissolve the last of tenuous form so that the spark can be released to make its way unencumbered to the pure freedom of Chokmah.

From the vigour and action of the red ray the spark is surrounded by the pure soft blue of Chokmah. Now the true wisdom comes through and the consciousness of the spark knows its own individuality and at the same time that it has no individuality but is a segment of the whole. Now it is face to face and as the pure soft blue merges with the red of the path and its astrological influence, the spark is bathed in the pure spiritual ray of amethyst.

The last imperfections are swept away and gathering together in perfect harmony and balance all the rays issuing from Chokmah's Mundane Chakra, the sphere of the zodiac, it blends them into the pure brilliance which fits it to go forward into the World of Atziluth.

In Atziluth

The red ray is still the predominant ray of The Star in Atziluth. The path itself is scarlet and the ray from the astrological influence is red, but surrounded with brilliance. The scarlet and red are so pure that they are beyond the conception of even the higher mind. It becomes through the action of the Brilliance upon it, an indefinable rose pink, the octave of the red ray that has the attribute of universal love.

This path in Atziluth is the archetype of perfected universal love, that love which is prepared to sacrifice for the true wisdom, not for personal advantage, but to see clearly so that help and guidance can be given to all life at all levels of being from Malkuth to Briah.

THE HIEROPHANT

In Assiah

The Hierophant joins Chokmah to Gedulah and so there is wisdom flowing along this path and meeting mercy that pours along the path from Gedulah. It can also be described as a path where spirit as individuality enters in the first and highest stage of personality.

Vau is the Hebrew letter for the path and this means nail, hook or peg, something on which to hang or link some other thing. Taurus is the astrological ruler of the path of The Hierophant. Through Venus, the ruling planet of Taurus, the solar energies of The Hierophant or the universal energy of Chokmah blends with the Venusian qualities of imagination and mental imagery. It is for these qualities that Venus is the Mundane Chakra of Netzach and not Gedulah.

There is a reference to the Inner Voice and the hearing of it, and there is clearly a contact being made here between the conscious and the super-conscious. The Hierophant is the super-conscious at the conscious level and remembering the nail or peg as something to hang on, this is what The Hierophant is to the student.

A path of communication is how The Hierophant can be described and it is communication at all levels and in every sense, verbal, mental and even that higher level already mentioned, the communication of the inner voice.

The Hierophant is indeed a path of learning, as all paths are, but in this case it is learning not by experience so much as by accepting teachings that are given in many varied and different ways.

In Assiah the student has a number of rays with which to work. The pure clear yellow – Atziluthic colour of Assiah, red, blue, green and more yellow from the elements which form the Mundane Chakra of Malkuth or Assiah on the main Tree. The path itself responds to a rich brown, a medium octave of the brown ray and from its astrological sign Taurus there is a further emanation of the blue ray.

Out of all this the ray most important to the student is the brown ray of the path, although blue and yellow are the predominant rays, through the effect of two emanations from different sources within the World of Assiah. The brown ray is the most important because in following or trying to follow the path the student is not just a student following a general way of advancement, but is a student Hierophant.

The yellow ray endows him with quick mental activity, the Mercurial messenger aspect, but that quick mental activity has to be channelled in the right direction. Because he is on the path of The Hierophant this does not mean the student is beyond error. He can still develop vices as well as virtues.

The yellow ray is also the ray whereby intuition can be developed, intuition being a higher level of communication than any of the psychic forms of communication, which do not go beyond the level of the astral plane, or the Tree in Yesod.

Intuition reaches outwards and upwards. It could be classed as the 'hot line' to God, but to make the link or connection the mercurial activity has to be controlled and this is where the student can make use of the brown ray and why, although not predominant, it is important at this stage of the student's development.

The rich brown not only contains the quality of intuition as the yellow ray but it also bestows the powers of concentration if the student will only draw upon it. It is the ability to concentrate that the student must first develop, then he can draw up the intuitive powers of both the brown and yellow rays.

Wisdom and knowledge are also available from the high octave of the brown ray. Wisdom can also be drawn from the blue ray of the water element. With knowledge and the wisdom of how to exercise that knowledge, the student is now in a position to handle the green ray and use just the harmony and balance aspect of it.

With a quiet calm confidence and in full assurance of where he is going, he employs the red ray just sufficiently to give him the vitality and will to move forward, realizing that without this spur he could forever bask in the calm and peace obtained from both the brown and green rays.

From the path of The Hierophant it is not a great distance to the top of the Tree in Malkuth, where he can leave behind the physical world and move into the World of Yetzirah.

In Yetzirah

Moving on to the emotional plane of consciousness the student steadily climbs the Tree in Yesod until he reaches the path of the Hierophant in that sephirah.

The colour of the path is now a warm olive, an octave of the green ray. The blue ray still shines out from Taurus and the whole is set against a background of indigo. Grey, a medium octave of the grey ray, also influences this path and has its source in the olive green.

At this high level of the Tree in Yesod the student has no difficulty in obtaining the balance and harmony required to cross this path in the world of emotions, and even then it is not easy because Yesod, the astral world, is full of an illusory glamour, part of which comes from Yesod's Mundane Chakra, the Moon. Here truly is the root and seat of astral glamour, the waters of the Moon with all its illusions.

From the mixture of the grey and green rays, which make up the olive green, comes the quality of deceit. There is no attempt to deceive others, at this level of consciousness the student is inclined to deceive himself, further encouraged by the waters of the Moon. The unfortunate aspect of this is that the student does not realize he is deceiving himself but does it in all sincerity.

It is in this situation that the student misses either consciously or unconsciously the use of the brown ray and it is only when he commences to utilize the blue ray of wisdom from Taurus that he can break the difficult cycle he has got into.

First he isolates the green from the grey, restoring his balance which had temporarily been lost, and then from the octave of the grey he draws in the influence that encourages him to struggle for his spiritual freedom.

Indigo gives him both fortitude and caution and both are essential when travelling through the Tree in Yesod, particularly the characteristic of caution, in this plane of consciousness where so much illusion abounds.

By maintaining balance and proceeding with caution the student Hierophant makes a firmer contact with the mental plane and so overrides the emotional body, thus completing the lessons of The Hierophant in Yesod he now moves forward to the Tree in Hod.

The path of The Hierophant in Hod is overshadowed by a violet/purple and from Mercury the yellow ray streams out, placing the accent once again on the intellect, which can be a dangerous procedure in Hod, the sephirah of form.

The student Hierophant is now in a position to rise to intellectual heights and achieve the true glory that is Hod, providing he uses the blue ray from Taurus and applies wisdom to his intellectual prowess.

From the violet he can obtain the true quality of spiritual dedication. From this ray he also obtains reverence, a fine characteristic to develop, but one that can be rather dangerous and subtle in its workings. So often at this point does a student Hierophant fail because of reverence for the intellectual instead of reverence for the intricate mechanism of manifestation and its creative force.

To help the student overcome this danger there is a further quality he can absorb from the violet ray, that is humility. It is when he combines humility with reverence that he understands how insignificant he is in the whole scheme of things in spite of his intellectual abilities.

Through applying the wisdom of the blue ray he also understands that even the most insignificant aspect is important to the whole without being important in itself. The real Hierophant is now commencing to emerge. The student is being superseded by the initiate as the end of the path of The Hierophant in Hod is reached and he moves his sphere of activity to the Tree in Netzach.

Netzach illuminates the Tree within it with an amber glow, a high octave of the orange ray, and from its Mundane Chakra flows the blue ray to supplement the blue from Taurus, astrological ruler of the path of the Hierophant.

In Netzach the initiate on the path of The Hierophant is facing the last stage of his journey through the lower mental plane of consciousness. The teaching and wisdom that he now has to absorb is on a different level. From wisdom and understanding of the material or physical nature of manifestation he now has to develop spiritual wisdom and understanding.

Lines of communication are still the same from consciousness to super-consciousness, but on a higher level of understanding. Spiritual wisdom appertains not just to the human evolution, but also to the evolution of nature; the initiate should be able to understand why a blade of grass can affect a star.

Victory on the path of The Hierophant in Netzach can only be obtained when he finds the secret of the link that binds nature and the different streams of evolution into one inextricable whole.

Mental vigour and wholeness are the attributes that come from the amber ray and it is the mental vigour that the initiate must take from this ray if he is to successfully learn the lessons of the path.

The green ray from the path itself not only gives him ambition, but also the love of nature, which is of vital importance on the Tree in Netzach, and from the grey aspect of the path there comes endurance and idealism. This latter quality also belongs to Netzach itself, so once developed by the initiate it brings him into complete harmony and creates the perfect link between path and sephirah.

There is, as with most paths, a snare for the unwary, which is the imaginative quality that belongs to Netzach. It is so easy for the initiate Hierophant – once he has a little spiritual wisdom added to his wisdom and knowledge – to imagine he is the Hierophant. Again the quality of deceit emanates from the olive colour of the path.

If he is to be successful on this path the initiate Hierophant must keep the grey and green aspects of olive separate in his use of them. Only through wisdom can he do this and so it is imperative that he makes full use of the two rays of blue and also the Chokmah wisdom that flows down the path.

With that wisdom and the balance of the green ray the initiate Hierophant gains a clear perspective and knows that he still has a long way to go before he becomes the Hierophant himself. He also realizes that he still has a great deal of spiritual wisdom to absorb and in spite of how much he already knows, acknowledges that he knows very little.

Now he must leave Netzach behind and make his way to the path of The Hierophant on the Tree in Tiphareth, where his training continues, but commencing on the higher mental plane of consciousness pink/rose is the background colour for the olive colour of the path and from the Sun an orange ray beams out.

Pink/rose, a very high octave of the red ray, holds within it the quality of tact; forgiveness is also a characteristic of this ray. These are two essentials that a Hierophant must have. Without them he is no Hierophant. This then is the lesson on the path of the Hierophant in Tiphareth.

From the influence of the orange ray he develops self-control which is the basis for both tact and forgiveness, and the trials that he faces in Tiphareth will test that self-control to the full.

Although the sephirah in itself is one of harmony, beauty and balance, it is also the sphere of the sacrificed gods. From the olive deceit again raises its head, but this time it is the deceit employed by the forces opposing the initiate.

At Tiphareth the powers of darkness make their last stand in an attempt to bring about the initiate's downfall. Here he is 'thrown to the wolves' and has to meet deceit, treachery and subtle temptations. To meet these on a physical plane is not easy. On the mental plane, where it is a contest between minds, the last ounce of self-control is required.

To aid him in his battle the initiate must again draw upon the wisdom of the blue ray and the balance from the green ray. The initiate must forgive whatever action is taken against him. He must also exercise tact. From the pink/rose he can also cultivate constant affection, which ensures full forgiveness.

This can be claimed, if he is successful, as the near-ultimate sacrifice which not only takes him beyond Tiphareth to Geburah but also raises him to the level of adeptship and it is as an adept that he enters the sephirah of Geburah to make his way up that Tree until once more he faces the path of The Hierophant.

At Geburah the energy is once again the enemy within, an old enemy that he met at the lower mental level, that of pride carried by the orange ray which covers the whole of the Tree in Geburah and searing through the orange glow is the red of Mars.

This particular octave of the red brings with it the qualities of will and power: vigour and energy are also attributes of this octave and combined with the pride from the orange can be a danger to the adept and could be the destroyer-agents that would bring all his previous efforts to nought.

Again he turns to the influences of the path and draws in the wisdom of Chokmah and also from the blue ray of Taurus, but he must also take from the blue its second aspect, that of love through which he can transmute the red and so produce an octave of the amethyst ray.

From the amethyst ray the adept can now develop mystical and ritualistic powers, some of the main tools of the Hierophant. He has now all but reached his goal, the conquest of the path of The Hierophant in Geburah is within his grasp. Pride and pride alone stands between himself and victory.

The success of all his training, experiences and hardships now depends on which way he develops the pride of the orange ray, either pride in himself and his achievements, or pride in the magnificence of the whole scheme of manifestation. By using the wisdom of the blue ray and employing it he merges it with the orange and produces an octave of the purple ray which gives him the quality of humility.

Pride cannot exist in the presence of humility and by drawing calmness from the grey aspect of the path itself he emerges from the path of The Hierophant in Geburah triumphant and ready to tackle the Tree in Gedulah where he eventually comes to the path of The Hierophant, but now no longer as an adept but as The Hierophant himself where now he has to put into effect all that he has gained on the way.

Gedulah bathes the Tree within it in deep violet, once more the use of an octave of the purple ray is available, as also is the amethyst from Jupiter. The path of the Hierophant still throws out the influences of olive with the blue of Taurus still in attendance.

The Master is now The Hierophant and so his experience on this path in Gedulah is now vastly different from the state of pupil, where he is accepting teachings. He is now in the position of dispensing the ancient wisdom and mysteries to those who come to him for guidance.

Discretion and right use of his powers are the lessons that he now has to learn and so the path gives a two-fold experience, that of teaching himself as well as teaching others. First he must use the blue ray and obtain from it the maximum amount of wisdom that it is possible for him to extract.

Not only is the wisdom required for himself, but also as an

aid in dispensing the ancient wisdom. Guidance must not be given to all who come to him and through wisdom he can exercise discretion, but even this is not sufficient because discretion can still be faulty on the odd occasion.

To supplement the wisdom The Hierophant must use the amethyst ray to increase his mystical powers whereby he can be certain of the integrity of those who come to him for guidance and training, always having in mind that the olive of the path still gives out the quality and influence of deceit.

Deceit is now active within some of those who come to the Master, but not within the Master himself, and it is these that The Hierophant has to watch for. Only the sincere followers of the ancient spiritual wisdom must be given the teachings. The true meaning of 'cast not your pearls before swine' now becomes apparent.

From the violet octave of the purple ray the Master draws true spiritual dedication and applies it to its fullest use on the task he has in hand. Other Hierophants should emerge from his teachings and when one or two pass from the final stage in Geburah, fully qualified to take over his position in Gedulah, the Master's task is completed.

The Hierophant has now proved himself on the path of The Hierophant. From student to teacher, and with the successful accomplishment of this last stage, he is now ready to follow once more the path of spiritual progression.

With Gedulah at one end of this path the Master is now poised in every sense to cross the abyss and follow the path of The Hierophant to the point of no return. Leaving his one-time pupil or pupils to carry on the work of The Hierophant, he not only leaves Gedulah, but also the realm of the higher mental plane of consciousness and enters the Briatic World.

In Briah

Indigo is the ray of the path of The Hierophant in the World of Briah with the blue ray of Taurus still penetrating through. Forming the background to these rays in the sephirah of

Binah, which is the next Tree of experience, is the Atziluthic ray of Binah – crimson; from Saturn issues forth the black ray.

Latent esoteric powers of the black ray are now aroused in The Hierophant and at the same time, also from the black ray, a meditative influence. Communication once more is in the depths of the silence and back to single contact with the ultimate.

Through the restrictive influence of the black ray all outside communications are cut off. In one sense this was where The Hierophant commenced in the studiousness of the brown ray in Malkuth, but with a difference, then a student Hierophant, now a Hierophant.

It is in this meditative mood that the full influence of the indigo can take effect, first with its quality of clarity of thought, at this level clarity of the intuition, and second characteristic of the highest octave of the indigo ray, devotion. This is devotion of the highest level and in many cases is devotion to purity.

The calming influence of the blue ray brings The Hierophant state of consciousness to perfection and in this ideal state he is inclined to stay. If he is not careful the worst aspect of the restricting black ray can take over, the vice of inertia.

Against inertia, or when inertia commences, The Hierophant must make use of the crimson octave of the red ray to give that essential stimulus that will urge him forward to greater efforts that he may move across the basic Tree to the Tree in Chokmah, to go through the final experience of his journey on the many paths of The Hierophant.

The pure soft blue of Chokmah irradiates the whole of its Tree including the path of the Hierophant. From the Mundane Chakra all the rays stream out, but the predominant influence is blue. The indigo of the path with the blue from Taurus merges into the pure soft blue of the sephirah.

Full, pure, ultimate wisdom, the main quality of

Chokmah, pours through to the spark on the path of The Hierophant in Chokmah and from Chokmah at the end of the path.

This is the last task on the path of The Hierophant to absorb all wisdom and in the absorption to retain balance and also to retain all past experiences and see them in their true perspective of the ultimate wisdom. No longer seeing through a glass darkly, but now face to face, and in direct communication with the archetype of the path of The Hierophant in Kether.

In Atziluth

The Brilliance of Kether highlights the red/orange of the path of The Hierophant in Atziluth, and the blue ray from Taurus scintillates in its full wisdom.

With the red ray of will and power giving active energy and the orange aspect exercising self-control, which would be expected from The Hierophant who sits between the pillars of balance, there is the ability to control in every aspect.

A mixture of the red/orange rays symbolizes the creative will expressed with full communication between the higher and the lower world. The perfect archetype of the path of The Hierophant.

THE LOVERS

In Assiah

The path of The Lovers is a path of decision and at the level of this path on The Tree it is instant decision. On other paths it may be next week, or the week after, but with the path of The Lovers it is now. The choice of ways. This also means the exercising of discretion, another vital quality that is required on this path.

Running between Tiphareth and Binah it emphasizes and has the influence of balance, harmony and understanding, but whilst these are the qualities of the path, they are to be developed by those who tread it.

The path in the World of Assiah is influenced by a reddish-grey that is inclined to mauve and from the astrological influence of the path, which is Gemini, yellow flows out.

At the level of Assiah, or Malkuth on the basic Tree the yellow ray is in predominance as it is the Atziluthic ray of Malkuth and also the ray of the air element, part of the Mundane Chakra to Malkuth.

With so much of the yellow ray making its presence felt there must be creative activity in one form or another, but mainly it is the mental body which in turn must express itself through the physical being. It is this mental activity that is required to make the instant decision, although the lower bodies, astral, etheric and physical do not always follow the decision taken by the mental body.

When it is said of someone, 'The heart rules the head', it

means that the astral or emotional body is overruling the decision of the mental body. The physical body takes its lead or carries out the activity dictated by either of the other two.

As the physical body makes no decision for itself it is at the mercy of the higher bodies and this makes the path in Malkuth perhaps the most difficult as it is the battlefield for struggle between mental and emotional decisions, which are more often than not completely different.

With all the activity that is taking place, decision after decision will be made at the instigation of the yellow ray, some right, but the majority will tend to take the wrong path, which leads further away from the goal.

It is in those periods when the right decision is made that for a brief moment the less predominant rays have an effect on the individual. From the grey ray aspect of the path fear is experienced and there comes the moment when it is fear of the path the individual has been following. From the red aspect he draws the stimulation to guide his own destinies, at least he becomes a plaything of the gods if he just allows fate or easy decisions to guide him.

Once this decision has been made he has become a student and as such commences to direct the activity of the yellow ray into different channels. At the level of this path on The Tree he can call on the medium octave of the grey ray for endurance to face the persecution which comes from the lower octave of the grey.

Struggle for freedom, a desire given to him from the medium octave of the grey, backed with the fire and enthusiasm from the red, sets him off on a spate of spiritual/emotional activity. Again he can make mistakes with quick emotional decisions, but at least the mistakes are in the form of taking wrong branch paths on the right road, which only delays his progress.

Prior to reaching this stage his mistakes were leading him further away from his ultimate destiny and so the return is a slow, laborious task. Once the right direction is taken the activity commences to increase and the next major step is to prevent the quick emotional decisions that lead to mistakes.

Through the mauve, a high octave of the purple ray, the student obtains the desire and quality of aspiration and now he tries to find the link between his lower and higher self and in this he can be aided by the medium octave of the grey ray.

Once the link has been made and the aspirational tendencies developed, the student sees the vision of the higher realms and this leads him to probably the last decision he has to make on the path of The Lovers in the World of Assiah.

One of the magical images of Binah, which is at the top end of the path, is 'the vision of sorrow'. This is really the realization of all that the student will have to go through as a separate individual. The decision he has to make is whether to follow that vision or once more turn his back on the path to his goal, and the decision has to be made instantly, he either goes forward or back. There is no standing still.

The decision made to follow his aspirations and vision, the student can now call upon the red ray aspect of the path and from it gain the strength and will power to continue, an enthusiasm to carry on against all obstacles because from the grey and yellow rays he has come to the conclusion that in the long run that is all there is to do.

Having made the final decision and applied himself to the task in hand, with the aid of mainly the will of the red ray and the activity of the yellow, the student completes the work of the path of The Lovers in Assiah and leaves it for the last time to enter the world of Yetzirah.

In Yetzirah

On the Tree in Yesod the reddish-grey of the path in Assiah now changes to a brownish-yellow; the yellow of Gemini is of course still there. From the Mundane Chakra of Yesod comes a silver ray, a high octave of the grey ray, and overshadowing the whole is the indigo of Yesod itself.

Brownish yellow sows the seed of discontent and in this world of emotions it has a great impact on the student so that one of the first decisions he has to make on the path of The Lovers in Yesod is to carry on though discontented, or give up the struggle and return to the World of Assiah at the worst, or return to the lower levels of the Tree in Yesod.

Through the indigo ray, which gives him devotion, he chooses to carry on and as his devotion increases, the discontent, though still there, diminishes in its existing form and gradually develops into what might be called divine discontent. Binah has close links with the Holy Guardian Angel. This is considered to be one of the spiritual experiences of Malkuth, but does not alter the fact that there must also be the same link in Yesod.

This Holy Guardian Angel aspect of Binah may be likened to that part of the student which shows him the real purpose for manifestation, that is, his true purpose in the vast scheme of things, so at this early stage on the path of The Lovers the student may glimpse a part of the plan as it affects him.

It is here that the divine discontent appears. He will try to see more and possibly want to hasten along. He is discontented with, what may seem to him, his slow rate of progress. The aspect of the brown ray from the path can give the student depression and it may affect him in this emotional part of the Yetziratic world.

To counter-balance the depression there is the mental activity of the yellow ray. From the yellow he also draws the inspiration to carry him along this path, which is essentially one of separation.

In the final stages of the conquest of the path of The Lovers the decision on separation becomes of utmost importance because it is the separation from his emotional body and this in itself arouses the emotions. In order to break free from this vicious circle the student must use the silver octave of the grey ray from which he can obtain the required qualities to take this step, those of tranquillity, balance and spiritual harmony.

Once full use of the silver has been made the emotions are stilled and with the realization that he is not his emotions the student can make that final decision and separation that leads him off the path of The Lovers in Yesod and on to the Tree in Hod.

The whole of the lower mental plane of consciousness ruled by Hod is permeated with an aura of violet/purple pierced by a ray of yellow from Mercury. It is into this field of the lower mental level that the student now steps and slowly progresses up the Tree in Hod until once more he finds himself on the path of The Lovers.

Making its influence felt in spite of the other rays is the combined ray of brownish-yellow. The yellow ray from the astrological sign of the path merges and strengthens the yellow ray from Mercury. This is now intense activity, not only because of the increase of the yellow ray, but also because at this one point Gemini on the path has a direct link with Mercury, its ruling planet.

Shorn of his emotional body the student now sees with an increased perception and through the yellow ray the emphasis is placed on the intellectual which he finds, strange as it may be, does not appear to help him overcome the path of the Lovers in Hod.

Quick decisions are now made as this path requires, each one of an academic nature, each one leaving him back at the point of the path where he commenced. Now the brown ray aspect of the path with its frustration is again felt. The student finds that mental frustration is even worse as an experience than the emotional frustration he had in Yesod.

Again discontent from the brownish-yellow creeps in at his inability to make progress on the path of The Lovers and he channels the yellow ray to help activate the mental body to find an answer. Once the student does this then the understanding he gains directs him to the use of the violet/purple ray.

From the purple comes forceful power, but it does not take him long to realize that power alone will not take him across the path that faces him, but turning to the violet octave of the purple ray he does find the key that he requires to unlock the door that academic decisions cannot open.

Humility with spiritual dedication are two aspects of the violet ray that the student can put to use. The spiritual dedication encourages him to press forward and the humility aids him in the recognition that progress requires more than the intellectual approach.

By combining the power of the purple with the humility of the violet, the student can apply the mental activity derived from the yellow into a different line of thought which leads to a quality obtained from the brown ray, that of philosophizing.

The student is now learning discrimination, a vital aspect of the path of The Lovers, and through discrimination he makes decisions, other than by intellectual application, realizing in humility that spiritual thoughts must also be applied.

With this last realization the initiate moves from Hod to Netzach, where philosophy at its highest level can have full play, and soon the initiate is floundering, philosophical decisions are not so easily made, being less tangible than the more logical findings of Hod.

Brownish-yellow of the path and the yellow of Gemini are now given a background of amber, a high octave of the orange ray, and this is interspersed with the blue ray from Venus.

There is still a reasonable amount of the yellow creative activity at the initiate's disposal, but he can now call upon the blue ray of love and wisdom to aid him in the conquest of the path of The Lovers in Netzach. His first task is to decide whether the love aspect be devoted to that section of life on the path he is following, thereby discriminating, or should he devote that love aspect to the whole of life.

To the initiate at this stage of his journey it is a crucial decision to make, but from the wisdom aspect of the blue ray he realizes it must be for the whole. To devote the love, a universal force, projected by the blue ray, to a specific section of life would be the use the quality of discrimination in a negative and possibly adverse manner.

One of the qualities he obtains from the amber is justice and another wholeness, as he absorbs these qualities and develops them within himself the initiate knows he is doing the right thing – to give love to all.

Now the initiate is faced with another choice. Must he discard all intellectual attitudes for the philosophical? Once again the depression of the brown ray takes hold at the thought of it. From the amber comes his salvation. The orange ray is the ray of the concrete mind which bestows an element of wisdom and, joined with more wisdom from the blue ray, he realizes that the two must be used and blended.

The task of the initiate is now to use discrimination between the two and be in a position to make a quick and correct decision. As he gains experience along the path the number of wrong decisions decrease until he reaches the stage where, at this level, his decisions are always correct.

With the perfect blending of these two aspects of the lower mental body, the initiate has now only one choice left to make, to leave the lower mental body altogether or to stay in Netzach indefinitely.

Mental vigour from the amber drives him towards the higher plane of consciousness. The blue ray shows him the wisdom of leaving the lower mental plane and the yellow activates the initiate into making a quick decision.

From the lower mental plane up to the higher levels of the Tree in Tiphareth and the higher mental plane of consciousness. With the transition from one to the other, the initiate has now become an adept and he faces the path of The Lovers with confidence which comes from the orange ray of the Sun, Mundane Chakra of Tiphareth.

The whole Tree at this level is bathed in a pure pink rose – Tiphareth's Atziluthic colour – which also gives the adept a calm with his confidence. This new-born confidence can, if he is not careful, be the means of his downfall. To be overconfident leads to careless decisions, particularly when those decisions are made quickly.

The brown must be used with its quality of studiousness and also its depressive action, not sufficiently to destroy confidence, but enough to unsettle and thereby create doubt within the adept of his ability and so removing his over-confidence. Once this has been successfully accomplished the yellow ray can again be used to counteract the depression by creative activity.

With full activity operating the adept must now turn to the pink rose for tact and the orange ray for practical knowledge and geniality. With these qualities well developed there is confidence to move forward, but without over-confidence.

On this path the adept reaches one of the most vital and difficult cross roads in his long journey through time and space. The choice is to remain in the balance and harmony of Tiphareth or move forward to the Tree in Geburah, knowing the difficulty that lies ahead in this sphere at this stage of his development.

In full realization that he cannot achieve the ultimate without going through Geburah, that his only choice is whether it be sooner or later, he decides to go forward in confidence that he is prepared to meet this next stage of his journey and is capable of overcoming all difficulties that he may meet.

Geburah sheds its orange ray over the whole of the area of consciousness it covers. The red ray from Mars cuts across the orange background. These two rays light up the rather drab brownish yellow of the path and to a great degree smothers the yellow ray from Gemini.

With the power of the orange ray there is a great deal of rigidity within certain areas and the rigidity of Geburah is the unbending universal law of pure justice, which decrees reward or punishment and can in many cases be both.

The adept must, on the path of The Lovers in Geburah, be prepared to accept his rewards and punishments, only by doing so can he safely cross and overcome the difficulties of the path. All the way up the Tree in Geburah he has been going through the process of purification and now at this high level of the Tree he comes to the point of decision.

At this point he has to be certain of just how much karma he can accept, if he feels he cannot bear all that might be placed upon him, there is no point in trying to conquer this path. The adept must also learn that he in turn must work with the Universal Law in his dealings with all life at and below his level of consciousness.

When the adept decides to move forward he must prepare himself for the trials that lie ahead and this is where he will find the red ray of great help to him. From it he draws the will and power, and the brown ray gives him the single-mindedness that is also required to go across the path of The Lovers.

The adept now learns the lesson of retribution, the remorseless grinding of the 'mill' that grinds slowly but exceedingly small. It is here that he realizes how, even in his evolved spiritual state, he has in some form or another deceived himself. Without realizing it he has to some small degree broken Universal Law on each Tree, mainly through the quality of discontent contained in the combination of the brown and yellow rays of the path itself.

Discontent is a quality. It is neither vice nor virtue, but can be either. This is one of the tools of this path, in fact it could be classed as the main tool in the World of Yetzirah and one of the reasons for the brown and yellow rays combining as the path colour in this world. Discontent is the thrust block and essential on the path of decision.

It is only discontent with his spiritual progress that makes the student or initiate take the decision to double his efforts to reach the state of spiritual wisdom and perfection. According to how it is used, discontent becomes a vice or virtue.

The adept, like most individuals, has used it both ways on his journey and now on the path of The Lovers in Geburah he receives his karmic account in accordance with his use and misuse of the quality of discontent.

Once through the path of The Lovers in Geburah his

adeptship is over and he can go forward in his new state of Master to the Tree in Gedulah, where he will in due course of time again reach this path and still have to contend with the brownish-yellow, but there is also the pure yellow that flows from Gemini still available for his use.

The overall ray of Gedulah is the deep violet octave of the purple ray and the amethyst ray is supplied by Jupiter. The Master now has at his disposal both the royal ray and the spiritual ray. In Gedulah he learns how to handle these rays, not only for the furtherance of his own spiritual progress, but for the benefit of all life at his own level of consciousness and at all levels below.

What the Master has to be careful of now is the very subtle temptation to use the cosmic forces that are within his reach and his power for his own progression only or putting his own progress first and the others last. Even at Mastership level this temptation can be very real and many having reached the elevated state of Mastership have succumbed to it, hence the Masters of the Black Priesthood.

Providing full, and not part, use is made of the violet octave of the purple ray the Master will be successful because amongst its many qualities is the virtue of humility. This, with all the spiritual attributions and the aspiration of the amethyst ray, will aid him in completing the journey across the path of The Lovers in Gedulah.

Discontent from the combined rays of the path can now be of use to the Master. First it arouses discontent of the progress or lack of it at all levels of consciousness and second, discontent with his own efforts. The result of this is that he applies himself more actively to the work by making use of the yellow ray from Gemini.

It is imperative that the amethyst ray with its high spiritual vibrations is not applied to the degree where it would blot out the discontent of the path and in so doing destroy what can be a useful tool for the Master's advancement and of those he desires to aid.

Having mastered the path of The Lovers in Gedulah the

Master must now make his last decision before leaving the path, either to stay and give further help to that which he has already given or to continue his progress. At this level the choice is his and a completely free choice.

From the amethyst ray he draws a vision of the mystical, and at the upper end of the path of The Lovers Binah is calling. The Master decides, with some reluctance, to go forward, realizing that he cannot remain in the present state of consciousness for eternity.

In Briah

The crimson glow of Binah irradiates the whole of the Tree within its own range of the Briatic World; cutting through like a knife is the black ray from Saturn. The combined ray of brownish yellow on the path has now changed to pale mauve, but the yellow of its astrological sign remains.

On the path of The Lovers in Binah the Master has to make a choice between unity and separation: either separation from Binah for unity with the Chokmah force, or retention of unity at the Binah level at the expense and separation from the whole as embodied in the unity of Chokmah.

Although there is always a unity with the whole because everything is part of the whole, partial separation from the true spiritual force is always possible because of form with its deviations.

The crimson octave of the red ray with its quality for love of life can create an illusory effect inasmuch that it can be the love of the wrong life. At this point in his evolution the Master has to separate from all life with form and the love must be directed to the true life free of form. It is in the latter direction that the Master must use the crimson ray.

From the black ray of Saturn the Master must draw its restrictive quality and use it to hold the crimson ray within bounds and so make it possible to turn it in the right direction. The path of The Lovers in Binah is truly the parting of the ways.

Once the crimson has been restricted the mauve octave of the purple ray can be brought into use and through this ray full tranquillity can be obtained and the Master can now make his choice in quiet calm and peace. In this state it is possible for him to exercise discretion and make the right choice. The decision made, all that is left for him to do is to call upon the force of the yellow ray to put his decision into active operation.

Having left Binah with all its tenuous form there is no longer the Master but a pure spark of the Ain force facing the path of The Lovers in Chokmah. A pure soft blue forms the background to the mauve of the path and the yellow of the sign.

Activity is the keynote in the whirling energy of Chokmah, but it is an activity guided by wisdom for in this sephirah is stored the wisdom of the ages. Again the choice is unity or separation; however it is easier in this sephirah of wisdom to make the choice.

From the separateness of the individual to an individual within the whole, so preserving the individuality, as at the same time the individuality is lost. It is, on a higher plane of consciousness, losing one's life to save it. With the tranquillity of the mauve octave, the spiritual sedative of the blue and the activity of the yellow, it is not difficult for the spark to end its separate individuality in Chokmah for individual unity in Kether or the World of Atziluth.

In Atziluth

With the orange ray of the path and the yellow ray of the sign shimmering from the background influence of the brilliance of Kether, the full perfection of the archetype of this path is displayed.

The orange ray gives its quality for firm decision and its immovable firmness, while the yellow ray activates the decision quickly, without doubt or hesitation, and the brilliance shows the purity required in those qualities.

THE PATH OF THE CHARIOT

In Assiah

In the world of Assiah The Chariot has the influence of two rays merged into one – which is a greenish brown – and from Cancer, astrological influence of the path, flows the grey, a medium octave of the silver ray.

This is the path of the warrior king, triumphant and lord of all he surveys; standing foursquare, confident and in perfect control. The yellow of Malkuth creates great activity which urges him on from conquest to conquest.

From the Mundane Chakra of Malkuth stream the three major rays and the fourth ray of balance, the merging of which produces other rays, so that at one time or another the path of The Chariot feels the influence of all the rays.

The warrior king rules with perfect justice or as perfect as it is possible to be. The path's own ray with its element of green gives this ray a predominance of the path shared only with the yellow ray.

Although the warrior king stands foursquare, it is not with ease. The green brings with it harmony and balance, but only through conflict and struggle.

When the warrior king learns to discriminate and blend the various rays one with the other, he is moving forward to the conquest of himself.

At the level of Assiah his conquests lie in the field of physical domination, but the high level of the path gives it a quality of integrity that would be expected from the Intelligence of the House of Influence.

With all rays playing their part and having an effect on the path it is one of controlled kingdom, driven on by the greenish brown, which contains the qualities of jealousy and envy.

The brown aspect of this ray has a studious characteristic, it also has the qualities of absorption and knowledge without wisdom. It is through the knowledge aspect and the absorption in prosecuting his affairs that the warrior king is successful in his conquests.

There is a further step he has to take for the final conquest of this path in Assiah, and the aid for this last step also comes from the brown ray, knowledge and studiousness. From this, with the small amount of blue ray wisdom, comes the first glimmerings of light that there are other kingdoms to conquer apart from the physical.

When this stage of knowledge develops the warrior king stands foursquare within his Chariot prepared to go forward and make further conquests, but now in non-physical realms.

In Yetzirah

Bright russet, one of the higher octaves of the brown ray, is now the basic colour of the path of The Chariot. With the move away from the tree in Assiah the ray is no longer mixed, the greenish tinge has dissipated.

Only two other rays apart from the brown now influence the path. Grey from Cancer and indigo, the ray of Yesod, the Moon, Mundane Chakra of Yesod, strengthens the grey ray by sending out a further flow of this ray.

From the russet the warrior king obtains quiet assurance, confidence and quietness in activity. These are qualities that he will have access to and which he will require in every sephirah in the Yetziratic World.

At this level of the Tree the grey ray is an octave that adds endurance and persistence to the warrior king's other qualities, and the indigo carries with it the characteristics of fortitude and blind devotion.

It is the characteristic of blind devotion in the emotional

sphere of Yesod, that is the danger. In most instances on entry into Yesod the blind devotion is followed. It is only after a number of incarnations, and with the use of the grey ray to stabilize, that the warrior king conquers the path of The Chariot in Yesod and prepares to move on to the Tree in Hod.

With the violet/purple, a medium octave of the purple ray, emanating from Hod and the yellow ray issuing from Mercury, its Mundane Chakra, the warrior king takes the first step towards the real purpose of this path. This first step is to become a priest-king.

The yellow ray with its powers of creative and spiritual activity commences to influence him as he realizes that he must stand foursquare in harmony with the spiritual aspects of life. The violet adds the influence of spiritual dedication.

He now turns away from his previous ideas and becomes centred on a spiritual kingdom and in the first flush of enthusiasm the dedication is single-minded and the restricting form of Hod holds the priest-king in its grip. This restriction is accentuated by the black ray from Saturn, Mundane Chakra of Binah, which is at the top end of the path.

It is only when the priest-king realizes the power and potency of the red ray issuing from Geburah at the bottom end of the path that the restriction commences to lose its hold. The grey ray with its influence on the 'spirit's struggle for freedom' and its characteristic of endurance now aids the priest-king in his breakaway.

Idealism, which is another quality of the grey ray, helps him to set his sights on the sphere of Netzach, where he eventually reaches the path of The Chariot, once more to follow this path, but for the last time at the lower mental level of consciousness.

Amber is the overall ray of Netzach and this high octave of the orange ray carries the spirit of geniality, and this is added to the quality of sincerity which springs from the blue ray of Venus.

Netzach is the sphere of the energetic principle, victory,

firmness, the sephirah of idealism, and widening of consciousness and it is within this influence that the priest-king now treads the path of The Chariot. It is here that he must learn to control the lower mental body. This is the commencement of his second step towards the reality of the path.

He must now leave the role of priest-king behind and seek the spiritual maturity that leads him to Tiphareth and the higher mental world. In this he is aided by the particular octave of the blue ray, it is one of its characteristics.

Were it not for the blue ray, combined with the grey from Cancer, the priest-king could easily fall into a state of complacency wrapped up in the idealism of Netzach. But once victory is obtained over this state of consciousness, spiritual maturity is developed and the sephirah of Tiphareth is attained.

At Tiphareth spiritual maturity is the keynote, and the priest-king becomes the sacrificed spirit. Now the true meaning of the path of The Chariot becomes clear. It is the harmonizing of the elements within and without.

Pink rose, the colour of Tiphareth, is a high octave of the red ray, carrying with it the quality of forgiveness, and from the sun blazes out the orange ray of self-control, an essential quality of the path of The Chariot.

With the assurance and quiet confidence obtained from the russet brown, the spark now stands firmly in the centre of the universe balancing the forces into perfect harmony within and without. From here, on the path of The Chariot, truly he is lord of all he surveys.

There are – even at this stage of the spark's progress – imperfections, and probably the greatest is spiritual pride, which comes from the orange ray. From the pink rose there is the feeling of well-being and the spark is now well satisfied with his lot.

It is from the grey ray sent out by Cancer that the disturbing of this feeling of well-being arises and the red from Geburah at the lower end of the path urges the spark to leave this centre of harmony and rise completely into the higher mental world.

In Geburah the pride and sense of well-being is quickly eradicated by the red ray, which is now at double strength from Mars, Mundane Chakra of Geburah, at the end of the path and from Geburah on the basic Tree. Here is the point of Geburah in Geburah.

Orange is the ray of Geburah on the basic Tree and were it not for the double strength of the red it is very unlikely that pride would be eradicated.

The quiet confidence and assurance of the russet aids the spark to withstand the forces of Geburah which flow down the path of The Chariot. The control and balance of the spark on this path is severely tested, but the spark has learned the lesson well and accepts the buffeting it receives from the sephirah Geburah.

Purified by the searing red ray, the spark is now happy to move on to the realm of the Masters, still in perfect control, even more sure of itself than ever.

Gedulah is the home of the Masters and it is flooded with the deep violet from Jupiter. The amethyst ray streams forth, blending with the violet to produce a different octave of the amethyst ray.

From this octave springs mystical powers and the quality to attain to the use of these powers, attributes very much in keeping with the sphere of the Masters.

The spark's task on the path of The Chariot in this sephirah is to attain to their use and in a balanced manner, so that their flow down to the lower sphere or planes of consciousness will have the right influence to those that tune in to them from the Tiphareth level down to Malkuth.

Now the spark finds the use of the russet that belongs to the path and the grey from Cancer the astrological sign, and with calm, quiet confidence the mystical forces are gathered together and he assumes perfect control, just as on the lower level in the role of warrior king he stood balanced and supreme.

With the conquest of the path in Gedulah the spark is now

ready to cross the abyss to the World of Briah, where he will eventually tread the path of The Chariot again.

In Briah

Binah is the first stage of the Briatic World where the path of The Chariot has to be conquered. With the change from Yetzirah to Briah the colour of the path changes and the russet gives way to maroon, an octave of the red ray that contains the quality of will and power, but due to a proportion of the brown ray in maroon there is also the influence of deep thought. At the Binah level it is the quality of quiet understanding.

Crimson and black are the colours that flow from Binah and its Mundane Chakra. The spark now finds the path of The Chariot one of restriction, but this is conquered by the balanced use of the maroon, employing the will and power with understanding to break through the last barrier with any semblance of form, and now as a pure spark of spirit takes the path on the tree in Chokmah.

The path retains its colour of maroon, but the background from Chokmah is a pure soft blue and from the sphere of the zodiac all the other rays stream forth. This is the last test the spark will have on retaining perfect balance and control and in the art of harmonizing.

Now it must exercise the will and power with the clear understanding from the maroon ray and with these qualities control and blend all the rays into a perfect whole so that they cancel each other out and become the perfect brilliance.

To help in the conquest of this last path of The Chariot the spark can have the full true wisdom which impregnates the whole of Chokmah in the pure blue, the highest octave of the love/wisdom ray.

In Atziluth

In the World of Archetypes the concept of this path is perfected balance and control and the harmonizing of the elements within and without to the point where there is full integration into the whole.

The path is amber in the Atziluthic World, but it is an amber which we know not. There is a purity beyond the visualization of man and a sparkling from the pure brilliance of Kether.

Perhaps this is the Golden Crown that comes to the victor, the spark that has brought the Archetypal concept into reality.

STRENGTH

In Assiah

The path of Strength is the Middle veil and connects Gedulah and Geburah, so combining within it the influences of these two sephiroth, namely justice and mercy; there is also the influence of the path itself.

Assiah or Malkuth on the basic Tree provides a background of clear yellow to the reddish/amber of the path and the orange ray that streams forth from Leo, which is the astrological influence of the path of Strength.

On this path one of the lessons the student or initiate has to learn is the correct use of Universal force or strength in all its differing degrees from a destructive and constructive angle, its work of integration and disintegration.

In the world of Assiah the student or initiate is inclined to be influenced a little too much by the red ray aspect of the path and works, not only with enthusiasm, but with fiery energy that can set up barriers of opposition.

The amber octave of the orange ray creates a great deal of mental rigour, this allied to the attributes of the red ray aspect produces within the student or initiate the zeal of the reformer who is determined to reform at all costs and in some cases will try the use of physical force to bring his brother to heel.

This is the path in Assiah where the student or initiate acts on impulse, which he receives from the red ray, and in this fiery impulse will sincerely believe that there is such a thing as righteous indignation, when it is simply the red ray influencing him to lose control of his temper.

With the yellow ray of activity stirring the student or initiate to a continuous striving, he is constantly on the war path against those who do not agree with his views; a spiritual gangster who believes that the end justifies the means and so brings into being the destructive aspect and force of the red ray.

This method of approach is purely destructive destruction, which not only brings down trouble on the head of the student or initiate but also brings him back into incarnation after incarnation.

Other qualities are also available from the amber octave of the orange ray, such as justice and wholeness, two qualities that can also be associated with Geburah and Gedulah respectively, and it is only when he draws upon this aspect of the amber ray that a more balanced outlook is adopted.

From the orange ray given out by Leo can be obtained self-control and reliance; now the path becomes more clear to him and the iron hand is exercised with greater restraint.

Activity from the yellow and mental vigour from the orange commences to change its pattern and the red ray is now used upon himself and less on others. Using the mental vigour the initiate directs the red influence within himself to give to his physical being what the orange gives to his mind.

The initiate now employs the force or strength to help him progress against all obstacles that the world of Assiah can place in his path and uses the justice and wholeness of the orange ray in his dealings with fellow human creatures.

Now that he has conquered the turbulent aspect of the red ray he is well on the way to conquering and using wisely the strength or force of the path for his own development. With this change of force direction he can now develop the activity of the yellow ray to the right end, that of conquering the path and leaving the Tree in the world of Assiah for the first Tree in the Yetziratic world.

In Yetzirah

In the world of Yetzirah the path of Strength responds to the grey ray, the orange from Leo still remains and on the Tree in Yesod the path is subjected to an indigo background.

Yesod is the Sephirah of the generative force and there is a great accent on reproduction. The concern with reproduction is typical and understandable as Yesod is the finishing stage of all forms going down to Malkuth.

Where reproduction in the world of Assiah is purely on a physical basis, or bringing life into the physical plane through a physical act, the reproductive faculty of Yesod is to apply the generative force in its own astral emotional plane to reproduce in a lower plane.

It is Yesod's generative force and reproductive quality that the initiate must now contend with as he steps on the path of Strength in Yesod. The major influence that he first meets is that of the indigo ray with its quality of blind devotion and for a time the initiate is caught up in this strong emotional quality.

Stubbornness is another quality of the indigo ray which makes for great difficulty in trying to break down the blind devotion. Control of the emotional force is the first step that the initiate must take and to do this he must call upon and use the orange ray from which he can develop the attribute of self-control.

From the grey ray the initiate can extract the attributes of endurance and persistence, he must now apply to these the quality of devotion inherent in the indigo ray. Clarity of thought is also an aspect of the indigo ray and the initiate must draw upon and use this aspect.

Through his clarity of thought the initiate understands how the reproductive force of indigo can be used to reproduce in a higher plane of consciousness as well as the lower and it is to this end the initiate must work. Always on this path it is a control of force in some way or another.

Control at the Yesod level must of necessity be more gentle than the pure brute strength of the path in Assiah and the grey ray can again be brought into play to use a characteristic that should seldom be called upon, that of hardness, but applied the right way it can control the emotional force without destroying it.

Once the initiate has control he can now apply the generative force in such a way that through its machine he can conquer the path and move further forward into the Yetziratic world until he reaches the Tree in Hod and the path of Strength on that Tree.

The only change in the rays at the disposal of the initiate are those of the Sephirah. The violet/purple of Hod replaces the indigo of Yesod and from the Mundane Chakra of Hod the yellow ray is available.

Hod is the first sephirah of the lower mental plane of consciousness and the initiate can find the path of Strength on the Hod Tree very tricky to deal with. The path responds to the Hebrew letter *Teth*, meaning snake. It is in the sephirah of Hod that the snake influence is most apparent.

A strong subtle power flows down the path, bringing through from the orange ray pride and ambition which joins with magnanimity of the violet octave of the purple ray. Here is a form of strength and power that in its subtle way appeals to the initiate, he finds it quite easy to justify the pride in his achievements and advanced spiritual teachings. It is right to have ambition for further progress along the occult path, a glow of virtue spreads throughout his mental body as he graciously or magnanimously helps life at a lower level.

What the initiate has lost sight of is that help is not given for the sake of it but to glorify the pride of his powers. To extricate himself from this situation he must take heed of the other aspect of the serpent, that wise old serpent who symbolizes the healing of all impurities and secretly holds the wisdom of the ages.

The first step to counteract pride and ambition is to use the grey ray of the path and allow or draw from its influence the quality of idealism. This will turn his mental body towards the violet octave of the purple ray with its virtue of humility. Pride now ebbs away but the ambition remains, touched with humility, therefore the ambition turns into an ambition to help, with any thoughts of personal progression taking second place.

The initiate has now balanced the serpent forces and brought them under control and in doing so has added strength to his own character, so fulfilling the purpose of the path at this stage of his journey.

From Hod to the path of Strength on the Tree in Netzach where the grey of the path and the orange from Leo has an amber background, this is an octave of the orange ray, thus giving this ray a predominance over the others, which includes the blue ray from Venus.

Netzach is the sephirah of the energetic principle and now there is a test of strength for the initiate, strength within his own mental body to keep pace with the energetic activity that underlies, not only the path of Strength, but the whole Tree in Netzach.

In the Yetziratic text the path of Strength is listed as the Intelligence of all activities of the Spiritual being and this is well emphasized on the path in Netzach. The initiate finds himself jumping from one idea to another with barely time to absorb or understand in full any single one of them.

From the grey ray the initiate can obtain endurance – which is one kind of strength – and making full use of this he carries on through the whirl of activity. The amber octave of the orange ray can, if he calls upon it, supply mental vigour. Turning to the grey ray once more, he calls from it much needed stability for his own use to enable him to withstand the tremendous amount of energetic activity that is taking place and of which he is part.

How to remain stable within a vortex of energy is one of the main lessons of the path of Strength in Netzach and having learned the lesson the initiate can commence to move forward again, soon to leave the lower mental body as he reaches the path of Strength in Tiphareth.

Tiphareth is the sephirah which joins the lower and higher mental planes of consciousness and the path of Strength is just above the dividing line between the two bodies. Now as an adept, the lower mental body discarded, the one-time initiate faces perhaps his most difficult test.

Added to the grey and orange rays connected to the path is the pink/rose Atziluthic colour of Tiphareth and orange from the Mundane Chakra of Tiphareth. As with Netzach, the orange ray is predominant and from its influence the adept develops reliance and self-control, two qualities which will serve him well as he walks the path of Strength on the Tiphareth Tree.

The pink/rose octave of the red ray gives to the adept the quality of constant affection, which in turn he bestows upon all life in the lower planes of consciousness where to his regret it is so often rejected. This is the adept's test, to have the Strength to keep giving and being rejected, a strength that will overcome his sorrow at the foolishness of those on the lower levels who refuse to accept the gift that would aid them in their evolution.

From the higher level of the Mental plane he can look down with pity on the strife and struggles taking place in the Astral and Physical worlds and yet he must carry on making the sacrifice, and it is to him a sacrifice until he gains that quiet strength of endurance and acceptance.

Although on a different plane of consciousness, the adept now knows what it means to be despised and rejected of man. From the grey ray he must draw the qualities of endurance and persistence and employ them both to the fullest extent. The orange ray, when he turns to it, will provide him with self-control and practical knowledge.

Once the qualities have been acquired, then the adept obtains that quiet inner strength whereby he can withstand all the failures of his efforts and still keep trying in face of all adversity. This is the true conquest of this path and he is now free when he so desires to leave the work he has been doing and resume the journey of his own personal spiritual progression.

Now a Master, he must face the path of Strength on the Tree in Geburah. Still available for his use are the grey and orange rays supplemented by a further orange ray from Geburah and the red ray from Mars, Mundane Chakra to Geburah.

A double Martian influence has now to be contended with through the Geburah influence at one end of the path and the sephirah in which the Tree stands. Now completely in the higher mental plane of consciousness the Master meets the fire of Geburah flowing down the path, that cosmic fire that sears and burns impurities, that creates a burning desire for justice and for perfection.

From this sphere also emanates all the effects of previous causes, it also creates mental consummation, through the red ray the generative strength of the path is transformed into a regenerative power. Fiery force, rigour and energy all stem from the red ray that streams out from two points, the only prevention from total fiery destruction is the transmuting powers of the more predominating orange and the subduing grey ray.

In this particular sephirah the path of Strength could be also called the path of the balanced force of justice. The quality of justice can give power and to some degree supremacy, and at this high level of the Tree it is cosmic power that the Master has to balance and he can be so easily overbalanced by the strength of this cosmic power. The grey ray must be called upon for stability if cosmic justice has to be used in a balanced manner.

Without proper care and with a wrong basic motive the force could be used as a weapon for vengeance by the Master, because of this the need to control the red ray is of prime importance.

Used as a regenerative force it can be of great benefit to all on whom it is applied. Justice can be carried out, the impurities burnt away and new life is generated by the recipient of the force. With fiery zeal the purified one commences a new spiritual phase, the whole being having been regenerated.

To apply this correctly the Master, after gaining stability, must turn to the orange ray where he can obtain justice and wholeness, and so bring to his own mental body the strength that is required, wholeness being an aspect of strength, to successfully gain supremacy over the path of Strength on the Tree in Geburah.

From the tree in Geburah to that in Gedulah, where a deep violet forms the background to the grey and orange rays connected to the path. Jupiter issues forth the amethyst ray with all its influences and so the Master has at his disposal all that he requires to face once more the path of Strength.

Gedulah, with its influence and characteristics, covers the remainder of the higher mental world and on the return journey contains the last Tree in the world of Yetzirah and with the path of Strength on this Tree there is a double Gedulah influence as there was with Geburah, due to these two sephiroth being at either end of the path.

For the conquest of the path of Strength at this particular point on his journey he must have perfect balance. This is the key point of the path, not just on the Tree in Gedulah but on the basic Tree, here is the main and vital position of the path.

In Geburah the red ray influence from Mars created a burning desire and now the Jupiter influence from Gedulah gives to him an expansive character which can be a vice instead of a virtue if it is not curbed. The amethyst ray of Jupiter contains the missionary quality which can be as expansive and sweeping as the planet itself.

Over a period of cosmic time the Master is constantly giving out through the effect of Jupiter and the amethyst, because he has not yet taken control of the amethyst ray or brought the others into use, he is fully caught up in idealistic thoughts, idealism being another quality of the amethyst ray.

Only when he realizes that a lot of ideals are quite impracticable at the lower levels does he commence to curb the expansiveness of Jupiter by the use of the orange ray. From the orange he uses the attributes of self-control and organizing ability; he now commences to take command of all forces available.

Deep violet – as a lower octave of the purple ray – produces forceful power which can be useful to use for curbing the too expansive attitude of Jupiter, and also the more impracticable ideals arising from the amethyst ray. Once this task has been completed it is possible for the Master to utilize the other and more gentle aspect of the amethyst.

With humility, true spiritual attainment and mystical powers, all obtained from the amethyst ray, the Master develops within his mental body not only a spiritual calm but a quiet spiritual strength that is far superior to all the force, energy and power of the path of Strength at the lower levels.

The grey ray adds to this quiet inner strength by providing the desirable qualities of tranquillity, peace and harmony. Perfect balance on the path of Strength has been achieved at this level of consciousness and as the path at this level indicates, justice with mercy is perfected through a quiet strength that is a combination of firmness with compassion.

Once the Master has reached this stage he is ready to complete his journey through the remainder of the Tree in Gedulah and then step out across the abyss to the world of Briah, leaving behind for all time the worlds of Manifestation.

In Briah

Across the other side of the abyss the sephirah of Binah with its Tree beckons the Master, the crimson glow of the sephirah reaches out to meet him and the black ray of Saturn awaits to enfold him in its embrace. The path of Strength on this Tree is attracting him with its deep purple ray illuminated by the orange of Leo.

On the Tree in Binah the forceful generative power of the purple ray drives him forward and from the crimson octave of the red ray he can call upon the force of that ray to regenerate him, but he also realizes that until personality disappears the regeneration cannot take place fully, only in Chokmah free of personality can he reap the full benefit of the regenerated Strength.

To achieve his final goal he must free himself from the ties and restrictions of Binah, which is not easy – even at his level of consciousness – and the strength required to release and destroy his personality must be obtained.

The Master's first step is to make use of the black ray with its restrictive powers to effectively restrain the personality. The meditative aspect, with its latent powers, must be drawn also from the black ray. It is in this quiet meditative state that he realizes the orange ray has the influence to make him purposeful, a quality he needs very much at this time.

This is the strength he had to develop on the path in Binah. A strength that would give courage to sacrifice that part of any individual at any level of consciousness that is most dear to him. To sacrifice his physical body or any other part of him is difficult, but to sacrifice that part of him that means he is no more as himself requires an inborn strength that is beyond comprehension at the lower levels of consciousness.

Only by this act can the true quality of the path of Strength in Binah be acquired, and until it is, the way to Chokmah is forever closed. As the Master reaches this stage he realizes in full the purport of this second barrier or veil on The Tree.

With the conquest made and the personality destroyed, the individuality is free to make its way through the Tree in Chokmah until it meets the path of Strength on the Chokmah Tree. Although the rays of the path remain the same the background has now changed to the pure soft blue of Chokmah.

Not only is Chokmah the Sephirah of wisdom, but also at the Atziluthic level its overall ray has wisdom for one of its qualities, the pure soft blue being a high octave of the blue, love/wisdom ray. On the path of Strength in Chokmah the spark in its universal consciousness goes over all its experiences on this particular path at the various levels or planes of consciousness.

The wisdom of Chokmah influences the path and the spark

knows what is the last aspect of Strength, it is strength through wisdom, but it is only recognized and known by the spark as it makes its way along the path in Chokmah.

Forceful power and Greatness come from the purple ray of the path, which is – on this plane – akin to the force of Chokmah. From the orange ray of Leo comes the quality of power and purposefulness; it becomes apparent in the new pure consciousness why this ray has been attached to the path through every Tree in every world.

From the Mundane Chakra of Chokmah, sphere of the Zodiac, stream all the rays and the universal spark of the Ain in his strength of wisdom recognizes in turn each ray that has borne some influence on the path of Strength in one Tree or the other, and recognizes its force or power aspect.

In the world of Assiah it was brute strength in Yetzirah, a mixture of emotional, mental and quiet spiritual strength, all governed by the various rays which are originated in their divisions through and by Chokmah. With the recognition of this wisdom and the strength of it the spark is ready to return to the world of Atziluth which it left aeons of time back.

In Atziluth

The path of Strength on the Tree in Kether is yellowish/green, a combination of the yellow activity ray and the green harmony through struggle and conflict. The latter ray at this level has the harmony prevailing. The yellow in the archetypal path of Strength indicates the activity of all Spiritual beings – the Intelligence of the path – and the green ray portrays the struggle and conflict each individual will go through until they reach that harmony of the quiet spiritual strength within which is the ultimate goal and archetype of the path of Strength.

THE HERMIT

In Assiah

In the world of Assiah the Path of the Hermit is a plum colour, which is one of the lower aspects of the purple ray. The astrological influence of the Path is Virgo and this also emanates a purple ray which is a slightly higher octave than the plum. The World of Assiah is completely over-shadowed by the yellow ray and from its Mundane Chakra flow red, blue, yellow and green rays.

This is a very solitary Path to tread, the one treading it may be surrounded by many of his fellow human beings, yet he is alone because it is a spiritual way and not worldly. It can be even more solitary if the plum octave of the purple ray is used too much. Over-bearing, pompous, a holier-than-thou attitude, these are qualities of the plum, that attitude that has full confidence in 'my beliefs are right'. The student or initiate on this Path needs to guard against these characteristics. Spiritual activity flows from the yellow ray but the ray does not choose the way or the means of following it. Whatever the individual chooses, so the ray activates.

Each man follows many spiritual ways along the Path of the Hermit during many incarnations. Some lean entirely towards the wisdom of the blue ray, others trying to use the calming influence of the green may become enmeshed in its conflict aspect, the red; both uncontrolled zeal and a burning desire to implant a belief by fire and sword if necessary. It is only when the student or initiate turns towards the higher octave of the purple and cultivates the qualities of dedication and reverence combined with the blue ray of love and wisdom that the spiritual creative activity of the yellow ray can play its full part and aid him in the conquest of the Path of the Hermit in Assiah.

In Yetzirah

In the Formative world this Path can bring many complications but perhaps most of all in the sphere of Yesod, the astral plane of consciousness. This sephirah of the emotions is governed by the indigo ray and from its Mundane Chakra flows the silver ray. The Path itself is now impregnated with the green/grey ray, which will be retained through all the Sephiroth of the Yetziratic world. It is from the green that all the struggle and conflict emanates and besets the Path with difficulty through the whole of the Yetziratic world.

The key-word of indigo is devotion and true devotion is essential if the Path is to be conquered, but in Yesod the devotion is of an emotional content that leads to a state of near fanaticism, which is checked by the conflict of the green ray. It prevents this state developing by causing the emotions to flow from one extreme to the other. Reverence and dedication are always present, due to the influence of the purple ray from Virgo, and it is by the combination of this with the Wisdom of the blue that stability and balance are attained.

Wisdom now goes hand in hand with devotion and the Path is followed with controlled emotions and full reverence until its highest point is successfully attained and the individual is ready to move forward ultimately to reach the Path of the Hermit in Hod.

Violet/purple is the colour of Hod with yellow from the Mundane Chakra, Mercury. Violet is a medium octave of the purple ray having the quality of magnanimity and in Hod this can be one of the pitfalls. From the fluctuating emotions of Yesod now comes the rigidity of pattern and conformity in Hod. It is so easy for the student or initiate to conform to the usual concept of The Hermit and withdraw to live in solitary isolation, once in a while deigning to come out of solitude and magnanimously give of his wisdom to those on his own or lower planes of consciousness.

In the sphere of Hod the efforts made for spiritual progression are very sincere but confined. The yellow ray pours out its force of spiritual activity within these bounds and it is only when the student or initiate heeds the call of the green/grey rays that he commences to make true progress.

The green stirs up a conflict within him to a point where he starts to rebel at some of the set ideas and the grey ray gives him the essential impetus to struggle for his spiritual freedom. On the Path of the Hermit it is never a struggle for a personal freedom to follow any Path other than that of spiritual progression.

Just as the individual was dedicated to the narrow, restricted spiritual Path of Hod, now he is dedicated to obtaining the freedom of his soul. It is no easy task to break away from the prescribed, strict rules that apply in Hod and the work and struggle may wage over many incarnations before he is successful in loosening his bonds and – stepping forward – reaches Netzach, where he moves on the Path of the Hermit with complete abandon.

In the sphere of Netzach time and energy and many incarnations also may be wasted by casting the net too wide; it is here that the student or initiate basks in the amber ray of Netzach. A higher point of the orange ray, it gives geniality, receptivity and mental vigour. The qualities of this ray give him a capacity for accepting all ways of an idealistic nature, and this can be emphasized by the blue ray beaming out from the Mundane Chakra of Netzach, which may cause a certain amount of diffusion of energies. Inherent in the blue ray is the quality of Wisdom as well as love and this with the discrimination of the green enables a balance to be struck through the grey ray.

Eventually by determination and the continual exercise of

Will, the Intelligence of the Path, wisdom, balance and discrimination are practised and the true idealism comes forth. Love and wisdom are balanced, conflicting ideas resolved and the energetic principle is channelled into a single direction, which then inevitably leads on to the sphere of Tiphareth.

Tiphareth with its clear rose/pink reaches the highest point of Universal love, not to be confused with the ultimate Universal compassion which lies within both the blue and the grey rays in differing degrees. It will be seen that there is on the Path of the Hermit a degree of compassion expressed by the grey but it is reduced by the merging of the green ray and this merging continues through the whole of the Yetziratic World. This implies that the lesson of love must first be learned.

On this Path in Tiphareth there is the opportunity to acquire this quality and from here it can be rayed out to the whole of Manifestation.

The orange ray streaming out from the sun gives the feeling of domination and this is the danger point of the Path at this level of consciousness. Domination over lesser beings on lower planes of consciousness or domination control over his own lower feelings, is the choice presented to the individual on the Path of the Hermit in Tiphareth.

In order to make the right choice, and having made it to carry it through, the grey ray and clear rose pink must be used to the fullest extent and only thus will the Path in Tiphareth be understood and conquered.

The orange ray of Geburah brings its power to bear on the student or initiate as he treads the Path in this sphere and from Mars, its Mundane Chakra, the red ray flows out. From time to time, as the red merges with the orange, the flames of Cosmic Fire leap forth.

It is at this level of consciousness that the student, initiate or even a Master understands fully the esoteric meaning of 'Forgive us our trespasses as we forgive them that trespass against us'. The mental body is now a mass of seething conflict as the searing fire penetrates, burns and transmutes. Only the Will, strong in its belief from the Intelligence of the Path and further strengthened by the red ray with a little pride from the orange holds the being steadfast to the Path he is working out.

Gradually the green ray from the astrological influence takes over and predominates and with the support of the grey harmony is established and the way becomes clear. The cleansed, transmuted mental intelligence moves forward to the higher goal, that of the sphere of Gedulah, where after many adventures on the lower Paths the Master reaches once more the Path of the Hermit.

Only a Master can go forward from the searing Cosmic flames of Geburah, here an initiate can become a Master and a student an initiate but they must each return in due course to fulfil their Karmic destiny in those roles and then they too may go forward to Gedulah, the Sephirah of the Masters.

Even at this high level the Master still has lessons to learn before the Abyss is crossed and the Briatic World reached. The Sephirah of Gedulah is bathed in deep violet, an octave of the purple ray and an octave that gives out the quality of true humility. From Jupiter streams the amethyst ray with its altruism and ritualistic tendencies and it is this latter which contains within it the last lesson the Master has to learn.

Through high Ritual of near Cosmic level at this point on the Tree great work can be done, which to lower states of consciousness seem to be miracles. With the expansiveness of Jupiter there may be the temptation to use the powers developed on every occasion, the sincere desire to help overriding other – and perhaps more important – considerations, cosmically considered.

The conflict of the green ray still has an influence, causing a difficulty between what he knows to be required under Universal Law and what his developed qualities of love and feeling may dictate. It is not an easy conflict to resolve. The Master must decide when to send down to the World of Assiah forces to relieve pain and suffering but which nonetheless may be interfering with the Law of Karma, or whether regretfully to withhold those forces until such time as he knows the Karmic condition has reached a point when it could be transmuted without causing future suffering.

Here again is the lesson of discrimination, now on a very high level and on the Path of the Hermit there is an isolation from kindred spirits and the choice of what should not be done is his alone and has to be made alone.

The grey ray helps the Master if and when he chooses to use it, its calming, balancing, compassionate qualities aid him in resolving his problems, and once he can do this the Master can then cross the Abyss and dwell in consciousness in the World of Briah.

In Briah

The Path of the Hermit in Briah is a slate grey, a medium octave of the grey ray. Universal Love is now being augmented by a full compassion worthy of the Great Mother, Binah, the first Sephirah of the Briatic World on the Path of Return.

In Binah the slate grey has a background of crimson, one of the higher octaves of the red ray, and from Saturn issues the black ray, while Virgo still supplies the purple ray to the Path. Comfort, tact and unselfishness are to be drawn and dispensed from the Crimson and this is the task that has to be carried out now. Combined with this is the all-enfolding nature of the black ray, restricting only in its embracing comfort and enfolding compassion.

On the return journey it is the negative side of the black ray that is predominant, whereas on the Path of Outgoing it is positive and restrictive. The task completed and the purpose fulfilled in Binah, the last vestige of form is disposed of and the Divine Spark moves on to Chokmah, where in due course of time it once again reaches to the Path of the Hermit.

Slate grey is still the colour of the Path but it is now against a background of pure soft blue, the Atziluthic colour of Chokmah and the highest octave of the blue ray, with its attributes of pure Wisdom and pure Compassion. The struggles of the spirit for its freedom are now over and the quality drawn from the grey is that of tranquillity. Now there is a deeper understanding of the words, 'The calm and peace that passeth understanding'.

From the sphere of the Zodiac sparkling beautiful rays shoot out to be absorbed and held by the Spark and with the intelligence of Will are merged into a glittering Whole that transmits the pure brilliance that is no longer a mere reflection but Atziluth itself.

In Atziluth

In the World of Atziluth pure brilliance envelops the Path of the Hermit so that the green/yellow colour is sparkling and alive. It is truly living colour. The octaves of the green and yellow rays denote the true archetype of the Path, and that the Spark has at last achieved its perfection.

This way is truly the royal road to self-achievement, discrimination, true spiritual dedication and the Will to acquire all these attributes, no matter what the difficulties on the way.

THE WHEEL OF FORTUNE

In Assiah

The Wheel of Fortune in many respects has a great affinity with Geburah and the path of Justice, but where they are operating universal law in assessing karma the Wheel of Fortune puts universal law into operation. Symbolized in this path is the whole cyclic law of life in all its aspects and the student as he follows this path should eventually come to the understanding of the cyclic laws with their continuous ebb and flow.

In the World of Assiah the path is bright blue with yellow rays set against the pure yellow of Malkuth's Atziluthic colour. From Jupiter the astrological influence of the path flows the amethyst ray and red, green, with further blue and yellow rays issue forth from the four elements. The Mundane Chakra of Malkuth or the World of Assiah on the basic Tree.

With five of the twelve rays operating at this level of the Wheel of Fortune the student or initiate will be in a turmoil until such time as he exercises control and makes use of the rays for his own purpose. In his early incarnations he is carried on the current and taken up to the heights, only later to be plunged into the depths.

The expansiveness of Jupiter, with the impulsiveness of the red ray and activity of the yellow, are the major causes of his downward plunge and remaining in the depths. The wheel will turn along the pattern of birth, death and re-birth, each turn of the wheel awakening a little more of the student's or initiate's consciousness.

Each further awakening of consciousness brings a greater realization of the ups and downs of life, and the purpose of The Wheel of Fortune, the idea of rhythm, ascent and descent or involution and evolution, how the wheel refers to the Law of Periodicity in mental activity. Mental states have a tendency to recur in definite rhythms.

It is the law of the involution of undifferentiated conscious energy and its evolution through a series of form and that evolution is entirely in the hands of each individual. The Hebrew letter for this path is *Kaph*, meaning 'palm of the hand'. It also signifies a curve.

On this path, perhaps more than on any other, the destiny is in the individual's own hand as he follows the curve of The Wheel. It is the path of the Intelligence of Conciliation and Reward, that is for good or ill, the wheel turning and rewarding good or ill. It also implies an adjustment, harmony and order or an agreement.

The reconciliation of apparent differences takes place on this path which, when accepted, will lead to a greater harmony and peace. Here the real self can be known by the unfoldment of certain inner senses that correspond with the outer ones. It is the real self that seeks, through the dense matter, the middle of existence and it is the real self that must and can answer it. What stands in the way is the personality. The Wheel of Fortune moulds, makes and breaks the personality in turn.

Whilst the individual is on the 'ups' of The Wheel all is well and he does not question or seek answers, but when he finds himself on the downward arc as The Wheel turns, then he may possibly begin to wonder why and how life keeps hitting him so hard.

This is his turning point, with curiosity aroused he will commence to seek the answer. From the yellow ray he will draw the power of mental activity that will help him in his search and from the red ray will come the enthusiasm. Also from this ray will arise the characteristic of impulsiveness which, if not guarded against, will send the student on the downward turn of The Wheel.

With the use of the blue ray wisdom can be developed and this will control the impulsiveness of the red ray. From the bright blue, a fairly high octave of the blue ray, the student can obtain patience and also aspiration, which sends him on the upward arc or curve. Struggle and conflict will still beset him through the action of the green ray, but having placed his foot upon the path he forges ahead, recovering from each fall and pressing forward again.

From the amethyst of Jupiter the student gains the visionary quality. This can, at times, get out of hand and he will spend much time and energy chasing visions of imagination, caught up in the glamour of illusion which contorts the inner vision until such time as the blue ray of wisdom can ride over the amethyst. If the student cannot or will not take the necessary action to invoke, through the blue ray, the wisdom that is available to him, then the Wheel of Fortune will turn and bring him down to the hard fact that visionary qualities must be handled with care.

This path is also called the 'Reversal of Fortune' and this can be a reversal in either direction. It is eventually from one of the downward turns that the student commences to use the mental activity of the yellow ray combined with the wisdom of the blue ray. From this stage he proceeds to draw upon both the red and amethyst rays with discretion.

A reversal of fortune in the right direction now takes place and slowly the student follows once more the upward arc of the Wheel until, with full employment of the green ray, he is poised with perfect balance at the top of the wheel watching the activities below.

From this vantage point he gains the vision of higher realms and moves towards them until he reaches the point where he leaves the World of Assiah and enters the Yetziratic World.

In Yetzirah

Rich purple is the colour of the path in the Yetziratic World and with it is the amethyst from Jupiter. The first background colour to the path is the indigo of Yesod, which overshadows the whole of the Yesodic tree.

When the purple ray and the amethyst meet and merge there is a resultant blue mauve, the basic quality of which is high ideals. As these two rays remain with the path all through Yetzirah it does mean that the initiate will enter on every path of the Wheel of Fortune in every sephirah with high ideals.

It may be that in his journey through the Yetziratic World some of the initiate's ideals will be misplaced and at other times he may not at first reach the ideal, but this quality of high ideal is the spur that keeps urging him on in spite of the ups and downs and a continuous reversal of fortunes.

On the path of the Wheel of Fortune in Yesod his highest ideal is to raise the consciousness of the astral plane to a realm of desire for spiritual truth, to see through the illusion of this emotional world. For aid in his efforts he calls upon the purple ray. This is one occasion where the high ideal is misplaced and instead of raising the consciousness of the astral world, instead he is drawn into – and for a time enmeshed in – it.

The purple ray he had called upon because of its forceful power, only increased the emotional atmosphere, but the strong desire will not admit to this and the other qualities of the purple ray now influence him. Pride, perhaps the worst of the purple attributes, will not acknowledge defeat and he becomes pompous and overbearing until overwhelmed by the astral desire of illusion and the wheel turns.

From the Moon the silver octave of the grey ray streams out, a clear symbol against the darker purple of the path and the indigo of Yesod. Through this ray he obtains balance and realizes where he made his mistake, making use of the amethyst ray he gains, with the balance of the silver, a true vision of the world he is in and now knows his task is to control his own astral consciousness and reach up to the mental plane. From this level he can then help those in the astral, but not the plane itself as this is an essential part of the cosmic scheme.

Once this is clear to him, the initiate calls upon the indigo ray with its caution and fortitude. Using both qualities he commences to control his emotional body and in the course of time after many reversals the Wheel turns and carries him to the top of the arc. Holding the balance from the silver ray he now takes perfect control and is ready to move on until he reaches the point on the Tree in Yesod where he can discard his astral/emotional body and move to the Tree in Hod, the first sephirah on the return journey in the lower mental plane of consciousness.

The violet of Hod and the yellow of Mercury supplement the purple and amethyst rays as tools for the initiate to use on the path of the Wheel of Fortune in this particular tree.

Violet, as a low octave of the purple ray, produces spiritual dedication and with the yellow giving a powerful intellect the initiate is now well and truly on a pure high level mental investigation of the world around him. 'Around him' in this context means not only the plane of consciousness in which he exists, but the planes both above and below him.

Visions of understanding the whole cosmic scheme through the intellect is implanted in his mental body by the visionary aspect of the amethyst ray, through the purple ray he develops a pride in his intellect.

Having reached this stage of understanding, the mental body crystallizes and for aeons of time he whirls round on the wheel in his fixed groove. So rigid is the mental body that the initiate accepts the downs as part of misfortune, but never connects it with his mental attitude.

It is only when the initiate reaches the ultimate peak of lower mental understanding, with many questions still unanswered, that the powerful intellect, bestowed by the yellow ray, realizes there must be something more than mind. With difficulty he controls the pride of the purple ray and turns his attention to the amethyst ray in an attempt to gain a new vision. He also takes from this ray its idealistic attribute.

Once he has the idealistic attribute of the amethyst ray the initiate is on the fringes of the Netzach sephirah, slowly a new vision appears before him and drawing upon the forceful power of the purple ray he surges forward and the wheel turns into the lower mental plane occupied by Netzach.

On the path of The Wheel of Fortune in Netzach the purple and amethyst rays are overshadowed by the amber of the sephirah and the blue from Venus. Amber is a high octave of the orange ray, giving mental vigour, and from the blue comes wisdom.

The initiate's mental body now takes on a different form, from the crystallized rigidity of Hod it assumes a fluidity that ebbs and flows from one vision to another, high ideal after high ideal. The blue ray influences him to struggle for spiritual maturity and to this end he employs the wisdom of the blue ray and the mental vigour of the amber.

In course of time he is drawn to the second aspect of the blue ray – love. This is a quality that the mental activity has been inclined to push to one side and it is one of the vital qualities he requires, not just in Netzach, but through the whole of his journey.

In Netzach the quality of love is mainly directed to the lower forms of life in Assiah and also to the creation of the cosmos. As the wheel turns the initiate views every aspect of the universe as far as his lower mental body will allow. When he reaches the termination with the mental body he calls upon the amethyst ray and its visionary quality.

Through the visonary quality the initiate projects his mind and touches the sephirah of Tiphareth. The vision awakens him more to the blue ray, but he also realizes that love without sacrifice is only going half way. To achieve the full expression of love, sacrifice must be made.

The initiate now reaches up to the Tree in the sephirah Tiphareth and to the path of The Wheel of Fortune. In this sephirah, which is the bridge between the higher and lower mental level, the Wheel of Fortune plays an important part as it also bridges the lower and higher mental levels.

On the path in Tiphareth the initiate feels the fluctuation of the Wheel, perhaps more than in any other sephirah, as it turns between the lower and mental planes, throwing him up and tossing him down as he wages a continuous struggle against the pull of the lower mental planes of consciousness.

Clear pink rose forms the background to the purple and amethyst of the path, with the orange of the sun putting out its brilliant glow. The initiate will require the use of all these rays in his efforts to conquer the path of The Wheel of Fortune in Tiphareth.

Balance of the opposites is perhaps more essential at this point than at any other point on the basic Tree. Tiphareth is the central point of balance for the whole Tree, and this applies also to the Tree in Tiphareth. To attain the point of the sphinx, which sits above the turning wheel of change, the initiate must learn how to be a King and a Child and hold these extremes in perfect balance.

Higher and lower mental planes of consciousness have to be brought into balance, and as this path covers the two planes, neither the higher nor lower should hold power over the other. This appears rather strange at first to the initiate and his inclinations are to subdue the lower mental plane to the higher.

Through the higher mental plane he can attain his kingship, but this is inclined to destroy the qualities of the child, just as the lower mental will give him the child qualities, but never reach to the level of kingship. Until he can balance the two, the wheel carries him up and hurls him down.

From the orange ray he develops the qualities of practical knowledge and receptivity and from the purple ray he obtains greatness and by blending and using these qualities the initiate develops kingship. Turning to the amethyst ray he finds the humility required to become a child, and this – combined with constant affection and unselfishness, both drawn from the pink rose – completes the character of the child.

With both characters developed, the initiate has now to balance them. This is done through the careful use of all the rays at his disposal and at the same time he is gaining perfect balance of the whole mental body, both higher and lower aspects. In the sacrifice of one to the other balance is obtained and retained.

The path in Tiphareth is conquered and the adept, like the sphinx, is now above the wheel at this level of consciousness and before moving on he dispenses those qualities of balance to all life still on the ever-turning wheel. Having achieved the object and learned the lesson of the path in Tiphareth the adept now turns his attention to the Tree in Geburah and makes his way through the states of consciousness on that tree until once again he faces the path of the Wheel of Fortune.

Geburah envelops everything with its orange ray and Mars sends out the red ray, cutting through the orange, and inside these two rays the purple of the path and the amethyst of Jupiter shine through. The symbol of the path Kaph does in truth apply more on the path in Geburah than perhaps in any other sephirah.

The hand of the adept now grasps the dualities and blends them into a perfect balance. This is the task now before him and should be the eventual outcome if he conquers the path that now faces him. The forces of the universe must be grasped and directed in such a manner that only perfect justice pervades through the whole system.

To dispense justice is a new experience for the adept, but until he can do this in such a way that it is pure justice, no further progress on his own journey can be made. From the orange ray of Geburah he can, and in course of time does, take the quality of practical knowledge, but he can also obtain an overplus of pride and this can be a very real obstacle if care is not exercised.

Force, vigour and energy come from the red ray, again power that must be handled with care, and it is through the practical knowledge obtained from the orange that these forces of red can be handled with discrimination and in correct proportion. To counteract the pride of the orange, humility must be drawn from the amethyst ray.

Humility can lead to a gentleness not applicable to the task in hand and the adept must learn to administer justice in humility, but nevertheless with firmness, so that justice is meted out in its true course.

The purple ray adds a forceful power to the adept's armoury and – operated through the practical knowledge of the orange ray, like the red – can serve a useful purpose in applying justice correctly. Once the adept has mastered the ray qualities he has mastered the path of the Wheel of Fortune on the tree in Geburah.

Once more the adept is balanced and poised above the wheel, beyond justice of the lower worlds himself, he has now to bow to the higher levels. At this state of consciousness he can say, however, that he has grasped the universe in his hands and there is justice throughout the whole of that universe.

Unrelenting, the cosmic laws impress upon him the need to move forward lest he slip back. Even a balanced state of consciousness above the wheel does not allow inaction, and so emerging from the Tree in Geburah, now a Master, he commences the journey on the Tree in Gedulah.

Overshadowed by a deep violet from the sephirah, the Master approaches the path of the Wheel of Fortune to find on that path in Gedulah his cosmic tools are restricted to two octaves of the purple ray, one from the sephirah and one from the path, and the amethyst which comes from the Jupiter of the path and the Mundane Chakra of Gedulah.

The Master is now on the Royal Road, once through Gedulah he crosses the abyss and leaves the Yetziratic world for good. But he has yet to conquer the path in Gedulah and the sephirah itself. Here can be found conciliation and reward, which is the Intelligence of the path, operating to the full and although he has passed through the sphere of karma,

Geburah, it is here that the Master finds ultimate conciliation and reward.

Once more the balance must be attained as the Wheel of Fortune turns and the balance is very fine, with only the royal ray, purple, and the spiritual ray, amethyst. From the deep violet octave of the purple ray he can adopt the characteristics of adoration, magnanimity and spiritual dedication and from the purple itself forceful power and greatness.

These are some of the rewards for his efforts up to this stage of his journey. Here in his hands are some of the most potent forces to be found in the ray qualities. Used in the wrong way the Master could turn the wheel on a spin of reversal which could set him back in Geburah.

To complete the balance and have perfect conciliation, he must make use of the amethyst ray qualities of humility and altruism, and most of all its spiritual quality. If he uses these there can be perfect conciliation and once more the true visionary powers are with him whereby he can see the use for his powers in aiding all life below through the direction of influences and he also has the vision of Daath with the world that lies beyond the abyss.

After giving service in the sphere of Gedulah for some period of cosmic time the Master turns the wheel himself and rises up into the World of Briah and a new state of consciousness.

In Briah

The path of the Wheel of Fortune now responds to the blue ray, from Jupiter the amethyst ray streams forth and this is against the crimson background of Binah with the black of Saturn sending its influence around the sephirah and the Tree.

A full understanding of The Wheel of Fortune awaits the Master on this path in Binah. One of the first lessons is the restrictive action of the black ray of Saturn from which stems the majority of 'ring-pass-not' phases, one of which is the Wheel of Fortune and only as and when an individual is ready can he go through a pairticular 'ring-pass-not'.

It is at the point when a 'ring-pass-not' has been gone through that for a moment in time the one passing through is in balance and sits above that particular circle or wheel until caught up on the new wheel or cycle just entered.

With this understanding the Master looks for the 'ring-pass-not' that has to be conquered to gain victory over the path of the Wheel of Fortune in Binah. From the amethyst he again draws upon the visionary power and through that vision he realizes the restriction exercised by the black ray; the 'ring-pass-not' of the path in Binah is personality.

With the blue ray influencing him to struggle for spiritual maturity and the realization that this can only be attained in full by destruction of the personality, the Master calls upon the crimson octave of the red ray for the courage to separate his individuality from his personality.

With the use of the black ray he develops the last of his latent powers and through them removes the restriction of the same ray. Truly he has balanced the basic force by using one of its qualities to offset the other.

On the removal of the personality the spark can move forward into Chokmah, where the blue of the path of the Wheel of Fortune has a background of the pure soft blue of Chokmah; the amethyst from Jupiter is also in evidence.

The spark now views the ultimate Wheel of Fortune, the sphere of the Zodiac, Mundane Chakra to Chokmah, but now instead of being launched through one of the twelve portals on to a path of outgoing, the spark is above the wheel, balanced, its journey completed, now part of the perfected force that turns the wheel.

On this path in Chokmah he draws upon the wisdom of the blue ray and the mystical powers of the amethyst, through which he understands the twelve aspects of the wheel as it turns, sending some sparks out on their journey down through the planes of consciousness and at the same time lifting other sparks up into the higher realm.

With the knowledge that the sphere of the Zodiac is the great wheel and that all the portals are wheels within wheels, the spark can now stop the world and get off, and make the last move from one tree to another as it moves to the Tree in Kether.

In Atziluth

The path of The Wheel of Fortune in Atziluth – Kether on the basic tree, is violet, an octave of the purple ray. The main qualities of violet are humility, spiritual dedication and reverence. From Jupiter, the astrological influence of the path, the amethyst ray streams out with its spiritual and mystical qualities. This ray also gives attainment in mystical powers.

Behind is the brilliance of Kether, giving the full purity to the qualities of the rays and also illuminating the first swirlings, the embryo of the first wheel of birth, death, life.

The first swirlings show the vastness of the archetypal wheel and the rays of the archetypal path show the qualities to be developed in order to attain that perfection which is above the ever-turning wheel, and with all four elements blended into the perfection of the sphinx, remains calm, aloof and yet in perfect one-ness with the whole.

JUSTICE

In Atziluth

In the Archetypal World the path of Justice is emerald green, one of the higher octaves of the green ray. There is also a further octave of green emanating from Libra – astrological influence of the path.

With the brilliance of Kether as the overall background, the green is pure and creates the perfect harmony, balance, and discrimination that makes this path the perfect archetype of universal Justice as it should operate on all the planes of consciousness below, both subjective and objective.

In Briah

The colour of the path changes to blue in the World of Briah. This is an octave of the love wisdom ray, the Libra influence of green remains the same.

Chokmah itself is the pure soft blue, the highest octave of the blue love wisdom ray. From the Mundane Chakra of Chokmah – sphere of the Zodiac – flow all the other rays, which include more of the blue ray. It is this predominance of blue that builds into the spark the love and wisdom required to conquer this path so that perfect justice can be accepted and administered at all levels.

The green ray, second only in predominance to the blue at the Chokmah level, gives the balance required to carry out without bias the work of the path.

Once these qualities have been absorbed by the spark and put into use it is ready to move over to the other phase of the

Briatic World – Binah – where understanding and form have to be accepted.

Crimson is the over-all colour of Binah and the black ray flows out from Saturn. The spark now is impregnated with high spiritual understanding which comes from an octave of the amethyst ray created from the merging of the crimson and blue.

The black ray brings the first restriction and the pure universal law has its first imperfections as tenuous form enshrouds the spark and although love, wisdom and understanding are still there, it has the first sign of distortion.

Impulsiveness is inclined to creep in from the crimson, which has the addition of a lower octave of the red ray that springs from Geburah at the top end of the path and also from Mars, the Mundane Chakra. It is only the restriction of the black ray and the harmony of the green that maintains a degree of balance, now a little removed from the perfection of Atziluth.

The spark now having absorbed the spiritual understanding of universal law, is ready to cross the abyss down into the formative world.

In Yetzirah

Gedulah is the first objective state in Yetzirah on the journey down through the worlds, and the spark now takes on the higher mental body.

In Yetzirah the colour of the path of Justice changes from the blue ray to a deep blue green. The qualities of this mixed ray are those of helpfulness, trustworthy and friendly qualities that are not only part of the path of Justice but also of Gedulah itself.

Deep violet, a middle octave of the purple ray, is the background colour of Gedulah and from the expansive Jupiter flows the amethyst ray.

The task of the spark is again as it always will be on this path, one of discrimination. Without discrimination the qualities of helpfulness and friendliness could be taken to the extreme, leading to more mercy than justice, culminating in dire results as the over-riding karmic law from Geburah brings things into line again.

Geburah gives out the orange ray, which has a similar quality to the black ray – restriction. There is, however, a difference in their scope of limitation. Where the black ray is the limitation of form, the orange ray is the limitation of the mental bodies, both higher and lower.

It is at this point on The Tree that universal law takes a concrete form of the lower levels of justice, although at this high level of the Tree there is not the distortion that appears at the lower levels.

With the red ray from Mars influencing the path of Justice in Geburah, it could be a harsh, unsympathetic form of justice and even at this level of consciousness the spark could develop the qualities of dictatorship.

The blue green, with its helpful and friendly qualities, helps to tone down the red ray, but the green from Libra can cause a certain amount of conflict in the attainment of harmony.

On the path of Justice in Geburah the spark learns to balance justice, and to bring to it a degree of Mercy. This is not an easy lesson to learn with Geburah at the top end of the path, and probably never would be were it not for the softening and balancing influence of Tiphareth at the end.

Tiphareth is the next sphere where the spark must tread the path of Justice and here the path is overshadowed by a clear pink rose, one of the higher octaves of the red ray.

There is here a double Tiphareth influence, that from the sephirah itself, and from Tiphareth at the end of the path.

Mingling with the clear rose of Tiphareth is the orange ray with the qualities of self-reliance and trust, both much needed qualities on the path of Justice, as this is a path where equilibrium has not only to be acquired, but be maintained. This is not easy because the path is one of struggle and conflict.

At the Tiphareth level it is an internal struggle, at the mental level including both higher and lower mental bodies.

Very rarely can true justice be meted out without mental conflict and this is an aspect of the green ray emanating from Libra.

Justice is a lonely path to follow and it is important that the spark learns at this level to be self-reliant. Help from the higher level of consciousness is not now so easy to call upon with the commencing enshroudment of the lower mental body.

Through all the struggle and conflict the spark draws up the harmonizing quality of Tiphareth and bathes in the warmth of universal love from the clear pink rose and it is with the aid of this that the conflict is resolved and the path conquered.

From Tiphareth down into Netzach the spark is now fully embedded in the lower mental body, but with a certain amount of flexibility and – to a major degree – the wider outlook.

Amber, the ray of Netzach, is a high octave of the orange ray and does not have the same degree of rigidity that is a quality of this ray at the lower octaves. This results in a speculative attitude towards life at all levels and in all aspects, with the amber ray producing the quality of receptivity.

Receptivity is a desirable characteristic to possess if the equilibrium of the path of Justice is to be maintained, but too much speculation can be detrimental to the conquest of the path. In this respect the spark receives help from the lower octave of the orange ray which flows out from the Sun of Tiphareth and if made use of, can bring the speculative attitude under control. Once this is done and balance achieved, the spark is ready to move on to the Tree in Hod.

The last aspect of the lower mental body is added in Hod and the pliable form of Binah now becomes rigid form. The spark now has the idea of fixed patterns built into the lower mental body, and just as Netzach was too pliable for the equilibrium of the path of Justice, so Hod is too rigid.

The ray of Hod is violet/purple, a middle octave of the purple ray. This ray gives to the spark the first idea of power, as this is the ray of rulership. The task of the spark on the path of Justice in Hod is to learn how to handle power in a balanced manner.

By the use of the green ray from Libra, balance can be brought in and with the creative ray of yellow streaming out of Mercury the mental body learns to use power in a balanced and creative manner.

Once this has been achieved the spark is ready to take on an emotional body and move forward or downward, according to the point of view, to the Sephirah of Yesod where the predominating colour of the sephirah is indigo and from the Moon beams out the silver ray. Although this is the highest octave of the grey ray, its power is minimized at this level by other rays intermingling and bring it down to a lower octave of the ray.

Fortitude and caution are two qualities of this octave of the indigo ray. Caution is a very essential quality on the path of Justice, particularly at the Yesod level. The spark will also find it a useful acquisition when, with the final body added, incarnation into the World of Assiah takes place.

If caution is not developed at this stage, the balance and equilibrium of the path could and would be so easily disturbed and justice be based on emotion.

This form of justice could flow between two extremes, either to the sentimental or to that cold, harsh justice which is so wrongly termed emotionless.

No action is without one of the two forms of emotion (*a*) uncontrolled or (*b*) controlled emotion. Emotions are the motivating forces at the lower levels and perhaps to a lesser degree at the higher levels.

The green ray from Libra is full of emotions, hence the struggle and conflict that exists in this path at all levels, as this is the one constant ray.

The grey ray gives the attribute of stability and it is only by acceptance of this, and the caution of the indigo, that the spark can conquer the path of Justice in Yesod, and even then it is not an easy conquest. It requires much fortitude, which can also be drawn from the indigo ray, to bring into harmony and balance the struggle and conflict of the green.

In Assiah

Now the spark is equipped with all the essentials of the path of Justice to tread it in the World of Assiah. In this lowest of the four worlds the path of Justice is pale green, and from the sephirah the yellow ray overshadows the whole.

Yellow is the ray of creative activity, but is also something more important, particularly at the level of Assiah. It is the ray of communications, at the lowest level of the physical world this can be radio, television, etc.

At the higher levels of the physical world it can be communications by means of telepathy and higher still the developed and trained intuition. This ray is the spiritual link or line of communication between Assiah and Atziluth.

There is no doubt that this long line of communication has its distortions and messages do not come through clear until it has been used sufficiently for the spark, now The Fool, to become used to it and to understand more clearly.

It is during the period from arriving in the physical world to the point where he understands the communications, that The Fool makes many errors as he takes and absorbs from all the other rays which stream out from the Mundane Chakra of Malkuth.

The sense of discrimination and true justice is lost in the maelstrom of influences, with the green ray bringing in the struggle and conflict aspect, but the high octave of the green ray that permeates the whole of the path holds within it, altruistic emotion, charity and understanding and with this and the aid of the yellow ray, which at this level is a middle octave, and contains the qualities of knowledge and justice, The Fool can eventually conquer the path in Assiah.

THE HANGED MAN

In Assiah

This path joins Geburah and Hod on the left-hand pillar. It is a path where the student has to constantly reorientate himself. The path has no astrological symbol of influence, but is instead influenced by the element of water.

In the Yetziratic text this path is referred to as the 'Stable Intelligence', a peculiar attribution for a path where the symbol is a man hung upside down and hanging by one leg. With the element of water bringing the ebb and flow movement it would appear to be anything but stable.

Although there is a continuous ebb and flow, the basis remains steady. Patterns may change, but the whole remains steadfast to the pattern or goal that has been set and the sum total of the whole never changes, hence the 'Stable Intelligence'.

It is from the element – water – ruling the path that the student obtains his first glimpse of what this path means, images in water are reflected upside down. This upside down aspect not only symbolizes consciousness but means its complete reversal. An entire change in the student's habitual way of thinking or viewpoint is indicated.

The student on this path must change direction from a worldly based way of thinking to a more spiritual way, to realign his personality and give it up to the direction of the Universal Mind.

With the path of the Hanged Man the feet are above the head. In occult teachings the feet of the Zodiacal Man, Adam

Kadmon, are represented as understanding, so this path symbolizes – and teaches the individual to use – the understanding he has previously gained.

Mem, the Hebrew letter attributed to this path, signifies 'seas'. What it is telling the student is, here are the seas of waters of the great unmanifest, the waters of wisdom which can be his once he has pulled his feet out of the mud of Malkuth and once this has been done he is in a position to have a much clearer understanding of his goal.

This is the path where the potential adept or potential Master can become an adept or a Master according to the level of consciousness at which he is working. Each step taken, first to student, student to adept and adept to Master, requires a change of the conscious understanding and reversal of processes and thoughts.

On this path many problems are posed for the student because all four elements are present, each making its influence felt. Although it is the water that predominates, the Hanged Man is the stable intelligence in this respect also. The student has to balance and stabilize these elements.

The element of air causes him to jump from one thing to another. The water element brings him into conflict with his own thoughts, torn between the waters of wisdom and the waters of the moon. The fire element fills him with the desire to surge forward into the adventure of the unknown and the earth element pulls him towards the material things of life.

In the World of Assiah the path of the Hanged Man is white flecked with purple. It would denote that this path – even in the realms of Assiah – has a certain purity and the purple indicates that it is a path that can lead to rulership at this level of consciousness. There is danger for the student with the purple ray because of the quality of pride that it contains. The influence of greatness the ray brings with it is a promise of spiritual greatness, but the student, if not very careful, can fall into the trap of material greatness.

It is from the white ray that he can overcome the adverse

side of the purple ray by drawing upon the spiritual philosophy that is part of that ray's characteristic; also through the white he receives the desire to struggle for perfection.

Concerning these rays that govern the path, in the World of Assiah, viewed cosmically it could be the illimitable ether of space, which is the white of manifestation and the purple fleck is the ray shooting down to the depths of space, the digging deep into life in all its aspects in order to experience.

In Assiah it is the eternal spark that has sunk deep into matter and has experienced many lives and innumerable events until, as the student, eventually he realizes that the way the world is orientated is not really to his liking, it is not his way.

The student finds he has changed his outlook. The honesty of the purple forces him to acknowledge this and once he has decided literally to turn his world upside down then he is ready to go on to the more spiritual side of life, because this is what he knows he really wants.

From the yellow ray, the Atziluthic colour of Malkuth on the basic Tree, which is also the World of Assiah, he absorbs the creativity aspect of this ray and by so doing is able to carry out his reversal of consciousness and gain the stability amidst his activity which gives him the victory over the path of the Hanged Man in Assiah.

In Yetzirah

On the path of return the first Tree to be conquered in the Yetziratic World is the Tree in Yesod. Throughout the whole of the Yetziratic World the path of the Hanged Man responds to a deep olive green. Embodied in this colour are two rays, green and grey, and in Yesod this combination of the two rays underline the turmoil that is present in the emotional body of the student.

Yesod's indigo ray surrounds the whole Tree in its sphere and so influences the path and the student treading it. Indigo has devotion as one of its predominant qualities, which does not help the student in his new sphere of existence and plane of consciousness. The devotion can still be towards the physical life he has recently left.

It is quite a big emotional upheaval, for some more than others, the leaving behind of an established way of life, the solid material world in which he could always find an anchor, and now he is in this world of fluctuating emotions which cause him to keep changing his desires and wishes.

The octave of the grey ray that is part of the path influence can create a feeling of insecurity and at the same time encourages the qualities of hardness and suppression. Whether he retards or expedites his progress depends a great deal upon the use the student makes of these qualities. If he uses the quality of suppression in order to suppress his doubts and feelings of insecurity – and through the hardness form a protective barrier against new thoughts and ideals – then he will fail to conquer the path of the Hanged Man.

What the student must do is to suppress his desires for the physical world that he has left behind and harden his emotions, for the time being, to the cries of Malkuth. The feeling of insecurity will then put the student in the position to seek further in order to find balance in this emotional sphere of consciousness.

From the green aspect of the path he meets more struggle and conflict and his emotional being moves in first one direction and then another as he searches for stability and harmony within his being. From the Moon of Yesod streams out the silver ray – a high octave of the grey – and it is when the student commences to use this ray that he can absorb its influences of tranquillity and balance.

Once balance has been achieved and the emotions stilled, then he can make full use of the indigo ray and the aspect of it that gives clarity of thought. Now he can see the folly of his desires for the material world with all its restrictions and temptations, which will take him deeper into matter if he returns again to that plane of consciousness.

With full realization of what reincarnating into Malkuth

would mean, the purpose of the path of the Hanged Man in Yesod becomes clear. The student commences to turn his emotions upside down, from a desire or pull towards Malkuth to a desire for higher planes of consciousness. When the reversal of consciousness has taken place, then the student's task on the path of the Hanged Man is completed and he can proceed on his way through the Tree in Yesod and in course of time come to the Tree in Hod.

Although the path of the Hanged Man in Hod retains the olive green, the background is now one of violet purple with the yellow ray from Mercury having an influence also.

On the lower mental plane of Hod this reversal of consciousness or change of focus must continue. On the path in this sephirah the initiate feels the double influence of Hod, first from the sephirah itself and secondly from the Hod at the bottom end of the path itself.

With this double influence also comes the double influence of Mercury. The mental activity from Mercury combined with the strong lower mind aspect of Hod quickly removes any Yesodic influences that may still be with the initiate.

The initiate's difficulty now is to change his mental outlook, and to conquer the path of the 'Hanged Man' in Hod his whole thought process has to be re-orientated, and although the yellow ray is creating mental stimulation it is in part blotted out by the forceful power of the purple ray.

There is at this stage the danger of the initiate becoming pompous and developing pride and a false conception of greatness. All these characteristics come from the purple ray and the lower mental body, not long freed from the emotional body, is very susceptible to these influences.

It is to the violet ray the initiate must look for his salvation and by the use of this ray develop the quality of humility to cancel out his pride and pomposity. From the violet ray he can also obtain the quality of reverence which overrules his feelings of greatness.

Once he has balanced the violet against the purple ray the initiate for the moment is in harmony and he can direct the yellow ray towards spiritual mental activity of a wider nature. The humility of the violet makes him realize that his knowledge and understanding is indeed very limited in the whole vastness of the scheme of life.

From the olive green there is turbulence and it is at this point the influence of this ray is important to the initiate. Having either subdued or completely overcome the negative aspects of the purple ray and through the violet gained harmony and balance, he might be inclined to stay at this point, which would eventually lead to retrogression.

The olive green disturbs the balance and from the grey aspect of this ray comes the urge to struggle for spiritual freedom, which the initiate realizes cannot be obtained on the Tree in Hod. This is the reversal or the turning upside down that had to be achieved on the path of the Hanged Man in Hod and now the initiate is ready to move forward on this Tree and complete the remaining paths with a greater degree of ease due to his changed mental outlook.

The next Tree the initiate has to face is that in Netzach, where on the path of the Hanged Man the olive green of the path has amber as a background with blue from Venus. Amber is a high octave of the orange ray, containing the qualities of mental vigour and wholeness.

Netzach brings him a stage nearer to his ideal of spiritual freedom. His eyes are upturned towards the higher influences. With the amber octave bestowing mental vigour, he surges forward without restraint, only to fall back through lack of discrimination. In Netzach he is receiving the influences that create a wider consciousness.

Having left Hod behind, the initiate is inclined to forget one of the lessons learned in that sphere, the discipline to channel his mental outlook. Netzach is the sphere of polarity to Hod and the initiate must learn to use its influences in that light and not just take the complete freedom of the lower mental body that Netzach offers on its own.

From the grey aspect of the path itself he must take the quality of self-control and then through the amber quality of wholeness realize that Netzach and Hod form the wholeness of the lower mental body. When this has been accomplished the initiate knows how to channel his mental forces.

The blue ray now brings in the influence of love and wisdom and it is with this influence a further struggle develops within his lower mental body. The love aspect, having been rather neglected as the lower mental developed its intellectual potential with the widening of consciousness, must now be taken into consideration.

It is through the wisdom aspect of this blue ray that the initiate eventually recognizes that further progress will be barred to him unless he develops the love aspect which will bring about a balance of the extreme intellectual forces established in his lower mental being.

By turning upside down his ideas of the lower mental plane of consciousness and bringing into it a quality beyond mental reasoning, that of love, a quality the mind with all its reasoning powers cannot define, the initiate can conquer the path of the Hanged Man on the Tree in Netzach and prepare to gain victory over the whole of this Tree and commence to move towards the bridge between the lower and higher mental planes of consciousness.

The bridge between the two planes is the sephirah of Tiphareth and the Tree within it. Here the initiate has not only to find harmony, but he must also understand how to bring about a balance within dualities.

A clear pink rose flows over the whole Tree in Tiphareth and forms the background to the olive green of the path of the Hanged Man. From the Mundane Chakra of Tiphareth the orange ray also sends out its influence over the path. It is this path, with these attendant rays, that the initiate now faces.

With the exception of Kether on the basic Tree, the World of Atziluth, Tiphareth expresses the path of the Hanged Man more than any other sephirah. The basic qualities of this sephirah can be related to the path. This is the sephirah that holds balance and expresses duality.

On the path of the Hanged Man in Tiphareth the initiate's

work on polarity continues, but the vision is now clearer and he realizes that polarity also means duality. The process of upside downness points out quite clearly that sacrifice has to be made.

The pull of the lower mental plane has to be renounced, all hindrances that this mental level contains has to be eradicated so that his higher mental body can be attained, at the same time he has to become as a child, simple and uncomplicated, but he must also develop a high degree of self-mastery and so become a king.

To become a king and a child at one and the same time is the near ultimate in balanced polarity and the blending of duality. The olive green of the path indicates that the way of this type of kingship is not easy because it is the way of the sacrificed God.

Inherent in the olive green is the grey aspect and this holds the quality of persistence. It is to this grey ray that the initiate now turns and obtains from it persistence for his efforts to attain to freedom. Encouragement comes from the green ray aspect of the path, giving to him the hope and promise that after the conflict is over harmony will prevail.

Green brings that harmony, although it is through struggle and conflict. The pink rose is also there, bringing to bear its healing power of magnetic nature; not only does it help the initiate in his struggles, but he also develops the power himself. Now he knows what it means to be a king and also turn himself upside down and be the child.

The power of healing he has developed is truly the power of spiritual king. To use it correctly he .must have the spiritual wisdom of a king and the simplicity of the child. From the orange ray he develops geniality and receptivity, which aids him in obtaining this force of healing and its distribution. He also obtains from the same ray trust and reliance.

Both trust and reliance are required to help him tread successfully the path of the Hanged Man in Tiphareth and again the qualities of polarity and duality. Trust is the childlike quality and reliance is the kingly attribute.

The initiate now goes forward to his sacrifice and with its completion he attains to adeptship and moves still further forward to the goal of full spiritual attainment, of which he had the first vision when he reversed his way of life on the path of the Hanged Man in the physical world of Assiah.

From his sacrifice on the Tree in Tiphareth he has learned another lesson, that each step forward can only be made by the sacrifice of preconceived ideas and that for each change he makes he must also sacrifice any part of his whole being that prevents him reaching the next higher state of consciousness.

The teaching, learning and full acceptance of this lesson is the fulfilment of the experience of the Hanged Man on the Tree in Tiphareth.

Geburah, sephirah of universal justice and assessor of karma, is the next sephirah in which the adept has to conquer the path of the Hanged Man. The olive green of the path is still there, but the overall ray of the Tree in Geburah is orange and from Mars flashes the red ray.

The adept is now completely on the higher mental plane of consciousness, his own lower mental body having been sacrificed and disposed of at Tiphareth. In this sephirah his intellect will be highly developed and polished.

On the path of the Hanged Man in Geburah the adept will co-operate fully with the laws of the cosmos because he has now gone deeply into them, penetrating into and learning many of their hidden secrets and workings. The adept has also by now learned acceptance of whatever comes to him.

Whereas at Geburah on the lewer levels he would have been inclined to rebel against the workings of Geburah and attempt to buck against cosmic law, now he plunges in with his eyes wide open. The intellectual Hod and the path of the Hanged Man gives him clear logical reasoning powers.

Knowing where he wants to go and what it entails before he can succeed in arriving helps to a great degree, but this clear view can also be very daunting. It is in this situation that the adept can call upon the red ray to give him courage and the necessary stimulation to go forward.

From the orange ray self-reliance is derived and from the grey aspect of the path itself the adept obtains persistence. When he combines these qualities with those from the red ray he is well equipped and advanced on the way to overcoming the path of the Hanged Man in Geburah.

Struggle and conflict can and will enmesh his higher mental body as he goes along the path in the sephirah of karma, but his clear and logical understanding aids him in his difficulties and by his reversal of attitude from one of resistance to one of acceptance he eventually emerges as victor.

Cosmic law having operated, and karma having been satisfied, the adept that entered Geburah now emerges a Master of cosmic forces, Master of his destiny and – most important of all – he is Master of his higher mental body.

Now as a Master he is fitted for the next stage of his journey, that of entering the sephirah of Gedulah and progressing through the Tree in that sephirah. For the last time he will tread the path of the Hanged Man with the olive green as the dominating colour of the path.

The Atziluthic colour of Gedulah which surrounds the whole Tree is deep violet and from the Mundane Chakra of Gedulah the amethyst ray pours out with the full expansiveness that only Jupiter amongst all the planets can bestow.

There is now a complete change. The violet of Gedulah spreads a peaceful atmosphere in marked contrast to the struggles of Geburah just left behind. Spiritual emanations from the amethyst, combined with the peace of the violet, create ideal conditions for the Master's next phase of his journey to the ultimate.

This is a consolidating or gathering together stage. Consolidating what he has learned on this path in all other spheres and gathering together all his spiritual resources. The Master is now above all other worlds and part of his experience on the path of the Hanged Man in Gedulah is to once more re-orientate himself so that he can not only be above the other worlds, but look down and help those worlds without becoming involved in them.

The world of cause and effect is now within his control. He understands more clearly ultimate causes and it is with this wisdom he can help the lower planes of consciousness, again the duality with perfect polarization. As he looks down, so at the same time he looks up. The Master is looking upon the created and the creative world at one and the same time.

From the violet octave of the purple ray he strengthens his spiritual dedication that he may work for the lower planes as well as preparing to reach the higher planes of consciousness. The amethyst ray provides attainment in mystical powers and the Master sees again the vision of the higher realms.

Now his work on the path of the Hanged Man in Gedulah is completed and he is prepared to take the step across the great abyss. Knowing, as he does, that once he leaves the security of Gedulah he has passed the point of no return, he calls for the last time on the grey aspect of the path for tranquillity and endurance and takes the step that leads him to Binah on the other side of the abyss.

In Briah

The path of the Hanged Man in the creative world is sea green and blue, the first of the two to be met in Briah provides a crimson background with the black ray of Saturn penetrating through sufficiently for the Master to draw upon as and when he needs it.

In Binah the upside down process carries on, now he must turn the values of personality and individuality round. Prepared for this as he now is, it is still no easy task, only so recently in cosmic time having developed full mastership, now he must sacrifice it, the personality must give way to individuality alone.

From the sea green of the path itself he can obtain the quality of discrimination which is an aid in making his decision. The next step is to make use of the black ray with its restricting qualities. Slowly, but surely, he restricts the personality more and more and finally through the energizing power of the crimson completes the disintegration of the personality.

After aeons of time journeying across time and space the spark is at last free of all lower entanglements and as a pure spark of the Ain force it moves to the Tree in Chokmah where, on the path of the Hanged Man, with the sea green of the path and the soft blue of Chokmah, the spark prepares itself for that final step to the World of Atziluth.

Here in Chokmah, where all the wisdom of the ages is stored, the spark finds the answer to many aspects of the upside-down values. Through the medium of the pure soft blue with its quality of faith and innocence, the spark understands their true meanings; faith born of wisdom and innocent of negative conduct; love that is completely selfless and wisdom which does not appertain to intellectual faculties.

From the green of the path the spark takes harmony and balance and again a reversal of what balance meant in other spheres. This is the true balance where positive and negative are not just balanced against each other, but integrated one into the other so that both are there and yet not there.

Now the spark is ready to take its place on the path of the Hanged Man in Kether.

In Atziluth

In Kether, the World of Atziluth on the basic Tree, the path of the Hanged Man is deep blue and this, like the rest of the Tree in Kether, is bathed in the Brilliance of Kether's Atziluthic colour. This is the ultimate ray which highlights everything it touches. The deep blue holds the qualities of gloom, melancholy and power aspiration. Once the brilliance interpenetrates the deep vanishes and in its place is a blue ray that is full of lustre, shining clear and beautiful. The negative qualities vanish and are replaced by spiritual aspiration, the joy of true life.

The spark takes this final lesson and through the wisdom of this same blue ray sees clearly the perfect archetype of the Hanged Man. The negative aspects are essential to the proper understanding of the positive qualities, and with understanding comes the complete reversal of values.

DEATH

In Assiah

This is the path of the Imaginative Intelligence with the sephirah Tiphareth at one end and Netzach at the lower end. In the World of Assiah the colour of the path is blackish/ brown, a combination of two rays.

The ray that will stay with this path through all the four worlds is the indigo ray, which emanates from Scorpio, the astrological influence of the path of Death.

Transmutation is the basic quality of this path and the lesson that the student, initiate, or Master, has to learn is the art of correct transmutation, and of making that transmutation, not just being transmuted.

It will be realized that actual progress on the path of return depends entirely on the ability to transmute correctly. This lesson, once learned and the attribute developed, transmission or transmutation from sephirah to sephirah and escape from the different paths should be that much easier.

To go from one sephirah to another or from path to path without correct transmutation means recapture by those sephiroth or paths until the lesson and attribute of the path of Death has been developed. Then, and only then, can the complete escape which means no return be accomplished.

The most difficult step of all is escape from Assiah, where the path of Death on the return is met for the first time. At this level the mixed colour blackish/brown gives out the influence of decay, which to the majority of people in the World of Assiah is misunderstood and looked upon as a finality, the end of the road.

Indigo at this low octave produces superstition, stubbornness and a religious outlook. It is the last quality of the indigo ray that can help in understanding this path and even this can take many incarnations because most of those who turn to religion have the other two qualities of the indigo ray, superstition and stubbornness.

Superstition that punishment will be meted out to them if they entertain any idea other than that taught by their religion, and a stubbornness to believe in any other religion than their own, is typical of the crystallization and density of Malkuth of the basic tree, or as we know it, the World of Assiah.

This first path of Death in the four worlds is difficult and the conquest is a slow process, but with spiritual activity from the yellow ray of Assiah the barriers of superstition and stubbornness are eventually broken down and the student or initiate can move on to the World of Yetzirah.

In Yetzirah

Yesod, the first sephirah in Yetzirah on the path of return, has indigo for its influencing ray, but from its Mundane Chakra flows the grey ray. It is the high octave of silver, but at this level of the Tree it is tinged with indigo and green, producing a medium octave of grey.

The path of Death is now dark brown, a low octave of the brown ray, and of course the indigo from the astrological influence. It will be seen that the indigo ray is very prominent and bound to have a great influence on the path in Yesod. It is however a slightly higher octave than the one met with in the World of Assiah.

The low octave of the brown embodies the qualities of selfishness and biased thought, amongst other things, and the indigo at this level has the characteristic of blind devotion, and this quality has to be directed into the channels of transformation.

Yesod being the emotional and desire world, it is no easy

task to accept transformation or transmutation. If desires are being fulfilled and the emotions fed, the student or initiate is quite happy with the situation and if at times through the mental body the emotional body becomes restless, the biased thought of the brown is inclined to overrule it and bring the student or initiate back to the state of acceptance.

Self-control and a feeling of insecurity are the influences of the grey ray, and it is from the use of these qualities, combined with the selfishness of the brown ray, that the student or initiate can learn the lesson, in part, of transformation or transmutation.

After many journeyings through the Tree in Yesod the desires begin to pull and the emotions commence to stir up a feeling of insecurity. With the selfishness of the brown ray there comes a yearning for the happy comfortable state first enjoyed in Yesod. Exercising the self-control of the grey ray to stabilize the emotions, the student or initiate comes to the realization that the only way to extricate himself from what has now become undesirable is to transform himself to a higher realm of consciousness. With the blind devotion of the indigo ray he sets about the task.

Having transformed his outlook, the conditions are now suitable to transmute or discard the emotional/astral body and to commence the conquest of the Tree in Hod, the first of the two sephiroth at the lower mental plane of consciousness.

Going forward with a blind devotion, the path of Death is eventually reached and here the dark brown ray is overshadowed by the violet purple of Hod and there is also a shaft of yellow from the Mundane Chakra of Hod.

Violet/purple, one of the lower octaves of the purple ray, carries a number of qualities including humility, spiritual dedication, pride and an inclination to be pompous. Spiritual activity flows from the yellow ray, but the biased thought of the brown is still there, with blind devotion of the indigo.

It is on the path of Death at the Tree in Hod that the first major spiritual battle is fought. The spiritual activity that flows from the yellow ray brings with it mental conflict, biased thought towards orthodoxy or the known, with all its pompous surety, the spiritual dedication that is followed with blind devotion. These are the mental states that have to be transmuted, not just as a temporary measure. This would mean return to Hod at a later period. It must be transmutation that brings with it a finality to the narrow form and outlook of Hod.

The one outstanding quality of the purple ray that can help the student or initiate to accomplish this is humility. Once this aspect of the ray has been absorbed and brought into use the mind discards pomp and pride with the realization that the knowledge gained up to this point is only a small part of the whole.

With true humility, the spiritual activity and dedication commence the stage of transformation and the quality of idealism provided by the indigo ray aids in the final stage of transmutation from Hod into Netzach.

Amber, a high octave of the orange ray, provides the main influence of Netzach with the blue love/wisdom ray issuing forth from the Mundane Chakra Venus. The amber has the effect of raising the dark brown to the higher octave of medium brown and thus changing the influence and qualities of this ray on the path of Death.

This middle octave of the brown ray provides the characteristics of studious thoughtfulness, quietness in activity, absorption and knowledge without wisdom. The amber provides a true quality of Netzach – receptivity.

It is on the path of Death in Netzach that the idealism of the indigo can run riot, with the receptivity of the amber and absorption from the brown, thoughts and ideas rush in and are absorbed without too much discrimination.

A great deal of energy is spent following many false trails. This is the effect of the first flush of enthusiasm at being free from the restrictions of Hod.

In due course of time and after many visits or incarnations in the objective state of Netzach, the studious, thoughtful quality of the brown commences to be effectual. Deeper thought and more discrimination goes into what is received and so false trails are eliminated. Wisdom is added to the knowledge through the influence of the blue ray and the idealism of the indigo is channelled into higher ideals.

With increasing awareness, keener discrimination and heightened discernment the initiate now hears the call and feels the pull of Tiphareth at the top end of the path and the full influence of the Imaginative Intelligence comes into play and transformation takes place.

Transmutation or complete death of the lower mental body only takes place in Tiphareth, which is the meeting point of both higher and lower mental bodies or states of consciousness.

Clear pink rose takes the place of the amber as the overall covering ray for the Tree in Tiphareth and from the Mundane Chakra comes the golden orange of the sun. The dark brown of the path and the indigo remain.

For the first time the initiate has a glimmer of what it means for the lower self to meet the higher self as he meets the conflict of the higher and lower mental bodies. With the lower mental at the bottom end of the path he needs all the help he can extract from the pink rose of universal love and it is possible that without the devotion of the indigo ray even the pink rose would avail him nothing.

With devotion and mental vigour from the orange he perseveres along the path of Death and fully accepts the quality of unselfishness from the pink rose. This octave of the red ray also gives him comfort as he prepares to make the transition from the lower mental body in a complete transmutation that brings him face to face with the crucifixion of the lower realms of thought and being so that he is free from return to the lower realms, unless by choice. At Tiphareth he makes the transmutation from initiate to Master and is now prepared to go forward to the Tree in Geburah.

From the Mediating Intelligence to the Radical Intelligence is the next step and on the path of Death in Geburah the

Master undergoes a radical transmutation. The orange ray of Geburah with the red from its Mundane Chakra gives stimulation and added zeal to the devotion of the indigo. Any desires for the things of the lower planes of consciousness, for the pleasure of those things, are now transmuted. This is indeed the sphere of Death to all desires below its own level of consciousness.

The only burning desire left is to help all life to attain to this level of consciousness, either by returning to the lower levels purely for this purpose or to direct influences from the higher mental level to those on the lower levels who are prepared to accept them.

By taking advantage to the full of the indigo ray the maximum devotion can be given to the task that lies ahead. The dark brown of the path is still there, but in the sphere of Geburah. This is also transmuted by the orange ray of the sephirah and the octave is heightened to a coppery brown with its quality of quiet confidence.

With the quiet confidence that brings the calm and peace beyond understanding the Master moves from Geburah to Gedulah – the sphere of the Masters – there to commence a fresh journey on the Tree in that sephirah.

The Tree is enveloped in a deep violet and from the Mundane Chakra of Gedulah flows the amethyst ray, so appropriate to such a high spiritual centre. Although not perfection, amethyst has the qualities of the visionary. It is idealistic and from the violet springs the influence of humility, reverence and spiritual dedication.

Indigo at this level gives clarity of thought and devotion to purity. The one adverse factor is the dark brown ray, and interpenetrated with the violet it becomes a bluish/brown with the qualities of selfishness and religiosity.

It is these two qualities that can bring a fall even at this high level, and on the path of Death in Gedulah the first task is to transmute these qualities to unselfishness and spirituality, as opposed to religiosity.

To the question, 'How can this .be at this high level?' the

answer is, Mastership is reached by many paths, some religious, some spiritual with occult teachings, and others by means of the occult. Some become Masters by a mystical path and all have their weakness. The most sure path is a combination of all and even here there is a weakness.

Even a Master, that high level of being, can fall were it not so, and had it not happened in the past there would be no masters of the black path.

On the path of Death in Gedulah, spiritual humility from the violet ray must be exercised to the full and with the clarity of thought from the indigo comes the full realisation of the danger that stems from a selfish attitude towards his own particular belief. The amethyst ray helps here, if used, and its visionary quality developed.

Armed with the tools at his disposal, the Master now sees clearly and the final transmutations in any form of body takes place. After serving his purpose and fulfilling his task at the Gedulah level of consciousness he crosses the abyss via Daath to Binah.

In Briah

On the path of return, Binah is the first sphere to be entered and progression of the Tree in this sephirah commences. At the path of Death different rays come into play. The whole Tree is bathed in crimson, a high octave of the red ray. The highest octave of the black ray emanates from the Mundane Chakra of Binah.

The path of Death has now lost its dark brown ray. This has been replaced with a dull brown, but the indigo from the path's astrological influence remains.

Now the black ray is making its last claim of Death on this path. Its all-enfolding absorbing potential waits for the Master to call upon its powers to absorb the last remaining traces of form that were given to him, as The Fool, on the outward journey, so that he may be transmuted from individual personality to individual individuality.

This is the esoteric ray at this high octave with a secretive quality. It is with the removal of the last trace of personality that the esoteric, with its last secrets, will be revealed to the Master. It is a hard decision to make and even a Master may hesitate, but Tiphareth at the top end of the path still calls for further sacrifice.

Drawing comfort and the magnetic healing power from the crimson ray, and fortified by the spiritual devotion of the indigo, the Master prepares for the loss of his personality. With the knowledge and concentration drawn from the brown ray at this high octave he now uses the power of the black and completes the transmutation of his personality, going on towards Chokmah as pure individuality.

A pure soft blue is the overall colour of Chokmah and it is this high octave of the blue ray that dominates the scene, although from the Mundane Chakrah of Chokmah, the sphere of the zodiac, all the flashing colours stream forth.

Now in Chokmah, on the path of Death, the individual spark has to learn the lesson of the last Death or transmutation, death of the individual individuality so that it may become part of the united individualities.

From the blue ray the spark can obtain the last and full quality of wisdom and also it is on the path of Death in Chokmah that the lesson of selfless love has to be learned and accepted. Up to this point the quality of love has developed through all the varying stages, from the lowest point of sex to the highest point of universal love. It has, however, at all stages included the self to some greater or lesser degree. At this point in the journey it must be pure love, without the self included in any shape or form.

Again the indigo ray is called upon and now the quality of devotion has changed. It is true spiritual devotion to the whole scheme of manifestation. The brown ray of the path creates a contemplative attitude with its quality of quiet confidence, and in this state – with full wisdom – the spark conquers Death as the final transmutation to conscious perfection is made.

In its achievement of selfless love it also takes its place in the collective individuality state of consciousness.

In Atziluth

The World of Atziluth is perfection. It is also the supreme ray – brilliance. The path of Death in this Archetypal World is blue green, the blue of pure wisdom and the green of perfect harmony united with the indigo, devotion to the whole.

This is the perfect archetype of true Death that brings with it the perfected consciousness and through true Death, true Life.

TEMPERANCE

In Assiah

The path of Temperance or the Intelligence of Probation, as it is called in the Yetziratic text, is perhaps the first path where the personality meets the individuality; and so it is along this path, where that first contact is made, that the student or initiate has the first intimation of a higher consciousness. It is the first step on the journey referred to as the dark night of the soul.

It is on this path that the student or initiate feels life has become arid and desolate and many are the times when he is thrown back on his own inner resources as he meets the storms that make his journey turbulent and the clouds of darkness envelop him.

On this path the student or initiate is stepping out into the unknown. Preconceived ideas are shattered. What the student or initiate in the past had considered firm foundations crumble beneath his feet. There is no longer any anchor to hold him steady or familiar landmarks to guide him. He is on an unknown path with hostile conditions all around him.

In spite of all the hazards the student/initiate knows he must follow this path if he is to progress to that ultimate goal which beckons him, a goal that is far distant and as yet one that he cannot describe nor understand. Probably he is not fully aware of why he wants to reach it. This is the first urge from the individuality, or the spark of the real 'I', making its presence felt through and to the personality.

The path of Temperance as the first stage of the dark night

of the soul is the most difficult stage on each tree in each sephirah, but even more so in the World of Assiah because it is the very first stage of all. Once he is beyond this hurdle, the student/initiate has gained some experience and he is less uncertain of where he is going, although conditions change from Tree to Tree.

To accomplish this first stage in particular, the student/initiate needs the quality of devotion to the task in hand, the form of devotion that is single-minded in its intent, and he can acquire this attribute from the dark blue octave of the blue ray which – in the World of Assiah – governs the path.

Sagittarius, the astrological ruler of the path, endows it with the influence of the amethyst ray. No other ray could be more appropriate to the path of probation or Temperance than the amethyst and this ray will be with the path on every Tree through every world. Behind these rays in the World of Assiah is the yellow of Malkuth's Atziluthic colour, and from Malkuth's Mundane Chakra flow the four rays of red, blue, yellow and green.

At this low level of the basic tree the far from experienced student/initiate has a considerable selection of cosmic forces or rays for his use. At this early stage the effect of the rays will be more through their influence on the student/initiate than his knowledgeable and actual use and direction of them.

From the amethyst ray he received the spiritual influence which, with the arousing of the individuality, is the unseen, and at this point of his journey, the unknown force that is urging him to take this way of life. This ray influence is the cause of his inner desire to look for a spiritual path beyond the bounds of the orthodox.

Yellow, apart from being the ray of creative activity, is also a purgative ray and here commences the first purging of impurities. Religious beliefs of the conditioned mind, which have lost their spiritual content, receive the attention of this yellow purging ray and at the same time it stirs and creates activity within the mental body.

Through the influence of this yellow ray over many

incarnations the student has tried many philosophies and followed many spiritual paths, gaining from each one a limited amount of experience, until at last he has reached the stage where he has found his right path and the door stands open before him.

As the student/initiate stands upon the threshold, doubts assail him, in spite of the devotion from the blue ray. From this ray he also receives fortitude, which is an essential for him in the step he contemplates. It is now that the red ray influence comes sweeping through to give him the courage to go forward.

Many are the times, perhaps, that he has reached this stage in other lives, but not being so sensitive to the ray influences he has hesitated and turned back. Now, through past experiences, he is more sensitive to the rays and with the power of the red ray surging through him, he takes that step into the unknown.

Once the student/initiate commences to tread the path he is being tried and tested all the way. The familiar things known for so long, all the comforts and pleasures enjoyed for years, are swept aside. In the early stages he finds it a very lonely and desolate way. It is the green ray that flows in to give him balance in his struggle and conflict.

After a period of time, sometimes longer than others, he meets or joins other wayfarers on this path of Temperance going through the same difficulty, and although in many respects he still walks alone, it is in company of all others who are also walking alone. There are new pleasures enjoyed in this company of probationers and each gains something from the others, until towards the end of this path some intimation of the necessity for it seeps through and the personality has made the first known contact with the individuality, that spark of the Ain, the real 'I', or the student/initiate's higher consciousness.

When this first known contact between personality and the individuality has been made, the student now can be classed as an initiate and is ready to move through the remainder of the Tree in Assiah and on towards the World of Yetzirah.

In Yetzirah

In the World of Yetzirah the path of Temperance is green. From its astrological ruler flows the amethyst influence, through the six trees that form Yetzirah these rays will remain unchanged; only the Atziluthic colours or rays of the Sephiroth with their Mundane Chakras will vary.

On his journey back to source, the first Tree in Yetzirah that the initiate has to content with is that in Yesod, with its indigo background and the stream of silver grey, high octave of the grey ray, from the Moon.

The initiate's trials on the path of Temperance are mostly concerned with emotions and illusions. Where in the World of Assiah he eventually found the path after much diligent searching, in Yesod finding a path presented no difficulty to him as so many paths presented themselves to him, and unless he could discriminate he would follow illusory path after illusory path.

His emotional body in a complete turmoil as time after time he loses himself in a sea of emotions, in these circumstances he becoms desperate to climb out of this stage of consciousness to the higher levels and it is desperation that drives him to the point of realization that he must work for his salvation and not be carried along on the tide of emotions.

It is only when he reaches this stage of realization that he stops to consider how he can extricate himself from the present position; then his thoughts turn to the rays. First he uses the silver grey and from it gains balance and tranquillity, which allows him to control his emotional body.

Using the indigo ray he strengthens his devotion to the task in hand and once again he develops the single-minded approach to the path of probation. The green ray is still bringing him conflict between his mental and emotional body, but he is now in the position where he can achieve harmony within if not without.

From the amethyst ray he takes his spiritual inspiration and onward looking for the next stage on this long turbulent path. Method is a quality that he also draws from the amethyst ray, and using this quality with the devotion of the indigo and maintaining an inner tranquillity he goes forward in spite of the distractions and turmoil without and with the quality of fortitude from the indigo he follows the path with more confidence than he did in the World of Assiah.

On reaching Hod, the first Tree in the lower mental plane of consciousness, he finds a marked contrast to the emotional plane he has just left behind. The initiate now has to face the cold mental logic and hide-bound narrow reasoning of this sphere of orthodox activity.

The violet octave of the purple ray, with a streak of the yellow ray, provides the background for the green of the path and the amethyst from Sagittarius. From the green ray the initiate still has the conflict that has raged around him on each stage of his path of probation.

On the Tree in Hod the initiate follows his solitary path of the dark night of the soul in even greater isolation than before, more solitary because his lower mental body is so rigid on whatever path he chooses, and as with the emotional plane of Yesod there are a number of them, mostly purely intellectual without any pliability.

Spiritual aspirations are still part of the initiate's characteristics as the amethyst ray influence is still with him, but the crystallized mind keeps his aspirations within very limited bounds. Although the path of Temperance is a difficult path and in one sense, narrow is the way, it must still have wider concepts than those at present held by the initiate.

The initiate's first task is to widen his view and break through the rigidity and this in itself creates conflict within his mental body aggravated by the green ray, which finds the mental conditions suitable for that aspect of its influence. Only when the initiate takes hold of the ray and uses it, instead of the ray using him, does he obtain the harmony aspect of the green ray.

Once harmony has been achieved and for a time the lower mental body is still and receptive, the initiate can again use the amethyst ray with its visionary quality that for a moment gives a glimpse of the goal he has to strive for. With spiritual dedication obtained from the violet octave of the purple ray he presses forward on his path of probation.

Taking the creative activity from the yellow ray his lower mental body now commences to expand in consciousness and with the quality of originality also from the yellow ray he commences to follow a wider range of mental activity. The main lesson he had to learn on the path of Temperance in Hod was discipline, an essential quality on the path of probation.

What the initiate had to come to terms with and what caused him so much conflict was to understand discipline in its true sense, which meant the discipline of and by the individuality. The rigid discipline of the crystallized mind was discipline of the personality.

As the initiate proceeds on his solitary journey he will find the conflict between these two parts of his being becoming more pronounced until he reaches the stage where his personality is kept in control by the individuality.

The path of Temperance on the Tree in Netzach presents problems completely opposite to those in Hod. The first flush of freedom completely overrides the lesson of discipline that he acquired on the path in Hod.

Netzach has imagination for one of its qualities and although very different from the illusion of Yesod it can still lead the initiate on to many false trails. With imagination running riot the visionary quality supplied by the amethyst ray tends to become distorted and the initiate succeeds in obtaining only false visions.

Amber, the Atziluthic colour of Netzach and a high octave of the orange ray provides mental vigour, but unless channelled in the right direction this can push him further along the road of imagination. With the blue ray from the

Mundane Chakra of Netzach the initiate follows the mental pattern of 'love is the only way'.

Although love is an essential quality to progress, love alone can lead to weakness and become a bar to progress, which the initiate in the course of time finds out and the individuality attempts to re-impose the discipline gathered in Hod and conflict once more commences to take place within his lower mental body.

The initiate reaches the point where he realizes that love is essential, but must be controlled through wisdom and he draws this quality from the blue ray and attempts to balance love with wisdom, not easy on this solitary path of the dark night of the soul, where this comforting quality is missing, inasmuch as it applies to himself being a recipient of it.

Using once more the green ray, with its aspect of harmony, the initiate again finds balance and harmony through the struggle and conflict and so is able to balance the love and wisdom of the blue ray. From the blue ray wisdom the initiate can now also control the imagination, sufficient for him to use it in correct proportion with the visionary quality of the amethyst.

The blue ray also keeps him struggling for spiritual maturity and at the same time bestows upon him the quality of patience, a quality very much needed as he struggles along the path of Temperance and the dark night of the soul.

It is through patience and spiritual dedication that he carries on towards that higher vision he has glimpsed, the end of his path of probation on the Tree in Netzach is in sight and he eagerly reaches out to the Tree in Tiphareth where he hopes to find refuge from the mental conflict that has been with him for most of the time from his entry at Hod into the lower mental world.

Tiphareth as the bridge between the lower and higher mental planes of consciousness does not offer the peaceful haven that the initiate had visualized. The green ray still exercises its struggle and conflict influence through the two planes.

On the path of Temperance in Tiphareth the initiate is being pulled two ways. His individuality, through the amethyst ray, with the desire for the higher planes of consciousness, and his personality pulling towards the lower mental, which now he knows and can deal with.

It is on the path of probation or Temperance in Tiphareth that the initiate realizes why he has to tread the path of the dark night of the soul. It also becomes clear to him that sacrifice is required on every stage of his journey. It is not just a quality of Tiphareth.

Tiphareth is the sephirah of the ultimate sacrifice as applicable to the two lower worlds of the basic tree and applied to the complete trees in those worlds, but from the time of placing his foot on the path he commences the path of sacrifice, building up to the Tiphareth level.

Sacrifice is the keynote of the dark night of the soul. It is only through this quality that unity with the whole can be made and true at-one-ment be achieved. The purpose of the spark's journey, from the time it leaves the Ain to its return, is the attainment of conscious perfection and this means being at one with all life.

The path of temperance at Tiphareth is probably the most crucial point of the initiate's probationary path and once he arrives at this point he becomes fully aware of it. The clear pink rose of Tiphareth aids him at this point because he can absorb its influence, the main aspect of which is universal love.

One of the tasks at this stage is to bring personality and the individuality into balance and to do this the initiate must overcome the struggle and conflict aspects of the green ray. This means more sacrifice, but this time not sacrifice for others but for himself.

Through the amethyst ray with its higher qualities he subdues his personality, not an easy sacrifice to make, but an essential one to the initiate's further progression. Once this act has been accomplished the struggle with the lower mental body is over and the harmony aspect of the green ray is captured.

The initiate is now in the position where he can, without effort, use both the pink rose and amethyst rays with their love and spiritual qualities to the full and in so doing can sacrifice himself for the benefit of the whole. The amethyst ray provides him with the quality of humility which prevents the personality becoming predominant again.

Justice and wholeness, which are also part of the state of consciousness required at this level of being, the initiate draws from the orange ray. This is the final stage of the transformation that must take place before further progression can be made. When this last task has been completed the initiate who entered the path of Temperance emerges as an adept.

The green and amethyst rays still influencing the path on the tree in Geburah are now joined by the orange ray, Atziluthic colour of Geburah and the red ray from its Mundane Chakra.

Consolidation of all his previous experience must be made by the adept on the path in Geburah and to do this he must draw upon the orange ray with its qualities of practical knowledge, receptivity and self-control. A further characteristic of the orange ray, which the adept will find of great use, is that of being purposeful.

Through this act of consolidation the adept can view the errors within his own personality that have still to be eradicated. This is not an easy task because, although errors are exposed, it is not always obvious to the personality that they apply to him. It is very easy at this level of consciousness to have a feeling of perfection, that little touch of pride that is an aspect of the orange ray.

It is the searing fire of the red ray that burns into the heart of the personality and the receptivity of the orange that opens up the adept to the reality of errors within himself. Once this happens then the humility of the amethyst can once again play its part.

With discrimination obtained through the green ray the

adept discovers the errors and with the justice of the orange ray commences the process of eradication, driven on by the power of the red ray until the adept has purified himself to the point where the aspect of wholeness from the orange ray illuminates, his entire higher mental body.

The other major lesson of the path of Temperance in Geburah has now been learned, that of self-correction or self-discipline, realization that the sephirah of karma can be worked through by his own efforts. With this understanding and practical experience of it the adept's wholeness is now complete and a new Master emerges from this probationary path.

Once Gedulah is reached the goal is in sight, but the green ray of the path still brings its conflicts which apply even at the level of Mastership. There is still a pull from the personality which desires to reach an even higher goal, whilst the individuality or the true spark of Ain, the real 'I', pulls towards the use of his now developed powers to aid those on lower planes.

There is a great temptation for the personality to follow the call of the individuality and then to develop into the great 'I', the first step towards becoming a Master of the black path. It is this conflict that the Master has to resolve.

Once more the amethyst ray must be called upon for the quality of humility to overcome this desire to be the great 'I', the Master. This same quality can also be used to repress or overcome the personality desire to reach higher levels.

The deep violet, an octave of the purple ray, provides also humility, but it also has the quality of magnanimity which can be of subtle danger to the Master whilst the personality is still pulling. There is, however, an extra quantity of amethyst to draw upon which flows from the Mundane Chakra of Gedulah.

With the balance of personality and individuality once more attained, the Master completes his work on the path of Temperance and through the use of the green ray plays his part in the sphere of the Master to bring about harmony in the lower planes of consciousness.

Now the Master can truly say he has served his probation on the path of Temperance in Gedulah and is nearing the stage where he can cross the abyss. Once the path of Temperance is conquered the Master finds the remainder of the Tree in Gedulah, although still difficult, comparatively easy after the path of Temperance.

In Briah

Over the abyss the Master commences to work through the Tree in Binah. The path is now governed by the yellow ray with the amethyst still playing its part. The whole Tree is encompassed with the crimson of Binah and through it there is a shaft of the black ray from Saturn.

Here the Master's task is to completely discard the personality and retain just the individuality aspect of the whole being. The one way in which he can accomplish this is to first use the restrictive power of the black ray to restrict the personality's activities.

Once the activities are restricted then the Master can bring the yellow ray into action and give added activity to the individuality. With the increase of creative activity the dangerous crimson ray can be used with confidence and the complete disintegration of the personality is accomplished. The individuality is now at last free and is very quickly in the state of consciousness where Binah can be left behind and the final stage commenced on the Tree in Chokmah.

The yellow of the path of Temperance with the amethyst from Sagittarius now has for a background the pure soft blue of Chokmah. The spark's journey on the path of Temperance commences here. The individuality has to maintain its discipline and adjust itself to losing its individuality in the whole, at the same time preserving its individuality.

It is from the desire to remain an individual individuality that conflict now ensues, but through working with the yellow ray the spark can conquer this desire. The yellow ray is the ray of communications at all levels as well as being the creative ray. The two major aspects of the ray can now be combined and the definite activity can work creatively at making the link with Kether or the World of Atziluth on the basic Tree.

Yellow is also a ray of unity and blue is the wisdom ray. The Mayas and the Egyptians both claimed that the Great Serpent of the universe, who symbolizes eternal mental activity and wisdom, was blue in colour and had yellow scales. Both of the ancient races had a knowledge of the meaning and symbolism of colour.

The spark through the use of these two rays now makes the link or direct communication with Kether. From the amethyst ray it draws the desire for spiritual attainment and realizes the final step can only be made as merging with the whole takes place, the individual individuality must go.

It is from the yellow ray that the spark can absorb that last final quality it requires to return to Kether or Atziluth, that quality of spiritual unity. This is the culmination of the path of Temperance, the probationary period is completed.

In Atziluth

Blue is the ray of the path of Temperance in the World of Atziluth and the amethyst ray still shines along the path. The whole tree sparkles in the surrounding brilliance, the Atziluthic ray of Kether. Brilliance is also the archetype of all rays and from it all others shine forth.

With the blue of love and wisdom and the amethyst with its humility, desire for spiritual attainment and the perfection of these qualities through the influence of the brilliance, the spark recognizes the perfection in the archetypal path of Temperance.

THE DEVIL

In Assiah

In Assiah the path of the Devil is slate grey, one of the lowest octaves of the grey ray and from Capricorn, the astrological influence of the path, the black ray flows out.

All this appears to be very appropriate for the path of the Devil and just as it should be. The black ray instils suicidal and murderous tendencies and many other unpleasant qualities, referred to in the World of Assiah as evil. It is perhaps for this reason that in the physical world black is looked upon and used as a symbol for evil, suffering, and by those with a wrong attitude to death, the symbol of mourning.

From the lowest octave of the grey ray comes depression which is in perfect harmony with the suicidal tendencies of the black ray. Deception is another quality of the grey ray and again quite in keeping with the Devil as most people know him.

These rays of the path are set against a background of yellow, the ray of Assiah or Malkuth on the basic Tree, and from the Mundane Chakra stream out the red, blue, yellow and green rays.

The combination of rays give a preponderance of the yellow ray, which is symbolic of the spirit even at this low level. It is also the ray of creative activity, whether that activity be good or ill.

Other qualities belong to the black ray that are not – or need not be – evil in intent. It is the ray that enfolds and comforts those who understand the ray correctly. But at the level of Assiah these qualities are difficult to discover.

It is the opposite of this path that the individual has not only to discover but also to experience and overcome, accepting the positive qualities and rejecting the negative. The student must also bear in mind that the grey ray symbolizes the soul's struggle for freedom.

How can the student or initiate accomplish this task of overcoming the negative aspects of the path of the Devil? It would appear that all the odds were weighed against him.

From the yellow ray he must capture the spiritual aspect of activity and draw upon the blue ray of love and wisdom, slight though it is in comparision to the grey and the black ray of the path.

The red ray, although on the low level, is an irritant with adverse fiery qualities, quick-tempered and heated emotions; it also has the qualities of force and energy, but the main quality of use to the student is that of an adventurous nature, the desire to probe into the unknown and it is with this aspect of the red ray correctly channelled that the student can make his first break from the fetters of the Devil.

If this ray is combined with the yellow of creative activity and the spiritual part of the ray is also acted upon, the student will find it possible to raise his level of consciousness, slowly at first but with an ever increasing tempo until he reaches the stage where the world of Assiah can be left behind and he is now ready to enter upon the path in the World of Yetzirah.

In Yetzirah

Indigo is the colour of the path in the World of Yetzirah and this ray, with the black ray from Capricorn, remains constant through all the six trees in the Yetziratic World. The only change in the rays to give the different effects on the path are those of the background colours of each sephirah that the student or initiate has to go through.

The first sephirah is Yesod, the world of desires and emotions, and there the ray is indigo. The student or initiate has only two main rays to deal with – indigo and black.

At this level of consciousness the indigo ray possesses the qualities of blind devotion, fortitude and religious instincts, while the black ray influences create a chaotic mind.

It is through this chaotic mental state that the opportunity arises for the religious influence of the indigo to work. Although the indigo ray is predominant at Yesod, if the mental body remained impenetrably black it would have difficulty in breaking through.

Fortitude, another aspect of this ray, is very much needed by the student or initiate at this stage of his journey, to withstand the chaotic emotions that surge through.

Helping to penetrate the chaotic blackness and bring a ray of illumination is the silver of the moon, the highest octave of the grey ray, at this low level it can be tinged with green and this brings the quality of envy, a useful influence to have at this stage.

Envy can be and does in many cases act as a driving force, a spur to reach the same high levels of others, and although the motive may appear wrong it can be the means of urging the student or initiate along the path of progress, always bearing in mind that this ray and – automatically – its quality is very minute in comparison to the other rays.

With the other influence of the indigo ray, that of blind devotion, he moves forward into Hod where the chaotic mind is brought under control and a rigid organized mind takes its place.

Now the indigo and black rays have the violet/purple of Hod overshadowing them and cutting through them the yellow ray from Mercury.

Added to the blind devotion collected in Yesod and remaining in Hod is the quality of faith which in many ways is just as blind as the devotion. Even here the Devil can still control, although the student or initiate is breaking loose from his shackles.

It is through the violet purple, a medium octave of the purple ray, that the shackles can once more be put on. The overbearing quality and the pomp and splendour of this ray are indeed tools of the Devil.

The yellow ray is the student's or initiate's safety-belt, and its illumination reveals the first true aspect of Lucifer, the light bringer, and apart from the spirit aspect of the ray itself, it highlights for the student or initiate the other qualities of this octave of the purple ray – spiritual dedication and reverence.

It is also the yellow ray with its aspect of creative activity that enables escape to be made from the rigid confines and conformity of Hod to the more open sphere of Netzach.

Amber, an octave of the orange ray, is the all-pervading colour of Netzach and from Venus flows the blue ray, which holds the love wisdom qualities. From the amber issues forth trust and reliance, qualities very much needed by student or initiate as he negotiates the path of the Devil in Netzach.

Netzach is the sphere of occult intelligence. The religious influence of Hod is now being left behind. The wisdom aspect of the blue ray is commencing to seep through, the devotion of the indigo is now devotion to the truth, the unravelling of the unknown.

The first glimpse of the Lucifer-wisdom has aroused the desire to know more and the student or initiate steps out on to an unknown path of spiritual progression and this is where he draws upon the trust and reliance of the amber ray, to have self-reliance and to trust his own judgement and to choose the correct out of the many unknown paths. It is so easy at this stage of the journey to slip back to the Devil aspect of the path.

The black ray is still there sending out its influences, for even here it is still the lower octaves that are operating and it only requires the slightest flaw in discrimination to overcome for a time the blue ray of Lucifer-wisdom.

Treading the path of the Devil in Netzach is indeed walking on a razor edge, but once the conquest is made the Tree in Tiphareth and the path of the Devil in that Tree offers further progress in the adventurous journey.

Tiphareth gives out a clear pink rose, a high octave of the red ray and from its Mundane Chakra streams out the orange ray.

It is on the path of the Devil in Tiphareth that the Devil aspect of the path can be completely conquered and the first step in this direction is to absorb and use the influences of the clear pink rose, those qualities of love and forgiveness. This is aided by the higher octave of the orange which gives geniality and receptivity for those who will take it.

Tiphareth is the sephirah of meditating intelligence and part of the task in this sephirah is to meditate, sending down love and forgiveness to the lower levels of consciousness. Here is an aspect of the sacrificial Tiphareth and to conquer the path of the Devil in this sephirah the initiate must forget self-evolvement and progress by mediating and sacrifice for all forms of life on lower planes of consciousness. Once this is achieved the initiate can move forward to the Tree in Geburah.

Orange is the background colour to the path of the Devil in Geburah and the red ray sends out its influence from the sephirah's Mundane Chakra.

The orange ray at this octave gives the qualities of self-control and orderliness, and on the path in this sphere these qualities are invaluable. Now is the point where the initiate clears up his outstanding karma and with perfect control brings spiritual orderliness to his being or – to be more correct – his higher mental body.

The red ray provides the energy, drive and courage to face the task of clearing up karma and the indigo of the path itself provides the devotion to the work of preparing for the step forward into Gedulah.

Only the Lucifer aspect of the path is left once the Geburah action has been completed. The black ray, now at this higher octave, takes on the qualities of protector as it enfolds the initiate in its comforting embrace.

Now enfolded and protected, the initiate commences the task of conquering the Tree in Gedulah. The path of the

Devil in Gedulah is overshadowed by deep violet, an aspect of the purple ray.

Humility and reverence are the two main qualities of the deep violet and it is as the spiritual wisdom flows in from the amethyst ray of Jupiter that the true light of Lucifer is understood. Now at Masterhood, the initiate develops and has the true humility and reverence associated with a Master.

The indigo now gives the devotion to serve humanity and the true wisdom given by Lucifer and on completion of the allotted task the Master is ready to cross the abyss on the path of no return.

There is no fear as the journey is prepared for; the all-encompassing and comforting black ray holds and shields from all fear with its protecting influence.

In Briah

On crossing the abyss the Master now faces the dissolution of his higher mental body and part of this process is carried out on the path of the Devil.

The path now is completely ruled by the black ray and this ray is predominant as it also issues forth from Capricorn, astrological influence on the path, and also from Saturn, Mundane Chakra of Binah, the sephirah in which the Master is now working.

The only other ray to penetrate this all-enfolding black is the crimson of the sephirah Binah, and just as the black gave the restriction of form on the outward journey, so the crimson is prepared to sear that form away, providing the Master is prepared to use it. To completely free himself from form he *must* use it as at this point on the Tree the black is the predominant ray.

Here again is the choice that is nearly always present on this path, to stay with the Devil on the lower part or to go with Lucifer on the higher.

The struggle that takes place in the higher mental body on the use of the crimson ray depends on the Master's strength to resist Hod, sphere of form at the lower end of the path, and hear the call for further sacrifice from Tiphareth at the upper end of the path.

Sooner or later the decision is taken and the power of the crimson ray is used. The last vestige of form is sacrificed and the spark is free to move into – and conquer – the Tree in Chokmah.

Now to a background of pure pale blue all the other rays send out their scintillating vibrations. The black ray still controls the path of the Devil and by the use of it the spark, now near to conscious perfection, keeps steady amidst the whirling mass of force that is Chokmah.

Ever seeking the true light of spiritual perfection as revealed by Lucifer, the spark attains the height of the path and with the perfect blending of all the rays it becomes the pure conscious perfection of brilliance that – from seeing face to face – ultimately leads to Atziluth.

In Atziluth

In Atziluth the path responds to the highest octave of the indigo ray and the black ray which scintillates with the true life of the brilliance that pervades the whole of Atziluth.

This path is the perfect archetype of caution, clarity of thought and devotion to purity, qualities of the highest octave of the indigo ray and the esoteric and secretive qualities of the black ray at its highest octave.

THE LIGHTNING STRUCK TOWER

In Assiah

This path joins together the sephiroth of Netzach and Hod and forms the last barrier on the downward arc and the first barrier on the return journey. On examination of the Tree of Life it will be noticed that the path of The Lightning Struck Tower crosses through the path of Temperance, which has already been mentioned as the path of Probation.

By virtue of the positions of these two paths a cross is formed and it can be truly said that the Lightning Struck Tower is a cross to the student, not only in the World of Assiah, but on every Tree in every World.

This path gives definite urges and proddings to the student that it is time to make a change or that changes are rather overdue, if he has ignored all the previous proddings of his higher self to change and re-orientate.

The student may find that if he remains stubborn to the hints given him, then the change may be made for him and it could be done rather drastically.

When it is said 'done for him', this only appears to be so to the lower self in his dense physical body and the changes brought about may be very upsetting and uncomfortable. Yet it is really the student himself who has initiated the changes and chosen the resulting discomfort, although his lower personality self may not realize this.

The colour of the path in Assiah is red with azure blue or emerald green. Red is the ray of ambition and so the student on this factor alone has one of two choices. The azure flecks would give him the ambition for spiritual aspiration, but if the emerald green flecks were used it could be ambition devoted to spiritual ends or it could be ambition for material success, as green is the ray of the planet earth.

If the student chooses emerald green with the red ray he is asking for trouble, even if the choice was for the ambition devoted to spiritual ends. Green as the ray of harmony through conflict would most certainly cause him conflict. The material would be forever tugging at the spiritual.

This is a rather drastic path to cross and with Temperance, the first path on the 'dark night of the soul' intersecting, it appears to be a path of trials where the old familiar things are swept away and the student feels completely forsaken.

These two paths do fit in with each other, and it is quite probable that the two are being trodden together, as everyone is treading more than one path or state of consciousness at any given time.

With Mars as the astrological influence of the path it is quite understandable why the path is called 'The exciting or active intelligence'. From Mars issues the red ray supplementing the red of the path itself. Creating more activity is the yellow ray of Assiah.

From these rays it is clear to see why the path of the Lightning Struck Tower is, particularly in Assiah, a path of disruption, destruction and re-building.

The student's one opportunity of passing through this first barrier lies in the use of the azure blue, which is a high octave of the blue ray. Once he uses this ray and gains the ambition for the true spiritual aspiration, then he can put to use the yellow ray of creative activity, which is also the ray of the spirit.

When the yellow ray influence has been directed into the right channels, more use can be made of the red, but now to be employed as a driving force and from it to obtain the will and the power to follow the spiritual path the student has chosen.

Until such time as the student does choose the right path

and adopts the rays to the use outlined above, all the schemes he builds up, either from philosophies or material ambitions will, as he reaches this barrier, come crashing down and be brought to naught.

In all probability the student will come crashing down many times, this is the main activity of the red ray, but it is this same ray that gives him the courage to try again, and the activity of the yellow ray which enables him to build up yet another material or spiritual edifice.

In Yetzirah

Arriving in the Yetziratic World on the Tree in Yesod the initiate meets the path of The Lightning Struck Tower, which now responds to a venetian red. Here there is, as in Assiah, a combination of two rays, the red and the brown.

Mars still gives forth the red ray and will carry out this function through all the four worlds. Yesod supplies a background of indigo to the Tree, which has its influence on the path and from the Moon silver, the high octave of the grey ray, it sets its mark also on the path of The Lightning Struck Tower.

One of the qualities of the indigo ray is fortitude and on this particular path in Yesod it demonstrates the accuracy with which these cosmic rays were allocated to their tasks in the archetypal World of Atziluth. It is the quality of fortitude that is needed so much by the initiate to aid him in withstanding the emotional shatterings caused by The Tower.

The action of The Tower is just as drastic in the emotional astral world as in Assiah, perhaps more so as there is no physical body to absorb the shock. The degree of severity in the action of The Tower depends to a great degree upon how much the initiate has allowed his hidden subconscious motives to dominate his life during his stay in Assiah and just before his departure from that plane of consciousness.

If the initiate has allowed his emotions to run away with him whilst in incarnation and not taken full command of them, then he is in for a great upheaval when he receives the destructive force of The Lightning Struck Tower.

It is again that the indigo ray can come to his aid with its quality of devotion. In spite of all adversity this aspect of the ray can lead him to pursue his object with a single-minded devotion, whether that objective is to leave the astral/emotional world and incarnate again in Assiah, or to leave this world of desires and travel with faith and idealism to the higher spheres of The Tree.

The brown ray aspect of the path holds the quality and the tendency to superstition. This can also be a characteristic of the indigo on the lower levels. On the higher levels of these rays, if the initiate calls upon them, superstitions can develop into aspirations, so that while the shock of the lightning flash can sear and burn the dross of the desire body, the red ray will drive him on and with the devotion of the indigo he can reach up to the sphere of Hod.

On the path of The Lightning Struck Tower in Hod all the same rays are at his disposal, except for the indigo which has given way to the violet/purple, Atziluthic colour of Hod. This particular octave of the purple ray carries the quality of spiritual dedication.

To the initiate who receives the new influence on his entry into Hod, spiritual dedication is just what he had been aspiring to in Yesod and the lower mental body rejoices at the achievement. This can be the initiate's undoing if he is not very careful.

The knowledge of his success in attaining to this level can so easily develop into a 'holier than thou' attitude and the quality of magnanimity becomes very strong. This is also part of the violet ray influence. If this does take place the initiate is well and truly caught in the groove of Hod.

As Hod is the sphere of form there is a certain amount of rigidity attached to it that holds all in the particular groove they fall into and once there it is difficult to become disentangled, mainly because the lower mental body feels that it is so right.

The brown ray aspect of the path brings knowledge

without wisdom on one octave and this places the initiate into an even deeper groove. The red ray, however, continues to stimulate and in due course of time creates a very disturbing feeling within the lower mental body. The power of the red ray is such that eventually the initiate finds the groove too narrow for him.

It is at this point, where he finds the groove too restricting, that the initiate commences the search for some way in which to break that restriction. Taking another look at the brown ray he discovers wisdom on the higher octave of the ray.

Armed with two tools, brown ray of wisdom and the red ray of will and its stimulating influence, the consciousness begins to widen and the restrictive practices of Hod commence to give way under the pressure.

The initiate now uses the yellow ray to create within his lower mental body a greater activity, and through this he sees the true glory of Hod which, through its Atziluthic colour, is humility and reverence. Now the initiate counteracts the magnanimity but, seeing in his humility that there is more beyond his present store of knowledge he retains the octave of the purple ray that gives him spiritual dedication and uses this to reach out for that greater glory.

If the initiate does not reach for that greater glory, but remains with his fixed ideas, the red ray of The Tower will not give a stimulating urge, but will completely shatter his rigidity and it would be such a shock to the lower mental body that the initiate would in all probability fall back into the sphere of Yesod.

Once, however, he does see the greater vision, it is only a short period of time before he moves into Netzach. In Netzach the atziluthic colour of the sephirah, amber, takes over from the violet/purple. Amber is a high octave of the orange ray, producing mental vigour and justice.

With the mental vigour of the amber and the energetic principle of Netzach itself, the initiate proceeds to rush forward, encouraged by enthusiasm stimulated by the red ray. Unfortunately the enthusiasm is not controlled and too much mental vigour and energy is applied without thought.

It is only when The Lightning Struck Tower halts the headlong plunge and brings the initiate crashing down that – by use of the brown ray aspect of the path – he subdues the stimulation of the red ray and brings his enthusiasm under control. From the brown ray he gains confidence. It also endows him with quietness in activity.

The initiate now proceeds with greater care, but still exercising the energetic principle with controlled vigour and – through the blue ray of Venus – an ever-widening consciousness of wisdom. It is by the use of all these rays that he can successfully conquer the path of the Lightning Struck Tower in Netzach.

When the initiate has negotiated the remainder of the Tree in Netzach he reaches Tiphareth and faces the struggle with The Lightning Struck Tower on the Tree in this sephirah.

The venetian red of the path and the red ray from Mars are now joined by the clear pink rose of Tiphareth and the orange of the Sun. The initiate has now entered the power house of the universe and from it he has many lessons to learn.

With orange ray increasing the mental activity, and the stimulation of the red ray, the initiate in most circumstances tries to follow the path of The Lightning Struck Tower on an intellectual basis with a predominance of his higher mental body.

This attitude of intellectualism proves his undoing. Pride creeps into the mental body from the orange as he reaches to levels beyond his present state of evolution in attempting to build the foundation of his Tower on a higher mental plane of consciousness before he has completed the control of his lower mental.

The path of the Lightning Struck Tower in Tiphareth – being completely on the lower plane of consciousness – his foundation, attempted at the higher plane, is very vulnerable and in course of time the Lightning Flash brings it toppling around his ears.

Rising up from the ruins of his Tower he commences once more to negotiate this path in Tiphareth. On his next attempt he has recourse to the brown ray aspect of the path, from which he can obtain the quality of absorption and become studious. In these circumstances he can now review what happened and see where he went wrong.

From the clear rose pink he takes and understands the quality of sacrifice. With understanding bestowed upon him by the brown ray he accepts the fact that he must first conquer and control his lower mental body, proceeding to the stage where he can attain perfect balance between higher and lower mental bodies.

When all this has been completed then – and only then – can he sacrifice his lower mental body altogether. Although in the first instance he had tried to operate through the higher mental, the pull of the lower is still very strong and he does not accept the idea until he draws from the pink rose the quality of magnetic healing. As this permeates through to the real 'I' the personality of the initiate accepts what he must do.

Turning again to the brown ray, he draws from it single mindedness and sets out upon his task. Now he can use the orange ray under his control, instead of being controlled by it. With the new attitude of mind he can now build his Tower on the correct foundation and successfully penetrate the barrier and so move forward into eventually the higher mental realms from which he can step onto the Tree in Geburah.

Geburah brings to the path of The Lightning Struck Tower the orange ray and Mars provides even more of the red ray. At this point on his journey the adept is surrounded with more of the red ray than at any other time on his journey.

Mars, as the Mundane Chakra of Geburah and also the astrological influence of the path, brings its full force to bear on the initiate, not only with the red ray, but also with all the Martian influences. In other words, it is the worst side of the red ray from the adept's point of view at that point in time, but the correct aspect for that particular phase of the adept's journey.

It is on the path of The Lightning Struck Tower in Geburah that many of his fixed ideas are destroyed. No longer does he dwell in an Ivory Tower. The destructive force of the red ray has shattered it. From the brown ray he draws a quiet assurance and confidence, and through the orange ray he sees the justice of what is happening.

From the searing experience he acquires the quality of wholeness, one of the orange ray's characteristics. This is the purpose of Geburah in its position in the sphere of karma, wholeness can only become a factual attribute after justice has been done and the purifying fires of the red ray have cleansed the whole of the higher mental body.

Truly the adept on the path of The Lightning Struck Tower in Geburah learns of fear and punishment, but this is not the purpose of the path or the sephirah. The lesson here is to destroy fear and to raise the level of consciousness to the point where punishment can be understood as a self-inflicted correction of deviations against universal law and that The Tower in Geburah is purely the instrument whereby the deviations are straightened.

To achieve this understanding, the adept again draws on the brown ray for knowledge and quiet assurance, and on the orange ray for self-control. He can then apply the red ray if he so desires to purify himself and work out his karma in full knowledge of where he is going.

When he can achieve this the adept can safely tread the path of The Lightning Struck Tower and – passing his first barrier – go forward to complete his journey through the Tree in Geburah from which he will emerge a Master at the end of his trials, and take his place on the Tree in Gedulah.

With Gedulah he has a complete change in the vibrations of consciousness, although still in the higher mental plane of consciousness. The quantity of the red ray has decreased, all that is left of this powerful ray is the aspect of the path that responds to it and from the Mars influence on the path. Gedulah provides the violet ray and from Jupiter flows the amethyst.

In Gedulah the Master faces a similar situation to the one he faced in Tiphareth. This time it is to prepare himself for the discarding of the higher mental body and it is on the path of The Lightning Struck Tower that he must commence this shattering or dissolution.

Now that he has passed through the sephirah of karma he is eager to aid with the lifting of universal karma and through the influence of the amethyst ray not only follow a spiritual and mystical path himself, but to use his influence and mystical powers to persuade others to do the same.

From the violet ray he receives the quality of spiritual dedication and if not careful this very dedication can lead to error, inasmuch as he may attempt too strongly to persuade people to follow his path, even against their will. He may to this end also use the mystical powers he has obtained.

It is only by use of the brown ray aspect of the path that he can prevent this and until he uses the brown ray he will find the barrier of The Lightning Struck Tower impassable. From the brown ray he can obtain wisdom, also concentration that will aid his powers of discrimination.

The Master now discovers that his task is to guide or lead with humility, another quality of the violet ray; to drive others is the wrong policy to adopt. The Master realizes that mystical powers are not to be used in exercising pressure but to aid all in trouble where aid is genuinely needed and trust that those who receive aid will put their foot on the path as a result of his example.

Now the path of the Lightning Struck Tower unfolds before him, the first step in controlling his higher mental body prior to dissolution. With quiet assurance and confidence, both qualities of the brown ray, he goes forward to penetrate this first barrier and so open up the way to ascent to the top of the Tree in Gedulah.

In Briah

Once across the abyss to the Tree in Binah, the Master finds himself in a different world. All the rays, except the red from Mars, have now changed. Binah embraces the whole Tree with crimson and the black ray of Saturn shoots through, influencing every part of the Tree and the path is now pure red.

It may be that at this level of consciousness, which is the Buddhic plane of consciousness, it will be the destroyer aspect of the red ray that will be the most dominant. With the sphere of consciousness being entirely red except for the black ray of Saturn, the path of The Lightning Struck Tower in Binah is going to be a difficult one for the Master to overcome.

The crimson octave gives forth the qualities of impulsiveness, a love of life and joy of life, qualities which at this level can be difficult to employ in the right direction. Unless the Master translates the love and joy of life to that life which is eternal he will find himself held back by the barrier of the lightning flash and the towers he builds will be constantly destroyed.

The impulsive influence can very easily lead him to jump to the lower interpretation of life in which he should now have ceased to take interest. Once he has crossed the abyss his duties to other life cease at an individual personality level and the duties are carried out in union with other individuals.

At this point in the Master's journey his concern is to fit himself for the full eternal life of love and joy through the destruction of his personality. All the force of the red ray is there for the Master's use to accomplish his task. To employ it in this direction he will have to use the black ray to its fullest extent, with its restrictive influence, in order to direct the full flowing force of the red ray power and also to restrict the impulsive influence in himself from the red ray.

It is, at this low level of the Tree, the lower aspects of his personality that have to be removed and with the successful conclusion of this task he can pass the barrier of The

Lightning Struck Tower to continue his ascent of the Tree in Binah and so move into the last stage of the Briatic World, the Tree in Chokmah.

Although the path is still dominated by the red ray the over-all background is now the pure soft blue of chokmah. Under the Martian influence of the red ray the individuality of the spark is inclined to go its own way. Full of its new-found freedom from all ties of form it goes round in a whirl of force, exercising that freedom until brought up with a jerk by the path of The Lightning Struck Tower.

The shattering effect brings the spark of Ain to a sudden halt, sufficiently for it to feel the influence of the pure soft blue, a high octave of the blue love and wisdom ray. From this ray the spark obtains both a spiritual sedative and wisdom.

In the quiet calm of that spiritual sedative the wisdom of joining its individuality to other individual sparks and operating in an at-one-ment for the benefit of the whole whilst retaining its individuality, is realized. The path now presents no difficulty to the spark and the barrier is passed. The spark of Ain now moves forward up the Tree in Chokmah towards ultimate eternal freedom.

In Atziluth

The path of The Lightning Struck Tower on the Tree in Kether is Scarlet and it is combined with the red from Mars. This demonstrates the latent qualities in the archetype of the path. There is an active destructive force there which recognizes that old traditions and customs have to make way for more advanced forms at stages of progress and planes of consciousness.

The active, energetic stimulation of the scarlet prepares the way for the changes that must come about in the world of form, whether that form be of solid or tenuous matter. It is a constructive destructiveness, a breaking down in order to rebuild.

With the brilliance highlighting the scarlet and red it

expresses in its searching penetrating ray that personality could not exist at this level of consciousness. This path in Kether or Atziluth is also the archetypal symbol that freedom is only obtained through discipline.

THE EMPEROR

In Assiah

The path of the Emperor runs between Netzach and Yesod and so has the influence of the energetic principle from Netzach and the generative principle from Yesod. These two principles are very important to the path and to the student treading it.

Aquarius is the astrological influence of this path, with its white ray which will permeate the path on every Tree in every world. It is an appropriate ray in many ways for the path of the Emperor, as it is the ray of the positive pillar.

Although on this path balance has to be attained, as on all paths, it has to be a positive balance, in other words, balance will only be obtained and maintained by a positive outlook and positive action.

The Emperor is the path of rulership in every sense of the word, rulership over other individuals and rulership over the individuals' own bodies. This is the path of a King, material or spiritual kingship. It is also the path of the dictator and the initiate on the spiritual path.

A royal path indeed and one that requires discipline in every sphere and in every sense of the word if true rulership is to be attained. Only by self-discipline can discipline be applied to others. Self-discipline does not of course mean disciplining the self to do what the self wants to do, but the form of discipline that not only helps the self, but makes the self carry out tasks at every level of being that it is disinclined to do.

With the influence of Netzach flowing along this path the

student in the World of Assiah is inclined to be self-willed and will not listen to the true 'I' within or to the entreaties of others. There is inclined to be a harshness there in order to subdue both inner and outer criticisms. This latter characteristic stems from the red ray of the fire element, which is part of the Mundane Chakra of Assiah.

From the earth element of the chakra flows the green ray which adds to the struggles and conflict that go on around the student ruler. The harsher he rules the more rebellious becomes the opposition, and the stronger the opposition the more the student draws on the will and power of the red ray.

A vicious circle develops and the student finds himself sinking deeper into the mire of the negative side of the path of The Emperor. There is a double influence of the yellow ray coming through, partly from the Mundane Chakra of Assiah where the air element sends out the yellow, but the main force of this ray comes from the Atziluthic colour of Assiah or Malkuth which surrounds the whole Tree in this sphere.

The yellow ray has many qualities, but in his present state the student finds the two qualities that come to him easily are those of impatience and irresponsibility, qualities that are part of the air influence as well as the ray influence.

Through impatience he is inclined to listen even less to the wise counsel and remonstrations of those he rules. In a similar manner he heeds not the warning from within that stems from the conflict, which rages between the different bodies.

It is from the white ray of the path that the student finds help, first he absorbs the influence of the ray and develops spiritual philosophy from it. His attention can be turned again to the yellow ray to use – this time for its more positive and helpful qualities – the main one being spiritual unity.

To achieve unity there should be harmony and the student must now call upon the higher aspect of this ray, first to gain his own harmony and then harmony between himself and those he rules. Now is the time to call upon the blue ray which is available to him through the water element of the Mundane Chakra.

Once the blue ray is harnessed, the love and wisdom qualities can be absorbed and in turn given out. The student's physical, emotional and mental vehicles, which have been his rebellious subjects, now find harmony under his rulership and – as the new-found unity increases, the student on the path of the physical and spiritual Emperor moves on towards the goal of integrated unity and the balance of positive rulership. He is in command of his vehicles.

The colour of the path in Assiah is white tinged with purple and this is truly expressive of the path of The Emperor. The purple ray is the royal ray and one of rulership. The white ray – as already mentioned – is strengthened by the white flowing from the astrological influence.

The student has to watch carefully the lower influences of the purple ray, which can bring out characteristics of pomposity and domination. Pride, another quality of the purple ray, is the most dangerous one, particularly when the student reaches that state of integrated unity. He can become so proud of his achievements that within a very short time he could lose all he had made.

Immediately the influence of pride makes itself apparent the student must call on the full influence of the wisdom aspect of the blue ray and through its positive aspect tune in to the higher qualities of the purple ray, lifting himself to that higher level of consciousness where he can obtain from this same ray poise and understanding.

Victory over the path of The Emperor in the World of Assiah is now within his grasp and after exercising wise rulership over a period of time and proving himself, the student is ready to move forward to meet his next challenge.

In Yetzirah

On the Tree in Yesod, first sephirah in the Yetziratic World on the return journey, the path of The Emperor is covered with the blue ray, and this will be the ray of the path throughout the whole of Yetzirah, but the white ray from Aquarius is still there and will be through all the worlds.

Indigo, the Atziluthic colour of Yesod, permeates the whole Tree and beaming through is the silver octave of the grey ray. This emanates from the Moon, Mundane Chakra to Yesod. All these rays are at the disposal of the initiate as he treads the path of The Emperor in Yesod.

In the World of Assiah part of the student's task on this path was the rulership of all his bodies, but this was at the physical plane of consciousness, where the physical body – to a degree – served as an anchor to the emotional body. Now the initiate has to control his astral or emotional body without the physical anchor.

Balance in an entirely emotional fluidic world is not easy to obtain. As this is also the desire world the slightest thought from either the higher or lower mental body is sufficient to set in motion a changing pattern within the Yesodic plane of consciousness.

From the plane of consciousness itself there are ever fluctuating emotional vibrations bombarding the initiate from the moment he moves into this world and that bombardment will not cease until the initiate leaves Yesod for either Hod or a return to Malkuth.

The indigo ray with its attribute of devotion which, even if the devotion is in the right direction, can play on the emotions, is no help to the initiate. He is faced with the task not only of rulership over his emotional body, but also of disciplined devotion.

Devotion is an automatic quality at this plane of consciousness but it can be in any direction. The first task, if he is to conquer this path, is to find the right goal on which to level his emotions. By turning to the silver octave of the grey ray he will find spiritual harmony and from the blue ray of the path the initiate can obtain spirituality.

Having discovered these qualities the initiate must now

develop them to the maximum and it is upon this that he can turn the indigo devotion. This in itself does not give control of the emotional body and this is the next stage on the Emperor's path now the devotions have been correctly orientated.

From the white ray comes the desire to struggle for perfection, and Yesod being the desire world, this triggers off the emotions towards that end. With the goal fixed and working for it, the initiate now uses the silver ray again, but this time it is the tranquillity of the ray that he calls upon and through this he obtains balance, another aspect of the silver ray, and the emotional body is stilled.

With the path of The Emperor completed, the initiate is ready to move on through Yesod to the next stage of his journey, the Tree in Hod, where the indigo of Yesod has given way to a violet, an octave of the purple ray. Once more the initiate finds himself surrounded by the royal ray. There is also the yellow ray from Mercury, Mundane Chakra to Hod.

The initiate finds, with his transference to the lower mental world, that he has moved from one extreme to the other and on the path of The Emperor in this sphere he is following a rigid mental groove with such firmness that for a time his consciousness is restricted and the lower mental body is the ruler with the real 'I' its slave.

Although in this unenviable position, the initiate does not realize it for some considerable period of cosmic time. It is only when he realizes that he is not making any headway on the path that the first thought of something being wrong enters his mental body.

By use of the yellow ray he brings in a greater creative mental activity through which he has the realization that control or rulership of his own kingdom, his different bodies, works two ways. Just as on the path in Yesod he had to learn a stricter form of governing, now he must accept the fact that too strict a control is equally wrong.

Calling in the violet ray he takes from it the qualities of

humility and dedication. With the combination of these attributes he commences a new and more balanced form of rulership. The humility releases the rigidity and the dedication to his task. From the blue ray of the path he develops further the love aspect of this ray, which also helps to loosen the rigid grip of his lower mental body.

At this stage of his progress along the path of The Emperor he sees the true glory of Hod, the ability to be dedicated to a spiritual path with full humility, but a firm quiet strength that helps him to overcome the restriction of his lower mental body and attain the at-one-ment of this level of consciousness.

It is in the full glory that he moves on now prepared for further conquests and in due course of time reaches Netzach and the path of The Emperor on the Tree in that sephirah.

Netzach with its amber ray covering all and the blue ray from Venus adding to the blue from the path, fills the initiate with joy and love for the whole of life, both in the planes of consciousness above him and those below. From the amber – an octave of the orange ray – comes mental vigour which has the initiate's mental body jumping from one thing to another, in a completely haphazard way.

Netzach is the sephirah of the energetic principle. It is also the sephirah of Victory and in this instance signifies victory over the lower mental body, providing the initiate with the experience of controlling and channelling energy so that the lower mental body can be a vital state of consciousness, but ruled by the 'I'.

Amber provides the qualities of justice and wholeness so that the initiate, through its use, can rule his lower mental body justly and with wisdom from the blue ray apply the mental faculties to the many aspects of the Netzach philosophies, which includes aid to those on and below his own level of consciousness.

The white ray endows him with expansiveness which – combined with the Netzach freedom of thought – allows him to give full play to his philosophies until the right path is discovered. It will be the right path in the fullness of time, though only when it is known to him through the 'desire for perfection' influence of the white ray will he move forward.

Once this stage is reached the initiate is in full command and victory on the path of The Emperor in Netzach is in sight. With the completion of this phase of experience the goal of Tiphareth is in sight.

When the tree in Tiphareth is reached and the initiate is on the path of The Emperor, he finds a completely different set of circumstances awaiting him. The task that now lies before him is the balancing of the lower and higher mental bodies and then the complete subjugation of the lower mental.

Clear pink rose is the all-pervading colour of the Tree in Tiphareth and from this high octave of the red ray the initiate can draw the attribute of tact and also healing of a magnetic nature. With these two qualities he is able to reconcile many differences and through the white ray develop a faith with reason.

It is through this faith that he can commence the task of the complete subjugation of the lower mental body and also see the reason for its subjugation at this stage of his journey through time and space.

From the orange ray of Tiphareth's Mundane Chakra he receives the power of receptivity if he opens himself to it. Self-control can also be obtained from this same ray. Now the initiate is in the position to move upward to the higher mental plane and with perfect self-control he overcomes the pull of the lower mental and makes the sacrifice of all lower mental activities to reach the state of adeptship and also the higher mental plane of consciousness, where he will dwell for a considerable period of cosmic time until he has conquered the next two Trees, namely Geburah and Gedulah.

On the path of The Emperor in Geburah the adept has the full benefit of the orange ray, the Atziluthic colour of this sephirah. He can also use the red ray of will and power from Mars, Mundane Chakra to Geburah.

Now is the time when, on the path of The Emperor, he

must learn to rule his karma, in other words control the actions of his higher mental body to such a degree that he can pay off his negative karma and receive the benefit of positive karma in such a way that no further negative karma accrues.

No easy task, even at this higher level of consciousness, but the adept sets out on this thorny path. First he draws from the red ray the will and power to help him both face the task and go through with it. Again the orange is there to aid him with the quality of justice and the receptivity from the same ray to see the reason for that justice.

Holding firm to his faith through reason, obtained from the white ray, he progresses along the path of The Emperor and emerges triumphant – karmaless – having attained to Mastership and prepared to go forward to the sphere of the Masters and tread the path of The Emperor on the Tree in Gedulah.

With the lesson of Geburah behind him the Master has now to learn how to control mercy and use this quality of Gebulah in perfect balance with justice. The Tree in Gedulah is bathed in deep violet, an octave of the purple ray and from Jupiter issues the amethyst.

Once more the royal ray of purple influences the path of The Emperor and from this particular octave he can and does obtain the qualities of spiritual dedication and magnanimity. These two qualities can be very useful, but also have their attendant dangers.

Even at this high level it is still possible to fall through lack of proper rulership or control of these deep violet ray qualities. Spiritual dedication can reach a point where the Master could become oblivious of all else around him and so fail in the duties that are expected of a Master of the wisdom. Magnanimity used the correct way can help him carry out the work appropriate to his level of consciousness, alternatively – without proper control – it can deteriorate to a form of condescension.

From the amethyst ray he must absorb humility. This will

then aid him in gaining a balance of spiritual magnanimity, also from this ray he can develop the quality of true spiritual attainment and with this his spiritual dedication will be to all life in the widest sense of consciousness.

Love and wisdom from the blue ray of the path itself completes his armoury and he is now fitted to complete his task on the path of The Emperor in Gedulah and make his way through the rest of the Tree in that sphere until he reaches the point where he is ready to cross the abyss into the World of Briah.

In Briah

The World of Briah contains two of the three supernals and on the way back up the planes of consciousness the Tree in Binah is the first challenge for the Master. All the rays he has worked with in Yetzirah are now changed except for the white ray which shines forth from Aquarius, still influencing him to carry on the struggle for perfection.

The Tree in Binah is clothed in crimson, a high octave of the red ray; from Saturn the black ray penetrates to all paths on the Tree. The path itself has changed to a sky blue, which is a high octave of the blue ray.

Once again the Master's task has changed. Now he has to learn how to rule or control restriction in such a way that the restriction and discipline both creates and gives freedom. The restriction he faces comes from the black ray and the first reaction, after the expansion period in Gedulah, is to break through this barrier.

The crimson octave of the red ray carries not only the fire of the red, but also the attribute of impulsiveness. From this it is quite easy to understand the first reaction. The Master soon comes to the conclusion that this restriction or 'ring-pass-not' will not be conquered by force.

Through the sky blue he obtains not just love, but selfless love, a far more powerful and penetrating quality. Also from the blue he adds to an already vast store of wisdom. He also resumes the use of the white ray with its expansive quality.

Now the Master is prepared and ready to merge himself fully into the black ray, an act only possible through selfless love and that love expands within the black ray until the whole personality is merged and absorbed. Through the 'ring-pass-not' emerges the pure spark of Ain force with a true freedom in its individuality.

Two lessons had been learned, that the true selfless love can overcome all barriers and the truth of the paradox that freedom comes from restriction, and with this new-found freedom the spark moves to the Tree in Chokmah and the path of The Emperor in this sephirah.

Only the overall colour has changed. The crimson ray of Binah makes way for the pure soft blue of Chokmah. There is, however, the added advantage that all the rays are available as they stream through the sphere of the zodiac, spreading out through the whole of the Tree.

The spark is now conscious near perfection and on the path of The Emperor in Chokmah the last great truths of wisdom are made known. The spark becomes perfection as from the sky blue it adopts the quality of innocence and a spiritual sedative so that it remains calm amidst the whirling force of Chokmah. The white is still urging it on to reach ultimate perfection and so the spark moves into Kether.

In Atziluth

The shimmering brilliance of Kether forms the background for the Atziluthic Tree and the path of The Emperor. The path is violet once more. The royal ray highlights the purpose of the path, but now with the ray of brilliance behind it the violet and the white ray takes on an added lustre.

This is the last stage of the spark's journey on the path of The Emperor and it now displays the perfect archetype of government and rulership. This is the essence of the perfected Divine ruler and it can be truly said at this highest plane of consciousness that 'I am pure justice with perfect control of the laws of the Universe, which are in complete harmony and balance'.

THE MOON

In Assiah

This path which joins Netzach and Malkuth, or part of the Yetziratic World to the World of Assiah, is a path of struggle for the whole of humanity. The path of the Moon is the first step man takes as he commences to extricate himself from the mud of materialism to follow the spiritual path.

On this path there is the influence of idealism that flows from Netzach and there is the pull of materialism which comes from Malkuth. The path itself is one of both inner and outer conflict.

In the World of Assiah the path is a stone colour. This is a high octave of the brown ray, and from Pisces, the astrological influence of the path, a middle octave of the brown ray issues forth.

A pure clear yellow envelops the Tree in Assiah and from the Mundane Chakra – the four elements – flow the red, blue, yellow and green rays. This mixture of rays, particularly on this low level of consciousness, adds to the conflict of the path.

This is the path where many students are looking for something without knowing exactly what. A few find their spiritual need, but the majority fall back and have to try again in another incarnation.

For those few who find their spiritual need it is a perpetual conflict with differing influences, reality and illusion, the pull of opposites as portrayed by Sun and Moon on the path; also emphasizing this pull of opposites are the two pillars through which the student must pass, and this requires the perfecting of balance.

The higher octave of the brown ray gives aid to the student if he will only take advantage of it. From this octave of the ray can be obtained wisdom, knowledge and concentration, also by the use of this ray the intuition can be developed.

Conflict is brought about by the lower octave of the ray. From its influence comes the quality of knowledge, but at this low level it is without wisdom. The intuition of the higher octave becomes clairvoyance at this lower octave.

In these two octaves of the brown ray can be seen the two sides of the Moon, reality and illusion; knowledge with wisdom – reality, knowledge without wisdom – illusion.

The higher octave – stone – being more delicate and subtle is not recognized at first by the majority of students and so the medium brown holds sway, and unless the student is careful he becomes absorbed in the glamour of clairvoyance – illusion – where he may remain for many incarnations until he finds the less spectacular and glamorous intuition – reality – of the higher octave.

Single-mindedness, another characteristic of this medium brown octave, holds him to his psychical course and the lower part of the Tree, where he becomes lost in the astral emotions.

Only when the student commences to use the higher octave with the combination of the yellow, creative activity, ray can he grasp reality and make the direct intuitive contact with Kether in Assiah and proceed from the path of the Moon up the Tree and forward to Yesod.

In Yetzirah

On the path of the Moon in Yesod the colour of the path changes to a light translucent pinkish brown, and this with the medium brown octave of the astrological influence will remain through the whole of the Yetziratic World.

Overshadowing the whole of this is the indigo ray of Yesod. The indigo brings in the influence of emotional ritual and worship. If the adage 'As above, so below' were applied, then this path in Yesod would bear a comparison with orthodox emotional religions of the World of Assiah, all heart – no head, the one difference being that in Yesod it would be full spiritual emotion, there being no material claims to detract from it.

Just as the emotions are freed from any physical restraint, so there is the compensating factor that the mental body is also free from physical distractions and can concentrate fully on control of the emotional body.

The pinkish brown ray of the path brings in more conflict. The pink aspect has the quality of affection, but with the brown merging it tends towards a selfish affection and the emotional aspect is emphasized once more. The only way these emotions can be stilled is through the use of the medium octave of the brown ray flowing out from the astrological influence and making full use of the knowledge aspect and developing through this knowledge. A rigid control over the Yesodic emotions is eventually obtained and the Hod plane of consciousness reached.

In the sphere of form – Hod – the rigidity developed in Yesod is in perfect harmony and the Fool on his journey through time and space now holds the conviction of rightness that for a period of time is immovable, the harshness of the rigidity being relieved slightly by a warmth from the pink aspect, and even this is an affection for humanity that emphasizes the narrow concept of view that one must follow this path for one's own progress and development. This is the right way, whether one likes it or not.

The violet/purple, which is the over-all colour of Hod, gives to the path of the Moon qualities of spiritual dedication from the violet aspect which could, if allowed, add to the rigidity of the mental concept 'I am right', but if the initiate grasps the purple aspect of the sephirah and wields the forceful power contained in this ray the spiritual dedication can be forced into the wider fields of mental consciousness, which can lead to greatness, another quality of the purple ray.

It is this quality of greatness that can break down the rigidity of form and this gives the spiritual dedication a new urge and fresh impulse, free from form, to aspire to the wider realms of spiritual consciousness. With the Netzach qualities and ideals at the top end of the path of the Moon it is now possible to make progress and eventually master the Tree in Hod and so move on the cosmic journey to the Tree in Netzach.

At this stage of the journey there is a double Netzach influence, one from the sephirah itself and the other from the sephirah at the top end of the path in Netzach. This is the point where the initiate meets with – and has to understand – the forces of Netzach in Netzach.

The path of the Moon at this point is one of great danger. The aspect of illusion is probably at its peak. Waters of illusion arise from the path itself, with a further flow from the mental freedom of Netzachian idealism.

From the extreme rigidity of Hod the pendulum swings to the other extreme, the fluidity of Netzach. Now the initiate must take a firm stand and strike a balance between the two extremes.

Venus, Mundane Chakra of Netzach, sends out the blue ray of love and wisdom. From the brown aspect of the path itself and from the brown ray of the astrological influence of the path comes the quality of knowledge.

By careful discrimination a right use of these qualities blends together wisdom and understanding; the understanding of Binah and the wisdom of Chokmah, the two pillars represented on the arcanum through which the initiate must pass.

With the blending, the waters of illusion recede and the waters of wisdom predominate so that progress along the Tree in Netzach can now be made and the Tree in Tiphareth attained.

Clear pink rose, a high octave of the red ray enshrouds the sephirah and the Tree in Tiphareth and blazing through it is the orange ray from the Sun, Mundane Chakra of Tiphareth.

Healing power of a magnetic nature flows from the pink rose octave of the red ray, also the qualities of unselfishness and the orange ray provides self-control and reliance.

The qualities from the rays of Tiphareth and its Mundane Chakra are much needed qualities in the struggle to master the path of the Moon in Tiphareth.

At this level of consciousness the waters of illusion can so easily creep back and needless sacrifice be made. Self-control and reliance can be developed to such a degree that pride and rigidity of the mental body can become a dominating factor. It is from the orange ray that the qualities of pride and rigidity emanate and the Sun brings in the quality of leadership.

To combat these qualities, so that the leadership aspect becomes one of guiding and helping rather than compelling and forcing, the pink rose octave of the red ray must be brought into full use so that the universal love quality, bestowed by this ray, can bring about this change and at the same time destroy the pride and break down the rigidity. It is in this process that the octave of the brown ray can help through its qualities of absorption and studious, quiet, keen perception.

Once these vices are overcome the next step forward to the Tree in Geburah can be taken.

The over-all colour is the orange ray and from the Mundane Chakra, Mars, streams the red ray. Here a difficult and serious situation can be built up. With the full strength of the orange ray overshadowing the sephirah, Geburah is rigid and unyielding in carrying out the task as formulated in and by Universal Law, and the initiate – using this orange ray to the full – can be equally rigid in this higher mental state and with the feeling that perfection was reached at Tiphareth will not accept for some time that there are still impurities to be removed.

From the brown ray issuing from Pisces, the astrological sign governing the path, comes the qualities of absorption and depth of thought which, when used by the initiate, gives knowledge and understanding that overcomes the pride of the orange ray and with the pink aspect, from the path itself, softening the rigidity of the orange, progress can be made.

The length of time taken, and the difficulties in moving beyond this point, depends entirely on the initiate with the reaction and use of the orange ray.

In Gedulah, the last tree and sephirah of the Yetziratic World on the return journey, the whole background and pervading ray is the royal ray of deep violet. At the Yetziratic level and a low octave of this ray, the quality of greatness can be tarnished by too much forceful power to influence or force others at lower levels and even at the same level to follow this particular path.

By drawing from the pink aspect of the path and merging this ray with the deep violet, the octave of the purple ray can be raised to a middle octave of lilac. Delicacy and sensitiveness are the qualities of this octave and they gradually replace the forceful power of the lower octave.

With use of the brown ray for the quality of true understanding, the work of Gedulah can now be carried out to the full and further progress made towards taking the momentous step across the abyss to the World of Briah.

In Briah

Now there is a complete change of rays for the World of Briah, except for the brown ray issuing from Pisces. The over-all colour of Binah is crimson, a middle octave of the red ray and the path is buff flecked with silver white. It is at this point that the final struggle for the conquest of this path commences and all ideas of any fixed form have to be discarded, that the truth of the ultimate may be known.

From the buff octave emanates the quality of spiritual philosophy. It also inspires the struggle for perfection and at this level of the path of the Moon it is a hard tough struggle, with the last nebulous vestige of form in the shape of the higher mental body trying to retain its hold. This comes from the brown ray, which is a ray of knowledge having a particular affinity to the mental bodies.

This is the point where mind or the mental body has to be overcome if the path is to be conquered and further progress made. From the silver white aid can be drawn. The combination of the highest octaves of the grey and white rays have a much needed influence at this point in the struggle for perfection.

The white aspect produces purity. It is also expansive and creative, and the silver aspect holds spiritual harmony and tranquillity. One great danger at this point is the crimson octave of the red ray. This octave instils into all it touches 'the love of life'.

If the mental qualities of the brown ray are allowed to impose their influence and the crimson is also used, disaster must follow and the stay on the tree in Binah will be long and arduous. But with the correct manipulation and use of the rays, that urge to struggle for perfection and the love of life applied to the true life, victory over the path can be attained and a further step in the conquest of Binah completed.

The last stage of the struggle to conquer this path in its entirety takes place in Chokmah. Here the over-all ray is the pure soft blue octave of the blue ray with the virtue of selfless love and pure wisdom.

Bathed in the influence of this blue ray the spark of spirit, or energy, can overcome the brown ray of knowledge by using it and merging it with the wisdom of the blue ray. Also, by the use of the silver octave of the grey ray, that final balance can be obtained that conquers the path of the Moon at this last stage and so creates the perfection of this path as first conceived in the Archetypal World.

In Atziluth

The path of the Moon in the archetypal world is scarlet and this octave of the red ray denotes and influences 'energies in lower directions'. Contained in Atziluth, which is the true archetype of the path, are the energies for man to draw himself up and out of the lower levels to see the vision of the two pillars and the path leading between them, symbolizing the Middle Pillar, with the Crown of Kether in the far distance at the end of the path, drawing him on.

The silver octave of the grey ray stabilizes to perfection the energies of the scarlet.

THE SUN

In Assiah

In the World of Assiah the path of The Sun is the path of promise and struggle, with Hod the sphere of form and restriction at the top end of the path and Yesod the sphere of emotions at the lower end, both having an effect on the path itself, the emotions struggling for freedom and Hod revealing its unbending form of concretion.

The yellow ray of Assiah forms the background for this struggle, with all the other rays or flashing colours bursting through intermittently. The path itself is amber, a high octave of the orange ray and this is streaked with the red ray. From the Sun, astrological influence of the path, flows another high octave of the orange ray.

With the yellow of creative activity and the orange of the concrete mind, the student or initiate is concerned with the conquest of life at an intellectual level, and even when he has overcome the material life and turned his attention to the spiritual path through the aid of the amethyst ray and the spiritual aspect of the yellow, his main idea is still the intellectual.

Through the intellect he feels he will conquer and overcome the mysteries of life and spirit, whereas the lesson he has to learn on this path is that the intellect can be the barrier to his freedom. The red ray gives him the urge to struggle along against all trials and tribulations. The orange holds forth the promise of freedom.

There is the characteristic of pride in the orange ray and it is this quality that prevents the student or initiate succumbing to the obstacles that strew the path before him. This is his struggle over many incarnations and it is only when he controls and uses the blue ray of wisdom that he overcomes the path and fully realizes that the promise of the Sun will be kept if he also carries out his part with true sincerity and conviction, and by his own efforts pull down the barriers that he himself has built in his journey through time and space.

This is a difficult path to conquer because there is so much of the intellectual ray and there is always the temptation to use it. Only when the intellect realizes that humility, the innocence of a child, is the key that the conquest becomes possible. At this stage of realization the student or initiate commences to draw upon the other less prominent rays at this level and by their use and manipulation frees himself from the path in Assiah and eventually the Tree in Assiah and moves on into the Yetziratic World.

In Yetzirah

Deep indigo pervades the whole of the Tree in Yesod, the first objective state in the Yetziratic World. The red ray has now disappeared from the path of the Sun and it just responds to the rich amber with the orange issuing forth from the astrological influence of the path.

Indigo is a cleansing purifying ray and the task of the student or initiate is to use that ray to cleanse the emotional vices. This is the first essential step in the emotional astral world. The orange mixing with the indigo creates an octave of the purple ray and a very low octave that brings with it overbearing and pompous qualities.

Once again the wall or barrier to his freedom is being built by his own hands through these wrong emotional influences. It is on this path on his return journey that the student or initiate has to learn the lesson of innocence and purity but, although these qualities are symbolized by a naked child, it must not be the emotional innocence that is prevalent with a child. Here the use of the orange ray can be of help through its quality of self-control.

Neither must the quality of innocence be that of a child – which is blind innocence – where the child can do wrong without realizing it. This must be the wise conscious innocence that is synonymous with purity.

Amber, with its quality of wholeness, and the indigo with its cleansing facilties, should now be called upon and made use of to attain this state. Drawing also upon the silver ray which emanates from the Mundane Chakra, the student or initiate can receive its calming influence, which helps in his task.

The silver, highest octave of the grey ray, also serves a further purpose, that of urging the spirit to struggle for freedom. As the silver merges with the other rays connected to this path it darkens to a grey and it is from this octave that the desire for the spirit's freedom emanates.

Through making use of the rays, and with the single-mindedness of the child combined with the purposefulness of age, the student or initiate presses forward to overcome the path of the Sun in Yesod and commence the task of working upwards until he reaches the path of the Sun in Hod, where a new experience awaits him.

The amber and orange remain with him but the over-shadowing ray of indigo gives way to the over-all ray of violet/purple.

Hod, the sphere of restriction and of mind – also the sphere of religious thought – adds to the difficulties of the student or initiate on the path of the Sun in this sephirah.

The orange ray of concrete mind is even more restricted to the realms of orthodoxy by the influence of Hod itself and the only way to break through this rigidity is to take advantage of the spiritual creative activity of the yellow ray which emanates from Mercury. It is a slow process because there is more of the orange than the yellow, but constant application and effort will eventually bring success.

With the influence of the violet/purple, a middle octave of the purple ray, there is the danger of a magnanimity that savours of the self-righteous. There is also the quality of spiritual dedication that can be exercised in one of two ways, either giving added influence to the wrong type of magnanimity or by being used in conjunction with the yellow ray and having that true spiritual dedication which in due course of time will, with effort, free him from the first objective phase of the lower mental world.

On the path of the Sun in Netzach the student or initiate will find – and in all probability go to – the other extreme and for a time lack the control that held him so rigid in Hod. This extreme swing will be the effect of the blue ray flowing out of Venus, Mundane Chakra of Netzach.

From a narrow religious basis to the open mind of finding the truly spiritual, the narrow bigoted ideas give way to the wide philosophy of the love wisdom ray, and perhaps more love than wisdom at this lower mental level. The safeguard is the orange ray from the path's astrological influence and once the initiate or student realizes it is there for use his wild extreme flow of love can be brought into balance by the concrete mind restriction of the orange ray.

The amber ray of Netzach gives the influence of practical knowledge with receptivity and mental vigour, all these qualities are invaluable if the balance and conquest of the path of the Sun is to be achieved.

In Netzach the quality of innocence as symbolized by the child is inclined to extend to the point of gullibility or blind innocence until such time as the orange ray is brought into use to place a curb on the lower mental body and so enable the quality of innocence to be retained and applied in a rational manner. This rationalized application of innocence is vital to the development of purity, the other quality of this path of the Sun.

After many profitable – and some trying – experiences the Tree in Netzach is conquered and in moving forward to Tiphareth the path of the Sun again stretches out before the initiate with the forbidding wall barring the way. This does not perturb the initiate unduly at first; has he not surmounted similar walls on the path of the Sun in other spheres?

The whole of the Tiphareth Tree is bathed in a pink glow from the clear pink/rose applicable to this sephirah. From the Mundane Chakra flows the orange ray, as also from the astrological influence of the path, and interpenetrating them all is the amber ray of the path itself.

From all these aspects it will be seen that the path of the Sun in Tiphareth has a near even balance between the red and orange rays, although there are two octaves of the orange ray operating, the amber being a high octave, whilst the two orange are on the medium octave.

The pink/rose.is one of the higher octaves of the red ray and from its influence flows the qualities of tact and unselfishness, also comfort.

Tiphareth is the sephirah of the mediating intelligence and to be able to carry out the task of mediation the initiate must develop the qualities of the pink/rose. All are qualities that demand sacrifice and it is not easy, because although this sephirah is the bridge between higher and lower mental planes of consciousness, the path itself is at the lower mental level of the sephirah.

It is the medium orange octave that can give considerable help at this point, with its quality of self-control and the amber octave gives the characteristics of geniality and receptivity.

Once armed with these qualities, the initiate is now in a position to surmount the wall that bars the path of the Sun in Tiphareth and proceed on his journey through to Geburah, where once more the path of the Sun with its barrier faces him.

Amber and orange from the path and its Mundane Chakra remain, but the over-all ray from Geburah is now orange and from Mars – Mundane Chakra of Geburah – flows the red ray of will and power.

With the development of innocence and purity, gained by experience on the path of the Sun in previous planes of consciousness, the initiate approaches the wall of the path full of confidence that it can be surmounted, as at previous levels.

Armed with the will and power of the red ray, the initiate proceeds to take the barrier in his stride and it is now that the justice of the red ray brings the initiate to a halt.

It is only when the initiate makes use of the amber with its quality of practical knowledge that full realization dawns. This time the wall cannot be surmounted but must be taken down brick by brick, just as it has been built.

Each mistake, each error, had added a brick to the wall; this was what remained of his karma. Drawing upon the orange ray for self-control, reliance and organizing ability, he sets to work, fortified with courage from the red ray, and will to accomplish the task. He commences to take down the wall that he had built.

From the amber he draws mental vigour and it is from this octave of the orange ray that he obtains the quality of justice and in so doing realizes the sense of justice that demands he carries out this task.

Once this understanding dawns he is ready to accept the quality of geniality from the amber octave of the orange ray and work out his karma willingly and with a desire to do so, and not because he has to do.

The wall taken down, the initiate can now claim his Mastership and continue his journey through time and space free and without, but not beyond, karma.

With quiet and calm and confidence the Master now enters the Tree in Gedulah. Here he is enveloped in the deep violet/purple of the sephirah with a streak of amethyst from the Mundane Chakra of Gedulah.

There is still a wall on the path of the Sun, but now it is a barrier of choice. One can surmount it and prepare to cross the abyss, or remain on one's own side of it and give service to those on the lower planes of consciousness. Neither choice is easy to make or to follow.

If the Master chooses to surmount it and cross the abyss, he is at the stage where he may do so without incurring any further karma. However it will be more difficult to conquer the Tree in Binah if he does not turn for a while and give service to the lower planes of consciousness.

From the purple aspect of the violet/purple ray there is a forceful power which urges the Master to go forward and cross the point of no return, and from the violet aspect comes spiritual dedication and reverence, which can also be an added incentive to go forward.

Counteracting this urge is the quality of the amethyst ray, which gives humility that softens the forceful power of the purple. From this ray also springs the talent for attainment in mystical powers, and a deep spiritual quality.

It is usually the amber that becomes the deciding factor in the Master's decision. This high octave of the orange ray has the quality of wholeness, a quality that is always uppermost in the higher mental plane of consciousness. Having attained to this state of wholeness himself he now seeks to bring that wholeness into the other planes of consciousness.

Most make the choice to stay on the life side of the wall and give service to those who follow, but a few take the direct step across the abyss to the higher realms.

Whatever the choice, the Master in due course reaches the end of his journey in Gedulah and commences to tread the paths in the World of Briah.

In Briah

The Tree in Binah is the first stage of the Briatic World. Here the path of the Sun works under the influence of golden yellow, a high octave of the yellow ray which has the quality of the creative active spirit.

Crimson is the overshadowing colour emanating from Binah and from its Mundane Chakra issues the black ray. As on the Tree in Gedulah the wall is not a barrier, but one of choice. To pass through the wall is easy enough. What deterrent there is lies beyond the wall.

The choice is to sojourn in Binah and retain the personality or to go through the wall and reach the ultimate in this sephirah, which leads to the extinction of personality.

The yellow ray holds the quality of well-being and tends towards remaining in the lower levels of the Tree, remaining in the known. One quality of the crimson is a love of life, which gives added support to the yellow ray.

It is the black ray that calls with its characteristic of secrecy. There is also the esoteric and meditative qualities that urge the discarding of the personality to reap the full benefit of enfoldment into the realms of pure individuality and to truly merge with the whole.

The spark – now on its last stage of the journey – enters the soft blue aura of Chokmah, where it is an individual individual. The last wall on the path of the Sun has to be conquered and the task is to leave the state of individual individuality to become an individual merged into full unity with other individual sparks.

From the pure soft blue there emanates a calming and soothing influence. The yellow ray imbues the spark with the desire of creative spiritual activity and the orange ray brings to the consciousness of the spark the practicality of merging into the oneness.

With the aid of these three rays the last wall is broken through and the spark draws into its consciousness all the rays emanating from the sphere of the Zodiac – Mundane Chakra of Chokmah.

Now the final and perfect blending takes place and the spark is ready to continue its journey through the remainder of the Tree in Chokmah and so reach its ultimate goal, the World of Atziluth.

In Atziluth

On the Tree in Atziluth the path of the sun is orange and so is its Mundane Chakra. The background to it is brilliance – Kether – the scintillating point of light. The brilliance gives to the orange a pure golden glow that illuminates the whole path, bathing it in cosmic sunlight.

The wall is still there. It too is bathed in the pure cosmic

Sun. This is the perfect archetype that symbolizes not only purity and innocence, but a golden promise that whatever wall is built by man can be overcome and that he may enter into the beauty and peace that lies beyond.

THE LAST JUDGEMENT

In Assiah

All through this path in every world the red ray on one octave or another is active. There is no astrological sign ruling the path of Judgement. It is governed solely by the element of fire and this aspect of the red ray is always there, enforced by the various octaves from the path itself.

In the World of Assiah the colour of the path is vermilion flecked with crimson and emerald. Vermilion is a mixture of two rays, red and brown, and is one of the lower octaves of the brown ray.

Vermilion – with its quality of sensuality – unless controlled will bring the individual up against the path of Judgement time and again, incarnation after incarnation. This quality is accentuated by the quality of 'love of life' which issues from the scarlet octave of the red ray.

This path can only be conquered, and judgement given to pass on to higher or other levels of the Tree, by bringing the vermilion under control and this can only be accomplished by emphasizing and making greater use of the brown aspect of the ray.

Brown, with its absorbing qualities, has the characteristic of single-mindedness. It is the single-mindedness of the student to overcome, with the use of the green ray to calm down the effects of the red aspect of vermilion and the scarlet love of life influence that will give victory over this path.

There is the religious (as opposed to spiritual) influence

from Hod flowing down the path with the yellow ray from Mercury, stirring the spirit to activity. Once the yellow ray is contacted then the scarlet love of life undergoes a change as the student takes hold and uses the yellow to activate the true love of life, the life that is beyond the physical and material.

From knowledge and understanding – qualities obtained from the brown ray – the student knows that the true life beyond the physical can only be attained by commencing the search and finding the path leading to this state of being in the physical world.

This change of outlook is not only the first step in overcoming the path of Judgement, but it also opens up the consciousness to the spiritual creative activity of the yellow ray.

With the ever-growing dominance of the yellow ray and full use of the brown, Judgement commences to fall in favour of the student and eventually the path yields to his struggles as a new way of life or cycle commences and the student moves on until he reaches the path of Judgement in the World of Yetzirah.

In Yetzirah

Through the whole of the Yetziratic World the path is scarlet flecked with gold. From the ruling element of the path flows the red ray and the whole is overshadowed by the indigo ray of Yesod.

This path has now to be trodden on the Tree in the sephirah of the strong foundation. On the outward journey it was the strong foundation prepared to take on the physical body. Now it is the strong foundation on which to build the basis for ascending to the higher planes of consciousness.

The scarlet ray with its love of life exerts its influence, but now it is a helpful influence due to the interpenetrating gold, high octave of the yellow ray.

Negating this helpful influence is the sway of emotions, chief characteristic of Yesod, and this can be accentuated by the indigo ray of devotion. Devotion is a good quality if rightly applied, but when it is based on an emotional urge it can run riot.

The indigo ray is just pure devotion with no bias to right or left and so it could be applied to evil just as easily as it can be applied to spiritual advancement.

If the student is to successfully traverse the path of Judgement in Yesod he must harness this ray of devotion to the spiritual aspirations and in this respect he can draw on the yellow ray, not just the gold flecks interpenetrating the scarlet of the path, but also from Mercury, Mundane Chakra of Hod, at the top end of the path.

From Yesod's Moon further aid can be obtained from its silver, a high octave of the grey ray. In this ray can be found the quiet calm that will help still the emotions. Once the emotions are stilled and the devotion fixed on the ideal, then the red ray from the fire element of the path can be brought into use and its will and power influence applied to attaining the ideal.

Once the correct application of the rays has been put into effect it should not take long to reach the right Judgement and resume progress through the Tree.

The next Tree on which the path of Judgement has to be faced is in the sephirah of Hod, where all is overshadowed by the purple ray. The yellow ray now has increased power through Mercury with its double activity, one from Hod at the top of the path, and the other from Hod itself.

Work on this path is now dealing with Hod in Hod and increasing the rigidity of form. At this point conformity is the key word and the traveller on first reaching the Tree in this sephirah is soon caught in the concrete form of Hod and falls into the conformity of all the sojourners.

The task on the path of Judgement in Hod is to learn how to make correct judgement, even though at times it means cutting adrift and going against the tide; to realize that form is essential, but not all forms, and to make a correct judgement on which type of form should be rejected.

Once the power of true judgement has been developed, through the aid of the intellectual yellow ray, the next quality required is that of courage to break away and cease to conform to the rigid patterns no longer required. It is from the red ray that this quality can be obtained and by making full use of this ray the traveller crosses the path of Judgement and continues the journey towards the ultimate.

From Hod to the Tree in Netzach, the sphere of victory, imagination, ideals and ideas. From Venus emanates the blue ray of love and wisdom, encouraging the idealistic quality to a greater degree than ever before.

Amber, the colour of Netzach in the Atziluthic World, surrounds the whole tree with a steadying influence and it is the octave of the orange ray that the traveller will require to use if he is to find the balance in Netzach that will enable him to make correct judgement.

In Hod the task was to break out of form. In Netzach the task is to prevent the lower mental body flying off at tangents. The scarlet of the path imbues him with enthusiasm that must have a certain amount of control.

Victory over the path of Judgement in Netzach results in the perfect balance and the right use of control. On this path in Netzach the spiritual traveller has the advantage of the three primary rays of the lower levels. Red from the element of the path, blue from Netzach's Mundane Chakra, and yellow from the path itself.

A number of other rays are available for use, but the opportunity to control the forces of the lower trinity should be given prime importance and conquest of the path be obtained through them with the minimum use of the green and orange rays.

The red ray gives the enthusiasm and will to do. The blue ray can channel it in the right direction and by correct use of the intellectual yellow ray the lower mental body can be raised to that high level of consciousness that leads to Tiphareth.

At Tiphareth the path of Judgement is surrounded by a

clear pink rose, a high octave of the red ray that spreads out through its influence the quality of universal love, a quality that has to be fully understood otherwise it could lead to weakness and grave errors of judgement, preventing the traveller reaching the higher mental levels.

The red ray is still driving and urging the traveller to even greater efforts of accomplishments. Just out of reach is the higher mental world with its wider expansion of·consciousness, the path of Judgement lying in the lower half of Tiphareth.

From Hod, at the top of the path, must be drawn the yellow ray from its Mundane Chakra. The lower mental body must be activated to the full, and the green ray must also now be used at this level of the basic Tree. The octave of this ray, issuing from Malkuth at the bottom of the path, is a medium octave combining the qualities of ambition and harmony. It is these qualities that in the end aid in making correct judgement and correctly directing the quality of universal love.

The yellow ray is used to make the correct analysis of when and where to follow the idealism which is also an aspect of the middle octave of the green ray. It is at Tiphareth that the struggle of the soul for freedom takes place and correct judgement obtains its release.

Now the path of Judgement has to be faced on the Tree in Geburah, but this time it is a double-edged judgement. Clear judgement has to be made of all reactions that will take place from the actions of the initiate, and judgement that is meted out to the initiate.

In Geburah the Tree is in the sephirah of punishment, fear, and death. Death at this sephirah can result in a new beginning on a higher arc or it can result in returning to the Tree at a lower level to commence again, a completely fresh start on the return journey.

Through Geburah the whole path is clothed in the orange ray and darting across it are fiery streaks of red from Mars and from the element ruling the path. The whole is an inferno of thermal rays.

From the red ray comes the quality of courage which must be drawn upon to withstand the searing experience of Judgement in Geburah. The yellow ray helps the initiate, once he draws upon it, to understand the reason of Universal Law within the bounds of judgement and in that understanding he draws upon the orange ray to aid in stabilizing his mental body.

Self-reliance and self-control are the two chief qualities for the initiate to draw upon from the orange ray. These are the stabilizing factors. He is now fully equipped to meet and accept the judgement and in so doing moves further along the road of spiritual progression.

The last Tree in the Yetziratic World is in Gedulah, where a deep violet forms a cloak, not only for the path of Judgement, but for the whole Tree. This octave of the purple ray has the qualities of humility, dedication, and spiritual devotion as opposed to just devotion of the indigo ray.

From traveller to initiate and drawing very close to the level of Mastership, the path of Judgement and its conquest presents the opportunity to go forward to this high state of being.

Now the real test of Judgement is before the initiate and one judgement to be made is how to use the scarlet with its quality of love of life. Love of life that will prevent him taking the final step to walking alone, or the love of life for all life that means spiritual devotion, and dedication.

With full use of the purple ray and its qualities the scarlet octave can be put to the right use and its highest level employed. By tuning in to the amethyst ray flowing out of Jupiter with its visionary quality, right judgement can be exercised and in turn he can pass across the path of Judgement and so make his way up the Tree in Gedulah to the point where he is ready to cross the abyss to meet up with Judgement in Binah.

In Briah

Binah, the first supernal on the path of return, sheds its scarlet colour over the whole Tree. The path itself is now vermilion and it is the brown aspect of this mixture that must be used to offset the predominance of the red ray.

The black ray from Saturn can also be called upon to absorb some of the fire element and restrict its quality of impetuosity. The lesson to be learned on the path of Judgement in Binah is control of the individuality.

One should be able to judge, as well as have Judgement pronounced on the amount of restriction that should be imposed on the individual spark once the restriction of Binah has been removed.

Knowledge with understanding can be drawn from the brown ray, a high octave at this level. The black ray also on the high octave has the influence not only to contain, but bring out the latent powers. This must be used to the fullest extent to bring out the power and judgement of true balance, which is embodied within every individual spark.

Only when the Master understands these lessons of the path in Binah will Judgement pronounce him fit to go forward with other preparations higher up the Tree for the transit to Chokmah, where all restriction is removed, except for that which is self-imposed.

Once in Chokmah the spark is soon meeting the path of Judgement once more. The path is now bathed in a pure soft blue which – merging with the red – produces an octave of the amethyst ray. At this high level of the Tree full mystical attainment can be reached, a quality of the higher octave of the amethyst ray.

From the blue the qualities of wisdom and altruism can be captured. The red ray is still providing a driving force of energy and on this Tree in the sphere of energy has to be carefully directed lest it get out of hand.

As the spark is now nearing conscious perfection, correct judgement on despatching the wisdom and mystical qualities in balanced quantity down the Tree with the right amount of energy is important. Failure here could result in reverting to unconscious perfection and commencing another complete cycle.

The Mundane Chakra of Chokmah is the sphere of the Zodiac and it is through the twelve signs that the Chokmah force is despatched through the four worlds, a task in which the near-perfected sparks take part.

With the differing signs following in their cycle, correct judgement of how to transmit in accordance with each sign is essential. Apart from transmitting the mystical quality and wisdom, the basic quality of the path itself – Judgement – has also to be sent out through the other worlds.

From the Tree in Chokmah the spark moves on to the Tree in Kether.

In Atziluth

The path of Judgement is now radiating in all its lustre from the brilliance, the overall ray of Kether. The path itself is now a glowing orange/scarlet highlighted by the brilliance of Kether.

Here is the perfect archetype of Judgement, of which the spark is now a part. The red ray as the ray of Judgement, and the orange ray, gives wholeness and justice to the perfect archetypal form.

THE UNIVERSE

In Assiah

This path is the last on the Tree. It is, in fact, a path of completion, the basic foundation or trunk of the Tree. The colour of the path in Assiah is black rayed with yellow and this is surrounded by yellow, the Atziluthic colour of Malkuth or Assiah.

The astrological influence of this path is Saturn and in this sense it is associated with Binah because through Saturn, common to both Sephiroth and the path of The Universe, there is restriction.

Throughout all the four, therefore, this ray will have its effect of restriction with, of course, the other qualities of the black ray that flows from Saturn.

It is significant that in The Fool's (or man's) journey through time and space, the pathway of the stars, the astrological influence to the path corresponds with the basic quality of the Hebrew letter attached to the path, the influence of the *Tau.*

This aspect of restriction is, however, rather different to that of Binah, which is a restriction of form in a limited sense, but the *Tau* is a symbol of the ultimate boundaries that man may travel. It is the twenty-second path and twenty-two is the number of the superhuman. It is also the number of the Sun.

This path is in itself the Tree of the Universe and conquest here is ultimate victory; although shown as the last path on the Tree it is in essence symbolic of the completion of the journey. Hence it stands alone, respresenting victory of spirit over matter on each Tree in each sephirah in each of the four worlds.

Let us follow this through in the power of the rays or colour symbolism, commencing in Assiah. Apart from the yellow ray of creative activity there is also red, blue, yellow and green flowing from the Mundane Chakra of Malkuth.

The only ray that is outside the major rays of the lower trinity is the black ray from the path itself and predominating over them all is the yellow ray of creative activity, the ray of the air element and also the ray symbolic of the spirit. This does not necessarily mean it is spiritual. It is just spirit, neither good nor bad, and only the ultimate outcome of treading this path will prove it one way or the other.

The red ray is there to create the adventurous spirit, fill the Fool, which he is in Assiah, with urge and desire for experience and the will and power to carry through whatever task he sets himself. From the blue ray can be extracted the qualities of love, wisdom and a calming antidote to the power and thrust of the red.

Mental activity and the powers of intuition can be obtained from the yellow ray if the Fool chooses to use it, and from these major rays, if he blends them, he can obtain the other rays. From the green ray, which is a ray of balance, albeit through struggle and conflict, belonging to neither major nor minor rays, the Fool can obtain stability.

These qualities can give him victory over the path of The Universe, but wrongly used – and all these qualities can be – the Fool can put his foot on the first incline down the slippery slope of the Qliphohic Tree. It is for the purpose of avoiding this that the black ray is there for use if called upon.

It is the restricting quality of the black ray and its power of absorption that can not only hold within the 'ring-pass-not', but also limit the qualities of all the other rays. If the Fool draws upon this ray and at the same time uses the green ray, he can find and keep an even balance, but if he just uses the black ray to its fullest, the restrictive negative aspect will be so great that regression instead of progression will result.

Here is the task that awaits the Fool, the correct manipulation of the rays and the conquest of The Universe in Assiah and so he moves onwards to face The Universe in the World of Yetzirah.

In Yetzirah

Yesod, with its all-pervading indigo ray is the first Tree in the Yetziratic World where the path of The Universe has to be trodden. From its Mundane Chakra streams out the silver, a high octave of the grey ray.

In the Yetziratic World the path is blue black, a combination of the black and indigo rays. At this low level of The Tree the octave of the black ray is also at a low level.

Obscurity and sorrow are two of the qualities emanating from this ray. The obscurity in Yesod is the emotional clouding and sorrow is a full and overflowing emotion. These emotional qualities must be mastered and controlled, in fact obscurity must be completely dispersed if the wayfarer is to have a clarity of vision that will lead him to the higher planes of consciousness in the universe.

Blind devotion, fortitude, and stubbornness arise from the octave of the indigo ray and these are qualities, if the ray is used correctly, that can prevent the restricting emotions from taking full control and also from setting up a restrictive barrier to the mental levels.

The silver octave of the grey ray can help if brought into use, through its powers of tranquillity. Where it merges with the black ray a medium grey is produced, the middle octave of the ray.

Endurance and one essential emotion at this level, the urge of the soul to struggle for its freedom, these are the characteristics that spring from the middle octave of the grey ray.

With the influences that are available, cosmic law has provided for the wayfarer to control the emotional universe and move upwards to a higher plane of consciousness, that of the Tree in Hod, still in the Yetzeratic World, but at the lower mental plane of consciousness.

In Hod the blue black of the ray is overshadowed by the violet ray, the Atziluthic colour of Hod. From the Mundane Chakra the yellow ray beams out.

Fresh from the conquest of the emotional universe the initiate is now eager to press forward and accomplish the next stage. With the emotions suitably controlled the initiate's lower mental body is in full control and merging with the lower mental consciousness of the Universe.

With the aid of the black ray all that this sephirah has to offer is absorption, all mental forms and concepts become such a living reality that he cannot, in fact does not, attempt to break through the 'ring-pass-not' of the Hod form.

Although the violet ray is sending out its influence of spiritual dedication, the initiate only directs it along his chosen path of conformity and though this violet influence urges him to break away, the stubbornness of the indigo ray resists any moves towards a wider viewpoint.

It is only when the initiate is so hemmed in by the form he has created and is brought to a halt by his own barrier that a search for further expansion takes place. At this point he commences to use the yellow ray of creative activity and with the spiritual dedication of the violet ray he ultimately takes control of the form and commands the universe of form.

From the extreme of conformity the initiate now swings to the extreme of non-conformity as he treads the path of The Universe in Netzach where the amber ray holds sway, not only over the path of The Universe, but over the whole Tree. From Venus the blue ray of love and wisdom streams out.

Netzach is perhaps one of the easier Trees on which to tread the path of The Universe. However much the blue ray leads towards idealism and however strong the devotion to the ideal from the indigo ray, the initiate in his new-found freedom cannot swing too far to the extreme from Hod as there is always the black ray to restrict.

It is the correct use of the black ray that determines whether the initiate suffers defeat or claims victory over the path in Netzach. If the ray is not applied but allowed to run its own course, then there is too much freedom, applied by the initiate too strongly, and progress is curbed.

Truly does the initiate learn the quality of discrimination on the path of the Universe in Netzach. It is from the amber, high octave of the orange ray, that the initiate can gain help; from this ray comes the quality of practical knowledge. There is also mental vigour with this ray.

By the right use of the amber ray and the full development of its qualities, a balance can be found that produces sufficient discrimination to gain victory over the path of The Universe.

The next stage in the battle of this path takes place in Tiphareth and this is the final struggle in the conquest of the lower mental universe. Overshadowing the blue black of the path is the clear pink rose of Tiphareth, high octave of the red ray.

From the pink rose ray flows the quality of universal love. This is the important lesson the adept has to learn. Combined with this is devotion coming from the ray of the path itself, and also love and wisdom from the blue aspect of the path.

True universal love, as expressed by the pink rose, means that the adept must have the same love for all of life, not just one section and no exception to the rule, not even himself.

Once tuned into this ray, and then combined with the love of the blue ray, the quality can get out of hand and love would deteriorate into weakness. The adept must now harness the wisdom aspect of the blue ray and the restricting influence of the black and, with true devotion to all life, give forth the balance and true universal love.

He can now fulfil his destiny and stand victorious over the lower mental universe as he conquers the path of The Universe in Tiphareth. The way is now clear to reach forward to the path in the Tree in Geburah.

Orange is the overshadowing Atziluthic colour of Geburah and from the Mundane Chakra pours forth the red ray. The path is still governed by blue black.

One of the qualities essential to this path, which is the Intelligence of Administration, is courage and it is even more essential at this higher mental level and in the sephiroth that lie beyond Geburah. It is at this point in his journey that the adept learns to administer under all conditions, even under the influence of fear and punishment.

The orange ray offers him knowledge and the blue aspect of the path wisdom to apply that knowledge. The black ray aspect of the path does, however, impose restrictions and with it fear and the thought of death.

It is in these circumstances that the red ray must be brought into use, first to give the adept courage to go forward and face death, that through it he may become a better administrator. This form of death means death to preconceived ideas of judgement and justice.

If the adept uses the red ray with care and blends it with the blue black he can bring into being an octave of the amethyst ray with the quality of ceremonial magic whereby he can rise above all his preconceived ideas and with courage go forward in the knowledge – and with wisdom – that he can become the master administrative intelligence of the higher mental universe.

The whole Tree at Gedulah is now flooded with a deep violet, an octave of the purple ray, and from Jupiter flows the amethyst. With the influence of these two rays the restrictive nature of the black ray is to a degree diminished and the accent for the path of The Universe in Gedulah is on expansion.

It is now imperative for the adept or Master to adopt this quality of expansion and administer correctly all the expanding qualities and the expansive nature of the higher mental universe.

From the amethyst ray full expansion and attainment can be gained in mystical powers and by correct use of the violet they can be wielded with reverence and true spiritual dedication.

Although the black ray is not now so powerful, it is still required to prevent the expansive qualities running riot and the adept or Master must bring this ray into use in order to hold both the amethyst and violet in correct bounds or proportion.

Once the full control of these rays has been accomplished, then the combined blue black rays of the path must be called upon, first for the quality of devotion to the work on the path of The Universe in Gedulah and then to draw upon the qualities of devotion to purity and clarity of thought prior to taking the step across the abyss to the World of Briah.

In Briah

The path of The Universe is now completely on the black ray, and this same ray emanates from Saturn, Mundane Chakra of Binah. The whole Tree in Binah is enveloped in crimson, an octave of the red ray. At this high level of the Tree it is the highest octave of the black ray that the Master has to handle and fully understand.

Contained within the ray are the latent powers, and secretive esoteric knowledge. Here is the last major 'ring-pass-not' and to break through this the Master must understand the reason for this black ray, which follows the path of The Universe through every Tree in every sphere.

From the merging of the crimson and black rays an octave of the amethyst ray comes into being with the qualities of spiritual mystical attainment. It is through the manipulation of these rays and the understanding given from the amethyst that the Master comes to the full realization for, and the paradox of, the black ray.

It is only through the discipline of restriction that true freedom is gained and it is with the acknowledgement of this that the restriction of Binah is conquered and the second half of the Buddhic Universe can be attempted.

In Chokmah the all-pervading colour is soft blue, but from

the sphere of the zodiac, Mundane Chakra of Chokmah, flow all the other rays.

On the path of The Universe in Chokmah the spark is now faced with the task of balancing to perfection all the rays. In this task the qualities of the soft blue can be drawn upon.

Spiritual sedative, which helps to maintain a balance in the whirling malestrom of the Chokmah force, wisdom, with which the eternal spark can handle the rays, and the last quality innocence through wisdom and understanding, not through the lack of it.

At last the Buddhic universe is conquered and the eternal spark is ready to move forward into Kether.

In Atziluth

Kether, the Atziluthic or Archetypal World, is just pure brilliance, the thirteenth ray. Here is the sum total of all, balanced to absolute perfection, both unconscious and conscious.

The path of the Universe on the Tree in Kether is now influenced by the indigo ray at the highest octave of the ray. It is shimmering with life as it reflects the brilliance of the sephirah. From the indigo ray at this level there are the qualities of devotion to purity, clarity of thought, and the ray is also constructive in all its aspects.

The meaning of the *Tau* is now expressed in full perfection. Here in Atziluth is the perfected 'ring-pass-not' or boundary. This is the archetype in all its conscious perfection, created by clarity of thought, devotion to purity and the ever-present principle of spirit over matter expressed by the *Tau*, with its ability also to keep the perfection of the limitless boundary of The Universe.

Now the state of existence The Fool has struggled to reach and create is accomplished, and what was The Fool is now a consciously perfected spark of pure brilliance, conquerer of The Universe in all its many planes of consciousness.